HARD CHECKED

ICE KINGS, #4

STACEY LYNN

Hard Checked

Ice Kings, #4

Stacey Lynn

Copyright © 2020 Stacey Lynn

Content Editing: My Brother's Editor

Proofreading: Virginia Tesi Carey

Cover Design: Shanoff Designs

Hard Checked is a work of fiction. Names, characters, places, trademarks, and incidents are used fictitiously or are the product of the author's imagination.

All rights reserved. No part of this work may be reprinted, reproduced, or transmitted in any form without written permission of the author, except by a reviewer who may quote brief passages for review passages only.

This purchased material is for personal use only and NOT to be shared. Thank you so much for respecting the author's wishes.

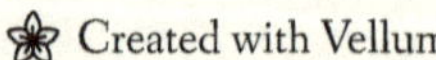 Created with Vellum

CHAPTER ONE

Sebastian

MY FINGERS TAP on my phone's blank screen, debating.

Is there any point in sending my wife another text?

My noise-canceling headphones aren't on, but I've been wearing them since before we stepped on our team's plane to bring us home from Nashville.

We just won the first game of the year. Professionally, I'm having one of the best seasons of my career as a defenseman for the Carolina Ice Kings. Our team is having the best season we've ever had. We're in first place by four games. We're gelling perfectly both on the ice and off. Our lines are perfection.

Our goalie, Byron Maddox, has allowed fewer goals than any other goalie in the league.

We are on fire. On top. Psyched to finish out the season strong for a good run at the Cup.

Personally?

Nothing could be going worse.

Madison hasn't answered a text or phone call from me since she left before Christmas. Spending the holidays by myself and then with the team on the road is not how I wanted to ring in a new year, but it was better than the alternative—home alone.

Even before she left to see her family in Minnesota, things between us were bad. In the weeks prior, she spent most of the days alternating between crying or in a zombie-like trance since we were dealt the latest blow to our medical struggles.

Low sperm count. Low motility.

In addition to the medical issues Madison has had the last couple of years while we've struggled with infertility, now I'm equally at fault. When we sat across from the doctor, barely acknowledging one another as he gave us that information, my wife's hope deflated as fast as a popped balloon.

I've promised her since we were fifteen years old I would always give her everything she's ever wanted. And this? The one thing she's wanted above all else... at this, I've failed her.

I'm no longer certain we can come back from it. And the way she looked at me when I broached the conversation about alternate ways to create our own family?

That didn't go so well.

"We can do foster care."

"Please. You're hardly home. Not exactly stable. And what happens if we get an emergency call for children when you're on the road? I can't do it all by myself."

"I've never suggested you would be." Sighing, I scrub a hand through my hair. It's long, but I never cut it during the season, so it flops at my shoulders and over my ears. *"Adoption. We never ruled that out."*

Tears swell in her eyes and she bites her lip. There was a time when Madison's bright, fiery red hair and pale blue eyes were the only thing I needed to see to get my day started on the right foot. There's still fire in her hair, but the pale blue eyes have lost their luster over the years. It kills me to see her constant sadness.

"Madison. We have options and the means to pursue them. Please, just think about it some more?"

"Okay, Seb. I'll think about it."

Her smile is faint and disappears quickly, but I lean in and kiss her. "Love you, Mads. Always."

"You too."

She steps back and I grab the handle of the suitcase. The car service has been waiting in the driveway to take me to the airport. I leave without another word and it takes me until I reach the airport to realize that it's the first time she hasn't said 'I love you. Be safe. Hurry home' to me like she's done before every trip since college.

Fear edged in when I realized she didn't tell me she loved me. I considered going back, missing my flight to the game to check on her. Instead, I brushed it off. Now, that fear is alive and thriving—that fear that if she left, she might not return.

"Damn it," I mutter and pull up the string of texts I've sent to her.

Hey honey. Landed safely. Love you.

Call me. Back at hotel after skate. Miss you.

Mads? Where are you?

Tell your family I said Merry Christmas. Hope you're having fun.

Tried calling. Heading to bed. Love you.

Happy New Years, honey. Love you. Always. We'll figure this out.

Good morning, honey. Sleep well? Heading to rink soon. Call me.

My knee bounces and my muscles are taut. My jaw aches from all the teeth gritting I've done to bite back a growl of frustration.

Why in the hell is she not answering a single text? What is going on in her mind? I need her home, so we can figure this out.

"Hey. You all right?"

I turn to my teammate and fellow lineman and defenseman, Sawyer. He's happy as a clam, recently getting married on Christmas Eve to his long-time girlfriend, now wife, Debbie. The fact they have a baby on the way hasn't made him my favorite person lately.

When Madison found out? She cried for a week.

I know what the guys think.

Madison's a bitch. She's rude. She hardly ever smiles and she always looks annoyed when she's around their families.

But she wasn't always like this. It's the stress. Seeing everyone we love get everything we want while month after month, we end up disappointed?

It's hard not to become bitter.

"I'm good." I turn back to my phone and the blank screen. I need to get home. Get Madison to talk to me.

"Looks like you want to punch through the airplane's window," Sawyer says, grimacing. "And I'm going to have to suggest you not."

He shivers, giving me shit. Normally I like his playful attitude, but tonight, I'm not in the mood.

Across the table from us are Jason and Jude Taylor. Not only are they brothers and two of not only the best wingers in the professional hockey league, they're the best men I've ever met.

Jude has his headphones on, head back, sleeping.

Jason has his headphones on, eyes on me with brows slightly arched. Great. How long has he been watching me? He's the only person who has any idea what we've been going through, and even then, he knows very little. Definitely not the most recent bad news.

"I'm fine, Sawyer."

I grab my phone and pull up my music streaming app, trying to ignore both of them.

"Really? 'Cause you had a couple more penalties than normal today and you've been playing crazy aggressive, so if something's going on..."

"Barthol deserved it." Drake Barthol is Nashville's most powerful center. He's also a damn good guy and a clean player. Which means I'm full of shit and Sawyer knows it. Someone had to be the focus of my frustration. Might as well have been him.

"No. He didn't."

I can barely hear Sawyer through my headphones, but I can't miss the tone in his voice. I turn to him, see his rarely used serious attitude, and sigh.

It's not *his* fault he can knock up his woman and I can't.

Or that Madison hasn't talked to me in over a week.

"Just a bad game. I'll get my head in it by the next one."

"I'm not worried about your game. If something's going on..."

"Nothing is going on," I hiss out through gritted teeth. The last thing I'm doing is spilling my guts thousands of feet in the air.

"All right." He lifts his hands and shoves off out of his chair, back to where he's been hanging with Byron Maddox and Duke Fletcher, other teammates.

I watch him go and when I pull my focus back to my table, I catch Jason still watching me.

"Don't start."

He pushes his lips out and nods. "I'm here. You know that, right? You were there for me."

Yeah, when I knew he was hesitating about going for a woman he wanted who wanted him back and both were too stupid to make a move. This is different.

I know what he wants to hear, so I give it to him. "I know. Thanks."

"Good."

An hour later, the plane has landed, I've grabbed my luggage and I'm in the back seat of a Town Car being driven home.

I pull up my phone again and hit call. My knee bounces while I wait...

"Hey, you've reached Madison Hendrix. I'm not available right now..."

I end the call. Try again. Four more times only to get the same voicemail message. It's not like her to completely ignore me.

Which means by the time the car pulls into my curved driveway in a suburb outside Charlotte thirty-five minutes later, I'm passed the point of slightly concerned or pissed off.

I'm getting worried out of my brain.

What if something happened?

I'M ATTACKED at the ankles as soon as I step inside the front door.

Scooping up Bruiser, our seven-pound Maltese fur ball I bought for Madison after her second round of fertility treatments didn't work, I slam the door closed. We have a housekeeper who helps Madison with the upkeep of the house and yard. If Madison's not home, Bruiser's usually kenneled in his own private dog room we made for him. I'd texted Cara earlier and told her she didn't have to wait for me and could leave him out. The poor guy's been kenneled way more than usual in the last week.

Once my cheek is covered in small doggy slobber and he settles in my arms, I set him down at my feet.

The house is quiet. Eerily so. Madison always has music on. She's not a huge television watcher but she loves books. I usually come home from a trip to see her settled in her pajamas, a glass of wine she's been nursing, her Kindle on the coffee table and some kind of music, either pop, country, or classic depending on her mood, filtering through our house system.

To come into the house and have it absolutely silent is nerve-wracking.

At my feet, Bruiser barks once, twice and then spins in three circles before taking off like a rocket for his food bowl.

"All right. All right, little man."

I'll feed the dog. Call Madison. Again.

And then I'm fucking going to bed to figure out what in the hell is going on and deal with it tomorrow with a clear head.

Once I've dished out Bruiser's food and made sure he has fresh water, I send a quick thank you text to Cara and open the fully stocked fridge. I'm rummaging through the contents when the doorbell rings.

Bruiser loses his shit at the sound like he always does and slips and slides on the tile floor as he races to beat me there. I scoop him up on the way, checking the clock above our fireplace.

It's freaking ten o'clock. Who in the hell could it be?

A large male figure dressed in what looks like a uniform through our frosted glass front door, makes the hair on my arms rise.

The hell?

As soon as I open the door, a man who was facing to the side turns to me.

Instantly, I take him in and double blink. The badge on his chest and the police car in my driveway make me freeze. In his outstretched hand, he's holding a manila envelope.

"Mr. Hendrix?"

"Yeah?" In my arms, Bruiser squirms, so I set him down inside, close the door behind me, and step on the front porch before replying further. "Can I help you?"

"Sheriff Butler, sir, and you've been served."

His words blur as he speaks. "Served what?"

"Dissolution of marriage. Now, there's a form on top in the envelope I need you to sign showing receipt of the papers. My suggestion, get yourself a lawyer, file a return by the date provided."

Dissolution... of marriage?

"The hell?" I rip the envelope out of his hands, shaking so hard as blood rushes straight to my brain and to my ears where my heart thumps. It takes me several tries to tear open the envelope before I find the metal clasp, flip it, and take out the papers.

"You're kidding me." Words stall in my throat and my chest grows unbearably icy.

She wouldn't do this. Would she?

At the top of the papers is a professional-looking letterhead.

Ritter Family Law Firm along with a second name I don't recognize. But the one I do know is enough.

Madison's uncle is a lawyer. Ritter is her maiden name.

Shit.

Right there, in black ink. The words, *Petition for Dissolution of Marriage* stare back at me, growing blurrier the longer I stare at them.

"Mr. Hendrix—"

"Sebastian." I glare up at him.

This isn't *his* fault but I'm pretty certain if it wouldn't get me sent to jail, I'd punch him in the face.

"I didn't come here to cause problems, and I'm not the reason for your understandable anger. I am, however, doing my job. If you could sign the acceptance."

I bite back a growl and clamp my teeth together. I'm vaguely aware his hand is at his hip near his holster and *holy fucking shit*.

She's doing this.

She's actually *left* me and she's doing this. My knees shake as I unfold the top sheet of paper, the acceptance the Sheriff has mentioned. Beneath it is another envelope. My name. Written in loopy, familiar handwriting, I want to tear it in half without reading. How kind of Madison to send me a *note* along with divorce papers.

A pen ends up in my line of sight.

"Fine." I take it without looking, scribble my name and hand the letter back to him.

"Thank you," he says, folding the paper and taking the pen from me. "Take care, Mr. Hendrix."

He turns and heads back to his patrol car. I'm frozen to my spot on my porch until it's far from sight.

Then, I turn and throw up into the bushes off our front porch.

SEBASTIAN,

I'M A COWARD FOR THIS. I know this. But you wouldn't let me leave and you wouldn't listen to me in all these years I've tried explaining. I want my baby. Ours. One I carry in my body and birth into the world. Now, we know with certainty that will never happen. I understand there are options. I've crossed those off. Please.

It's over.

Let me find my peace adjusting to the latest news. Perhaps this way, we'll both eventually get what we want but there's no hope of it—

THE PAPER CRUMPLES in my fist. I pull my arm back and fling it, unsatisfied it only bounces off the kitchen island before dropping to the floor. A scream tears from my throat and I look for something more substantial to throw. Something that will shatter like she's just done to me.

"Fucking bullshit. All of this is such bullshit."

The final flames of my marriage ending is going up right in front of me. I pull out the papers she had dropped off like she had it timed to do as soon as I got back home and read them.

Every minute that passes burns the hole she's creating brighter and bigger.

Twenty minutes later, I am *pissed.*

A few thousand dollars a month until she lands on her feet and finds a job to support herself along with the rest of her clothes and personal items in her closet and our house. She'll arrange for movers to come pack her things. That's all she's asked for.

No money for a down payment for her own home.

No Bruiser.

No insisting we sell the beach house on Sanibel Island where we've lived for thirty days every summer to relax before training camp. And she gets half.

There's no half of nothing.

After all she's been through. After all the dreams she put on hold for me, insisting it was worth it. After all the years she spent crying in my arms, hurting she couldn't carry our own child... and she's asking for fucking pennies.

It's almost more insulting than demanding everything. She walks away with my name and the salary of what my father makes teaching and she doesn't want a damn thing else from me except for my signature.

And fuck this.

Fuck it all.

CHAPTER TWO

Gigi

MY GRANDPA always said when life hands you lemons, make lemonade. When life handed me lemons, I stomped them into a pulp and bought myself a one-way ticket to Turkey where I spent a year and a half traveling Eastern Europe before spending another six months traversing through Western Europe, ending in Scotland before the weariness of traveling finally started getting to me.

My heart started missing my dad and home.

Despite my homesickness that took root, it still took a phone call from my aunt Pamela to tell me my dad was in the hospital with chest pains to finally get me back on the plane and on American soil. The moment I hit town, I headed to his bar to drop off my luggage in the apartment above his bar and clean up before heading to see him. I figured with what Pamela said, he'd be home and resting.

Imagine my surprise when I walked into the bar to grab the key for upstairs, and there he was.

All hefty, full stomach and thick head of graying hair and second chin, booming his standard and well-known laugh with a bunch of male customers.

I'd leaped over the bar, not caring about the drinks I probably spilled in my wake, and slammed my much more petite arms around him in a hug.

Since that day barely over a year ago, I've come to know the guys that were there that night were for the most part, team members of the Carolina Ice Kings, North Carolina's professional hockey team.

At one point, Dad pulled me aside and said the guys found his bar a year earlier, sauntering in after a loss at home with some of their wives and girlfriends. There'd barely been a body in his bar because most young people liked to head into Charlotte to the cooler clubs. Apparently, they liked the quiet so much they kept coming back. He told me I was never to tell anyone they came in. They liked it here, they tipped well and didn't cause problems, and he liked their company.

I know this because Dad introduced me to most of them that night in between the sassy shots he took at my colored hair, the mermaid tattoo I'd picked up in Germany, and the tiny nose piercing I got in the French Riviera.

There was one among them who stood out. He came in with his shaggy, dirty-blondish brown hair that had a slight wave to it. It flipped over his ears and curled over his collar. His beard was scruffy, in need of a trim. But it was his smile that pulled me in. Thick, light pink lips that were almost too feminine on his buff frame. Lips that smiled easily with a top lip that often disappeared beneath his mustache when he did.

So. Damn. Sexy.

Seeing him, I considered ignoring my dad's warnings

about them, jumping back over the bar top and planting myself in the man's lap when I caught sight of the shimmering black ring he wore on his left hand.

His ring finger, to be exact.

Sebastian Hendrix was one of the hottest men I'd met in all my travels, and he was married.

Since I wasn't that kind of girl, not ever, I tamped down my crush and my blooming lust for him and did my job. And I'd been doing my job for well over a year for the Ice Kings, pouring them drinks, telling them stories about my travels, some exaggerated for comedic effect.

In the meantime, I chopped eight inches off my hair, got rid of the hot pink tips and went to a deep, dark purple and then red, before going back to my current vibrant purple. My studs in my nose changed much more frequently from tiny jewels to silver balls to a gold hoop depending on my mood.

And through it all, I saw Sebastian laugh less and watched his smiles decrease in size to where now, I rarely see the guy smile at all anymore.

Which means I'm not the least bit surprised when the door opens, a brisk breeze from the cold January air comes through, chilling me through my cardigan and George's Bar tank top, and Sebastian walks in, shoulders hunched, eyes so sad it almost hurts to look at him.

He walks straight to the bar, not giving any of the few people in the place a second glance and pulls up a seat at the corner of the bar near where I am.

He's wearing a faded, old white ball cap with the Alabama logo on the front pulled down low. I lose his eyes as soon as he sits, but his hair would be enough to give him away from a distance. The curls flip at his neck and his ears, his beard is short but thick and I know it will only continue to grow longer through the season. The first time I saw Sebastian without a beard, my jaw dropped to the bar top. I'm not sure which way he looks better, displaying his square, carved chin or hiding it. Either way, the man simply does something to me.

I head toward him, dropping my black towel to the counter.

"Hey, hotshot. Happy New Year."

Other than his strange and morose demeanor, I'm more surprised his teammates aren't with him. Or that he's here at all. It's New Year's Day and they haven't been in since the week before Christmas.

"Shot of something strong, Gigi, and keep 'em coming."

He doesn't look at me. He barely acknowledges me, although I'm used to it. From what I've gathered, Sebastian Hendrix isn't the kind of man to look too long at any woman not his wife. Admirable. All women want to be married to a guy who's so devoted. With his money, his looks, and hell, even with just his personality, men like him are rarely as faithful as he is.

I brush off how his request stings while I grab a bottle of Maker's Mark bourbon. It's not the most expensive bourbon we have, but I know he likes it.

I fill two shots and slide them both his way.

He takes the first, tosses it back and slams it to the counter with a heavy thunk.

"Hey. You okay?"

His head lifts minutely and slowly, like the small move takes massive effort. "No. Not really."

He takes another shot and slides both shot glasses my way. "Like I said, Gigi, keep them coming. Or better yet, I'll take the bottle."

"Sebastian—" I'm not sure I've ever called him by his

name. Not since I nicknamed him. Oddly, he's the only guy on the team who I have nicknamed.

"Don't, Gigi. Not tonight, k? Just want to drink my bourbon and not be alone. Can you give me that?"

Someone at the far end calls my name and I glance their way, seeing Steve Shaw holding an empty bottle. Older than my own dad, I know him well enough to tell him to serve himself. Hell, the man changed my diapers in this very bar when I was that little. He likes to remind me of that frequently.

I tell him I'll be right there and look back to Sebastian. "I'll leave you alone and get you the bottle, but only if you give me your keys."

"Took an Uber here." He still reaches back into his pocket and tosses a set of keys to the bar. "But have them, in case you don't believe me."

"All right." I palm the keys and drop them by the cash register just in case he *is* lying. He wouldn't be the first drunk to do so and then sneak out. There's no way a drunk driver leaving my bar and possibly hurting someone or themselves is going on my conscience.

That done, I slide the bottle of Maker's Mark in front of him and grab a fresh and local Olde Meck pilsner for Steve.

I stay on his side of the bar for a while, talking to the guys I know and watching whatever game is on television. I only head back Sebastian's way when another customer needs something and to slide a glass of water in front of him, just in case.

But an hour later, when the bourbon is quickly disappearing from the bottle and the water glass has gone untouched, I make my move.

"Need me to call someone for you, hotshot? Looks like you might need to get some things off your chest."

He fills another shot glass, but this time he sips it slowly, sucking it in and hissing through his teeth. "No."

A twitch in his beard covered cheek tells me I'm pissing him off.

"Hey." I lean forward and rest my elbows on the bar. I've known these guys for a year. Granted, it's not like they're frequent regulars, but regular enough to know a few have gotten married, Sawyer's having a baby. I know their stats only because I started watching hockey after the first time they came in and Sebastian grabbed my attention.

Shameless and pathetic, maybe, but I like having something to talk to them about. Which means I've already checked my phone and I know they won a game earlier today so he can't be pissed about a loss.

"Seriously, hotshot. You okay? Because this doesn't seem like you, and if you need someone to talk to—"

"You offering?"

"Well." I scan the bar and return to him, smirking. What else do I have to do? "Bartenders end up being like therapists, you know? Trust me, I've heard it all. Seen a lot more. Nothing you can say would surprise me."

"Shit day. Shit year."

"The year's just getting started."

"It'll be shit," he mumbles, finishing his shot and quickly pouring another.

I slide the glass of water closer to him and he sneers at it. "You've been hitting the bottle pretty hard. Take a break, yeah?"

He glares at me, tipping his head up just enough to do so. Tortured, ragged green eyes meet mine and without taking his eyes off me, he drains the water glass.

It's shameful, more than learning about hockey because this guy is hot, but more so the way I watch his throat work as he swallows. My core sparks like I've been zapped with a live wire. Thankfully, I've gotten good at hiding the physical reactions I have when I'm around him.

Although in his current state, I doubt he'd notice.

"There. Happy now?"

"Much." I refill the water glass and set it next to the bottle. "Need food? Kitchen's still open."

"Not hungry." He fills another shot glass and this time, I watch as he takes another small sip. Then I grab a lowball glass, fill it with ice, and set it next to the bottle. Perhaps if he can water down his bourbon with some ice, he won't get so shitfaced he passes out right where he's sitting.

It's a pain in the ass to handle.

"All right, hotshot." Not so much as a muscle moves at his nickname. I'm used to smiles. Smirks. Friendly glances. Tonight, his face is as empty as the shot glass he's drained.

Because I'm me, also because I'm trying not to let the guy's blood alcohol content surpass maximum levels, I check to make sure everyone's taken care of, and scoot out from under the bar back. I clean up empty bottles on my way to the kitchen and put in an order of tater tots and nachos. Maybe if they're there, Sebastian will munch on them in between his sips of bourbon and scowling at me.

Everyone needs a night to blow off steam. I get it. Hell, I've been there. I took two years to blow off steam after my marriage ended, even if it ended amicably. I get having a bad night. However, it's not only my job to try to encourage responsible drinking, I like this guy and seeing him so upset upsets me.

After I take a quick trip to the restrooms and clean up trash and wipe down counters, I swing back and pick up the food and say goodnight to Max, the last cook who will be leaving soon.

Back at the bar, Steve asks me to tell him again about my experience in Amsterdam's Red-Light District. I slide the food onto the bar without looking at Sebastian but feeling his smirk as I pass him without a glance.

It's a common story, and really not all that exciting, but Steve likes imagining all the drugs you can buy from coffee shops and hearing about the night I spent in the Red-Light District.

Typical man stuff when in reality, the coffee at the coffee shops is shitty, and usually in the most popular tourist areas. There were very few locals when I went into one once, and once was enough for me. As for the Red-Light District?

It was an experience, and nerve-wracking, not because it's dangerous but because I am a female, a relatively small one, and I was terrified something could happen to me. In truth, it wasn't anything like I expected with the workers in windows they rent from brothels. Sure, there were workers on the street, but the ones men mostly went to see were safe behind a building's glass window in tiny alleys that curved along canals. The area was patrolled to make me feel safe enough and even though it isn't *my* thing at all, it was interesting.

I repeat all I remember from the time there, the drunken bachelor party, or stag party, who were all escorted away for not being respectful. The women's outfits. The music. And of course, the red lights shining from windows indicating someone was available.

"Gigi."

Sebastian calls my name like a bark and I shift, arching my brows at him.

I get a chin lift and a tip of his head in response, asking for my attention.

I tap the bar. "Be right back, guys."

"Ain't got nowhere to be, sweetheart."

I roll to my toes and kiss Steve's cheek. His wife Amy died from brain cancer a couple years back and since then, he almost lives at the corner of this bar. I've teased him about making him a nameplate so he can have an assigned seat. Sadly, he's here often enough assigning him a chair is unnecessary.

Making my way back to Sebastian, I fill a glass of soda for myself and prop my hip near the cooler across from him. "Something I can get for you?"

A ride home? Ibuprofen for the headache you're going to have?

He shakes his head and sips more from the shot glass. "You ever get lonely?"

"Excuse me?"

"When traveling. You ever get lonely?"

There's a strange look in his green eyes. He ditched his hat at some point so I can see him clearly. It's almost painful to look at someone as beautiful as he is. I want to slide my hand through his hair, brush my thumb along the deep lines on his forehead to smooth away his stress.

"If I want company, I can find it."

His eyes widen and it takes me a second to realize how that sounds.

Still a true statement, but embarrassment floods my veins, heating them. *He's not flirting with you or propositioning you, dumbass.* Right. Of course not.

"I meant—"

"I like being alone," I cut him off. I know what he meant. "I like the quiet and the peace that comes with it and I figure if you can't be happy alone with yourself, you'll never really be happy around another person. You know?"

"No."

He sighs and drains the shot glass. When he reaches for the bottle, I take it from him, holding it out of his reach. He eyes the bottle of bourbon like I imagine he focuses on the puck during a game.

Softening my voice, I ask, "I know I've asked, and I know you lied. You can tell me what's wrong. It's not like I'd repeat it to anyone."

His thumb on his left hand twirls his black, thick wedding band, but he doesn't take his laser-focus off the bottle in my hand. "Just a shitty time, Gigi. Can I have my drink now?"

I debate. He's had enough. At this point, even getting his drunk butt into an Uber will be difficult. At five-two, I'm not exactly big enough or strong enough to carry the guy out if need be. Plus, who's to say the Uber driver won't figure out who he is and I don't know... kidnap him? Steal his wallet?

The poor man is screaming sadness.

"Sure, hotshot." I pour his glass, clean up the bar, and say goodnight to Steve when it hits one o'clock in the morning. He and his old war buddies take off with a wave and a concerned look at Sebastian still hunched over my bar.

Then we're left alone, which he doesn't seem to mind ironically given his earlier question and I'm left to figure out what in the heck to do with him now.

CHAPTER THREE

Sebastian

"FUCK." I press my hands to my temples to try to settle the thundering in my brain to no avail. Holy shit, I got trashed last night. I don't remember much after the short conversation I had with Gigi. Like, how I got home.

I roll over and the scent of something minty makes my stomach roll and forces me to open my eyes. Madison doesn't wear anything minty. She's more floral and elegance.

Two things become immediately clear as I peel my first eye open, feeling like I might have scrubbed my eyes with sandpaper before passing out. One, the harsh reminder of Madison immediately brings to the forefront her stupid, fucking insensitive *note* she had delivered with the divorce papers.

And two... where in the hell am I?

I'm staring at some bright, psychedelic colored wall-hanging. It looks like it was tie-dyed by a small child. The sheets I'm on are most definitely not the white linens I'm used to from either my home or my experience in hotels. The lemon-colored sheets are almost blinding and with all the bright colors, I squeeze my eyes closed and roll to the other side.

Nope. The view is no better on this side where the only thing in front of me is a dresser that looks to be fifty years old and is covered with all manner of jewelry and trinkets flung all over the top, barely hiding the thin layer of dust I can see from this angle.

"Holy shit. What the hell happened?"

I sit up and scrub my face.

If I wasn't feeling two seconds away from emptying the bottle I drained last night, I'd be up on my feet by now. Or hell, if I didn't drink that entire bottle, I'd probably know where in the hell I was or what happened or how I ended up here.

A scent of something else filters in and I crack open my eyes.

Damn, I hurt.

There's no door to the bedroom I'm in that isn't only full of bright colors and loud wall-hangings, but clothes and knick-knacks in every corner.

If I was in my home, I'd think I was robbed, but since this is most definitely not any home I've ever been in, I cautiously peek beneath the covers. I'm wearing the same shirt I threw on last night after I worked out for hours and I still couldn't get rid of the permeating anger coursing through my system. My boxers are on too, and I tip my head back and stare at the ceiling.

A shaky sigh of relief flows through my parched lips.

There's no way I screwed some random woman last night. No way. No way I could have been that drunk and even pissed off at Madison, there's no way I'd cheat on my wife, if I can even still call her that.

Shit. I should probably figure this out. Apologize to the woman whose home I'm in and hope like hell she doesn't expect anything from me for whatever fool I made of myself last night.

Gingerly, I swing my legs to the floor and find my jeans and sweatshirt tossed in a pile on a small clean area of the floor.

I have my back to the opening, clothes in hand, and I recognize the sounds of cooking from the kitchen. Pots clanking. Water running. Quiet footsteps...

I pause at the sound.

"Oh. You're awake. How do you feel?"

Like I got hit by a truck. I vaguely recognize the voice so I turn cautiously, shoving my arms through the sleeves of my sweatshirt.

"Gigi," I sigh. "Thank fuck it's you."

She smirks and holds up a glass of water and a bottle of pain medicine. "You were out. I hope you didn't have to get up for practice or anything today. I was going to leave these for you on the nightstand."

I peer down at the piece of furniture she's talking about and arch a brow when I look back at her.

She laughs, and there's something about her voice I like. It's low. A little husky. Definitely not high pitched or whiny or refined. It's nice.

It's at least not making my hangover worse.

"Okay. I'm a lousy housekeeper and I despise cleaning. But here, do you need them?"

"Yeah." I shrug my sweatshirt over my head and yank it down, dodging high-heeled shoes and boots and jeans and sweaters on the floor while Gigi grins at me.

I take the pills and the water from her.

Thank you. I think there might be parts of the night that are hazy to me—"

"No need to freak out. I slept on the couch. Barely was able to get you up here. And before you ask, there was no way I was putting you in an Uber in your condition, and as much as I tried to get you to stop drinking, well, it seemed like you needed it."

"Good." I sigh and then cringe. "Not that..."

"You're married and a good guy, Sebastian. Nothing happened and you didn't try, and even if you had, I would have still slept on the couch and tossed you into my bed. No harm, I promise."

Something settles in my stomach. Except for the fact I'm not married. Or won't be soon. "Thanks, Gigi."

"No problem, hotshot. I've made some sausage and eggs and toast. Want anything?"

My stomach turns at the thought of putting anything into it. "Actually, I could use the restroom. And then I'll decide."

"No problem. Right that way." She flings out her arm and gestures to a door beyond the curved entrance to her bedroom area.

I step around her, scrubbing my hair and trying to clear my throat. It's almost as dry as my eyes.

This isn't me. I don't get passed out, blackout drunk with a woman who isn't my wife. Hell, I don't *with* my wife. I have an excuse, but I hate this feeling. Even more, the awkwardness of knowing for the first time since I was fifteen years old I've spent the night with another woman... sleeping arrangements aside, I've done it.

That thought alone makes me want to puke more than the alcohol still sloshing in my gut.

I FEEL SLIGHTLY BETTER after using the restroom, washing my face with some bright orange face wash bottle on Gigi's tiny bathroom counter and hijacking her toothpaste so I can give my teeth a quick scrub with my finger. I still taste and smell the bourbon seeping through my pores, and my eyes are still killing me. A quick dig through a basket of products she has on the floor beneath her sink tells me she doesn't have eyedrops, so I'm out of luck there, but at least when I give myself a quick glance in the mirror I look slightly more human than before.

All I need to do is get home and spend the day sleeping and I'll be back and ready for another game tomorrow. Thank God I at least have today off other than a workout I'll throw in later—puking or not.

Heading out of the bathroom, I catch sight of her messy, open bedroom again before turning to the other direction and seeing quite possibly the world's smallest living area that contains a loveseat and a chair.

A bookshelf is next to the chair, filled with so many books the shelves heave from the weight of the mismashed stacked books facing every which way. There are piles of books on the floor, several of them. A few litter the small round coffee table in front of the couch and I'm pretty sure next to the loveseat, she's using another stack of books as a side table.

There are more bright colors, something that surprises me about Gigi. She's always dressed in black. The only color she wears on her is in her hair and a tattoo on her upper arm.

With her penchant for traveling frequently, I would expect her apartment to be bare-bones, ready to empty at a moment's notice, not packed to the gills with knick-knacks and posters and artwork and photos all over her walls... and books. So many books.

Not that I've spent a lot of time thinking about Gigi and where she would live, but I've come to know her some over the last year since she showed up at George's Bar and pole vaulted herself over it to hug her dad who was giving her shit, squinting at her in a teasing way and asking, "Do I know you?"

At first, the guys on the team who were there that night braced to peel some crazy girl off him until she told him to shut up. He'd given us a round of drinks on the house, plopped his daughter on the bar, introduced her to everyone and kissed her cheek, saying, "Tell me everything."

She regaled us for hours that night with the Red-Light District in Amsterdam. The beaches in Denmark which brought Mikah Lutzgo, our Center who's from there, into the conversation. They'd talked and laughed for hours, bonding over her trips through Europe. Hell, I'm pretty sure she might have gone to Africa, too. But where she didn't go? To the touristy spots. She's never once mentioned Big Ben or the Eiffel Tower or a gondola ride in Venice. The mention of Amsterdam was as touristy as she got.

She's interesting, to say the least, and apparently, she's nice as hell to help a drunk jackass like myself.

It's quiet in her living room, and while there is a small kitchen, blocked by a row of upper cabinets, I catch sight of her small frame and head that way where I find her, plating up eggs, buttering toast, and lip-syncing to whatever music is coming from the white earbuds stuck in her ears.

Gigi notices me, tugs out an earbud, and smiles. She's always smiling. So damn happy it's almost offensive given my current state.

"Feeling better?"

"Almost." I scrub my eyes and cringe. "Any chance you have some eye drops? My eyes are killing me."

Her head tilts to the side, and she says nothing for a second before dropping the knife she was using to butter the toast. I swear I see a pink fade across her cheeks before she shakes her head.

"Sure. I probably have some in my purse."

I step back to give her room to get around me while she heads toward a small eating table for two with chairs that look like they could collapse under my weight. I grab the plates and silverware she already has set out and follow her there.

To my complete non-surprise at this point, she's digging through a purse the size of Massachusetts.

"They're somewhere in here," she says, face down, purple hair hiding her face from me. I watch as papers and receipts and pens go flying. There are hairclips and sticks of gum and Chapsticks and lotions. There are other knick-knacks I can't decipher. Business cards. I'm anticipating her pulling out a floor lamp like Mary Poppins when a condom wrapper gets tossed to the floor.

My gaze spears that thing with eagle-eye precision. Hard to miss the bright red, square piece of foil that plops down inches in front of my feet.

Cherry-flavored.

The hell? There's only one reason for a flavored condom and it's been so long since I've had that done to me, my dick, I swear, against my will also seems to notice.

Shit. I turn and head back to the kitchen. Thank freaking hell she has a coffee maker with boxes of pods stacked next to it. Her upper cabinets aren't cabinets but shelves, so I grab a coffee mug and hiss in a breath through my teeth.

Do not *dare* think of Gigi on her knees with a dick in her mouth. Don't even fucking think…

"Aha! Here they are!"

"Shit," I whisper. Once my mug is filled, I take a healthy sip so quick it burns my throat. Which I need. The pain helps clear the completely insane and asshole-ish visual still lingering in my brain.

I head back to the dining area, coffee in hand, keeping my eyes up so I don't spy anything else that might be on the floor. In her small hand with dark purple fingernails are two bottles. She examines both again and holds them out to me. "I don't think they're expired."

I'm too hungover to care if they are. "Thanks."

She surveys the mess. "Looks like cleaning out this purse got added to my list today." She swoops it all up and dumps it back inside.

It's none of my business. I definitely shouldn't ask. My mouth moves before my brain sends the memo.

"What else are you doing today?"

"Ordering for the bar. Maybe a hike if I feel like it. That's usually all I do on Sundays."

A quiet life. A simple one. Without traveling and hassles and constant *go, go, go*. I might envy her if I didn't love my job so much.

I put my back to her and flood my eyes with eye drops until they finally feel like they have a minuscule amount of moisture in them. Then I wipe my eyes and turn back, where Gigi is already sitting, digging into her food, acting way too interested in her toast on her plate which makes something perk up inside of me.

Was she checking me out?

It doesn't matter.

I wobble the chair across from her, testing the weight of it which makes her giggle.

"It won't break. Dad comes over and eats here all the time. They look more breakable than they are."

"Sure?"

"I'm sure."

"All right." I take a seat, not surprised at all when it creaks beneath me. "If I fall flat on my ass and bust something though, I'm telling the team trainers it's all your fault."

She shoves a bite of toast into her mouth and chews. "I'll accept that. You feeling okay?"

"Like I got ran over by a truck."

"I don't mean to pry and you can tell me to mind my own business, but last night really didn't seem like you. You sure you're okay?"

"Madison left me." It's out before I can suck it back in and it takes me a minute to realize what I've said, and to register the look of surprise on Gigi's face. "So no. I'm not really okay. And yeah, last night wasn't me. Any of it."

I'm pretty low-key. Mads and I grew up in a relatively small town in Minnesota where we went to high school together. Our families went to, and still attend, the same large Lutheran Church. I've known her since we went to Sunday school together. The first fight I ever got in was because I beat up a kid in middle school for yanking on her bra strap. One of my oldest sisters was best friends with one of her older sisters all through high school and even roomed together their freshman year at the University of Minnesota shortly after Madison and I started dating.

We spent our weekends fishing and swimming at our families' lake houses, because that's what you do in Minnesota in the summer. We spent our winters skating on the ice rink my parents built for me in the back yard every year.

We drank some, tried pot, but mostly, ever since I was fifteen, I was focused on three things: school, hockey, and Madison. And definitely not in that order.

"I'm sorry, Sebastian. Is it…"

Over? She doesn't ask. I shrug and swallow a large bite of eggs. "We've had problems for a while and the divorce papers made it seem pretty final. So yeah… it's over."

Admitting it to someone else makes me feel worse and I focus on my eggs, which are really damn good, so I don't have to see her expression. Why I'm confessing this to Gigi and not one of my friends is befuddling. What'd she say last night? A bartender is like a therapist? Maybe there's truth in that.

"Again, I'm—"

"Sorry. I get it." And I really don't want to hear apologies for things that aren't anyone else's fault. Or see pity in their eyes.

"Sebastian."

I act like I don't hear her and when she says nothing else, silence descends. It's thick and it's heavy and I have got to change this subject. I gesture to the wall where she has one huge area covered with neatly arranged canvas photos. It's vastly different from the chaos with the rest of her apartment. I can't help but notice how precisely arranged they all are. And how vastly different all the photos are.

"What are those from?"

"Oh." She smiles softly, and even her blue eyes seem to sparkle. "Dad gave those to me as a gift when I returned. They're pictures I'd texted him and emailed him when I was gone."

I stare at her for a moment. Then two. Then I realize I'm *still* fucking staring at her mouth and God damn it.

I focus on my sausage and my breakfast while she babbles on about Turkey and Hungary, pointing out where some of the photos were taken and I'm glad she gives me that play, knowing I was getting the attention off myself. But truthfully, Gigi is easy to listen to. That husky voice of hers is calming, melodic with softness and it's all things I should definitely not be noticing about the bartender who helped me to her apartment and let me sleep in her bed but it can't be helped.

Gigi might be the most interesting woman I've ever met in my life. That she's beautiful and I'm noticing shouldn't make me feel like such an asshole, and yet I can't stop it.

I finish my meal with gusto, shoving down how it threatens to revolt in my stomach and when I'm done, I stand abruptly. "I should get going."

For a brief moment, she looks stunned. I swear her face turns sad before she nods.

"Sure. Okay."

I pat my pockets and come up empty.

Gigi points to a spot on her kitchen counter. "Your keys and everything else are over there."

I remember the shit she gave me when she took them from me. Along with the question I'd asked her.

Does it ever get lonely?

If I want company, I have no problems finding it.

Yeah. It's definitely time to go.

I'm now remembering that response with her holding that cherry-flavored condom in her hand, and I'm pretty damn certain that's not how it actually happened. I also remember her saying something else wise about needing to be happy with yourself but I was already too drunk to appreciate it.

"Thanks for everything," I say once I've slid my keys into my pocket and tugged my hat down low. I don't look at my phone screen. I don't even want to know yet if Madison ever called me back after the dozens of messages and texts I sent last night before getting shitfaced, blackout drunk seemed like the perfectly reasonable solution for my problems. "Honestly Gigi. I appreciate your help last night. And this morning."

She grins up at me, pink lips in a tight smile. "Anytime."

"I'll just..." Be awkward and make this suddenly ten thousand times worse. "Wait outside for the Uber."

She points to a door beyond her kitchen. There are two that are facing in an L-shape before the short hallway that leads to her bathroom. "Door on the right will take you down to the alley. Take care, Sebastian."

Right. Somehow, I like hotshot instead of my first name coming from her. Especially with the strange look she's giving me. Like I've upset her somehow. Or disappointed her. I know the look well from the last few years of my turmoil with Madison.

"See you around?"

"Whenever you guys stop in, I'll probably be here."

"Right. Thanks again."

"Bye, hotshot."

She turns back to her food and grabs her phone at the table. I've done something wrong. Only I can't figure out what. Which means when I leave, carefully trudging down the rickety metal steps outside to the alley and out to the street, my mind isn't on the lack of texts from Madison, it's on the look Gigi gave me when I told her I had to leave.

And that's not cool.

CHAPTER FOUR

Gigi

IT'S NOT the first time in the last week that I've walked into my bedroom, such as it is, and my gaze has gone immediately to where Sebastian passed out on Saturday night. It's not even the first time I've scanned the area and been embarrassed for the mess he so politely called me out on— it only took a slowly arching brow.

It *is* the first time I've walked in, cleaning bucket in one hand, vacuum in the other, determined to clean up my mess.

I've never been great at cleaning or picking up. It's easier to sweep all my dirty clothes off the floor and dump them in the basket I take to the laundromat. Since that's all a pain in the butt, I'm more likely to go buy new clothes than shuffle everything down the stairs, through the alley, and across the street to my parking spot in a private lot.

My mind constantly runs with a hundred things on my to-do list. I'd rather sit and read or go for a walk or spend an afternoon at a museum or strolling through the farmer's market than I want to be stuck inside, armed with a dusting rag and mop bucket.

While I know Sebastian's teasing of me was playful, watching him hop and skip around my mess was mortifying. I shouldn't even care what he thinks of me. I've never cared if people see me as I am before. And truly, his opinion of me shouldn't matter.

I'm the girl who helped him out. I'm the girl who serves him drinks with a smile. And I'm the girl who will never, ever be on his radar for a woman.

Besides, he's still technically *married*.

I'm being stupid. I haven't yet washed the sheets, mostly because I like the gentle waft of his body wash or cologne when I roll onto the pillow he slept on. And that's just gross.

Not at all me.

I don't get hung up on men. Or at least I haven't since Evan and I divorced, and even then I'm not all that sure I was hung up on him.

We dated in college for a few years and when our friends started getting engaged and married even before graduation, I think we both felt like it was the next step. The problem is Evan's an accountant and back then I was an art major. I'm art and colors and constantly reinventing things, even if it's only living spaces. He's straight lines and black and white and neatly pressed button-down shirts and slacks with the perfect seam ironed into them. Seams. He's the only guy I know under fifty who still insists on them.

I'm different colored hair and tattoos and Evan has always been, and always will be, short, conservatively styled haircuts, perfect posture, and content to drive a simple Ford Escort the rest of his life because it's practical. Yet somehow, for years we worked together. We partied and had great sex and he helped keep me focused on my studies and I forced him away from Excel spreadsheets. We worked... until we didn't.

I'm still pretty sure that day came when he came home from work and I'd painted a wall in our small living room in our first townhome a dark, very dark, purple.

He'd dropped his briefcase, ran a hand through his hair that didn't even move it was so gelled into perfection and sighed. "That's going to kill our resale value, Georgia."

I remember turning to him, head tilting to the side. There was still paint on my cheek and my T-shirt, and he'd cringed when he saw the splatters on my white shirt.

It was the cringe, the startling revelation of how vastly opposite we were with what we wanted out of life that made me ask, "Do you really think we should be married?"

It took him approximately two days and I'm still certain a half-dozen spreadsheets before he came home, with flowers—because he's *such a nice guy*—and a sad smile and agreed. "It's possible we made a mistake."

Months later we were divorced. I'd been the office assistant at an interior design firm at the time, a job I absolutely didn't want but made decent money.

Once the divorce was final, I was over all of it. I quit my job, looked at my dad and said, "I need to see the world."

He'd hugged me, cried, and replied, "Then spread your wings, butterfly."

That was my dad. It'd always been my mom, too. They were full of encouragement and love and laughter and dances in their kitchen and kisses when they knew it skeeved me out.

I'd been back for a year and my apartment still didn't feel like mine. This life didn't feel like mine and I had noth-ing... absolutely nothing I loved inside of it except for the prints I'd started to tell Sebastian about the other day. They were the only important thing in my life outside my dad. He'd cut me off, jumped like I'd electrocuted him while I told my stories and he'd hightailed it out of there so fast that me still enjoying the freaking scent of him on my pillowcases is borderline crazy.

It's time to clean. And armed with a fresh supply of heaving duty cleaning supplies, I get to work.

I hopped on a plane three years ago to see the world and figure out who I was.

I might not have figured it out in my travels, but the one thing I do know is that I am *not* the kind of girl who gets hung up on a married guy, gets a crush on him, and then refuses to remove the scent of him from a pillow.

The sheets get tossed off the bed first, thrown on a pile of my clothes and then I head to my kitchen where I fill four garbage bags with all my dirty clothes.

Once those are filled and my floors are relatively clean, the job seems much less daunting.

I spend the next three hours cleaning my room, scrubbing every inch of my floor. I get on Amazon and spend way too much money on bathroom and bedroom organizing shelves and bins and drawers. Any second-guessing myself is thrown to the curb along with the rest of junk I don't need.

No way am I stopping to consider I'm doing all of this on the off-chance Sebastian Hendrix ever steps foot into my apartment again.

By the time I'm done cleaning, sweat clings to parts of body where no sweat belongs. My hair is a ratted mess. Cleaning chemicals are my new perfume and my muscles shake so much I can barely start my Jeep Wrangler. The garbage bags filled with my clothes I've tossed into the back will take me a day and a half to finish at the laundromat, so I pick up the phone and call my dad while I'm on my way to his place a few miles away.

"Hey Dad... any chance I can swing by and cook you a good meal before you head into the bar?"

He laughs into the phone. "Let the laundry get away from you again?"

He knows me well.

"Something like that." I can't even see out my rearview window the bags are piled so high.

"Anytime baby. You know that. Besides, I already have a roast in the oven."

"Even better." My dad's cooking is kick-ass.

MY DAD IS one of the best men I've ever met. He's always seemed to understand what I need in my life before I realized I needed it. When Evan and I told him we were separating and divorcing, that we realized we'd made a mistake, I can still see the way his shoulders slumped with relief. When I decided to pack a large traveling backpack and go see Eastern Europe, those shoulders had tightened, with that fear and worry I assume all awesome fathers have for their little girls. Then he nodded, smiled that scared, small smile of his, and said, "Go then. If that's what you need to fuel your soul."

That's my dad. Always encouraging. Always understanding. When my mom died in a car accident during a brutal rainstorm on her way home from her work at a nearby hospital, my dad never once faltered in his love and support for me. I would hear him crying at night, missing the greatest woman I've ever known. His love for her was a palpable thing, as was his grief. Yet during the day, his red, sad eyes would crinkle when he smiled at me. He made the worst period of our lives only slightly bearable because of his strength and love.

He took what they always wanted for me—for me to be happy, to find my passion and my drive and live it to the fullest—and he never once tried to hold me back. He's always the guy I can go to. I can talk to him about anything and everything. Even boys. Somehow, he made that okay and safe for me. He never once balked at anything girly, like buying me tampons or asking if I needed to go on birth control.

He did all the things moms do and as a guy, a man's man with a slight beer gut and running a rundown bar that was his pride and joy, I always came first.

George Barnes likes the simple things in life, and he wants me to have everything I want and need.

It's what makes me feel like dirt for hiding the fact Sebastian spent the night in my apartment when he asks if Sebastian got in a cab all right that night.

"I should have known Steve would call you."

"You know he doesn't like you being alone at the bar with customers."

"Yeah. I know." I slide my fork through my dad's pot roast. Somehow, he makes a simple meal so tender and juicy, the meat melts in your mouth. "But Steve should also know I'm comfortable with it, and I'm a pretty good shot with the gun. He *is* the one who taught me how to use it."

We keep a nine-millimeter handgun behind the bar, loaded. My dad hates the reminder I might need to use it someday. But in all honesty, I've never been frightened when I'm there late. Our bar is south of Charlotte, skimming the suburbs. It's off the beaten path, but not an unsafe path, and most of the men who come in are guys like my dad. Many of whom I've known since birth. Also, the Ice Kings. Obviously, we have other customers, but while we turn a decent profit now, I know that if Dad hadn't paid off the mortgage on the building right around the time I graduated college, we'd be struggling to stay afloat.

I like the slowness of it. The family feel of it since I know most everyone. Charlotte's one of the top fifteen largest cities in the country, and yet our bar has a small-town, know everyone who enters, feel to it.

"You give any more thought to what you want to do now?"

Not this again. He's been asking me for the last few months if I'm looking for other jobs. I haven't once had the urge to try to find something.

I duck my head. "Not really. I'm happy where I'm at. You trying to get rid of me?"

"Never, Georgia. You know that. But that don't mean your old man likes the idea of you tendin' bar the rest of your life. Not sure it's gonna give you the passion you need."

See? Such a good dad. I get his concern. I'm the girl who always needs the next greatest adventure. I get bored sitting still and even while we're eating dinner my knee is bouncing. I need to be moving, reading, dreaming and then *going*. Spreading my wings.

Helping him run the bar is the exact opposite of me.

There's no way I'm leaving. Not with my dad's health issues in the last year.

But he doesn't want me to stay for him. He doesn't want me having those regrets. What he hasn't yet realized is that I'll never, ever regret a single moment where I stay and help him with something he loves and spending this time with him.

"I'm staying busy. Taking pictures. Doing what I love, but mostly, I'm loving being home for a spell."

"Don't ever hold yourself back on my account."

"I won't. I promise. And I'm not."

Dad doesn't know I've started a photography account on social media. It's mostly me, walking around Charlotte. The trails. Day trips to Kings Mountain and other places I can get to and back easily. He'd hate to know I'm off on trails alone, even if I stay armed with pepper spray.

He also wouldn't understand, but in the few months since I've started, I already have over forty-thousand followers and every time I post I get hundreds of comments from people with their excitement of where I've been, what I've eaten.

For now at least, if I can inspire others to travel and pursue new sights, that's good enough for me.

"So what was wrong with Hendrix, anyway?" Dad asks.

Dad's come to care about the guys, though. He's a huge fan, although I know he's never let on. When they first started coming in, he'd text me, even if it was the middle of night where I was, he was so excited. He didn't want to act like it since he was afraid they wouldn't come back. After a while, he got so used to acting like he didn't care who they were, it actually became not a big deal.

It helped that when they started coming, they weren't dicks with big egos. They drink a lot. Tip even better. And they're nice to everyone.

"Had a bad day, I guess." It's not my story to tell, but I hate lying to my dad. It's not like he'd say anything.

"Odd. He's playing well. Team is doing good, too."

"Yeah." I shove a bite of potatoes into my mouth.

"Careful with him, butterfly."

"He's married."

I haven't hidden my crush on him that well if my own father can tell.

"Exactly. That's why I'm telling you to be careful."

Yeah. It's good advice. If only my hormones would get the notice and react accordingly.

"I was there for him during a bad night, Dad. That's all. I swear."

Dad's eyes narrow on me and I feel like a teenager who broke curfew all over again. Luckily, the buzzer on the dryer goes off on my last load and I'm saved from further inspection with the lame excuse of gathering my things before they get wrinkled.

Later, when I'm back in my apartment, and I'm putting the freshly cleaned sheets back on my bed, I hate that I miss the smell of Sebastian on the pillow next to me.

Which definitely means he's trouble.

And I need to stay far away.

CHAPTER FIVE

Sebastian

"COME ON, Ben. I just want to talk to her."

"You know I love you like a son. You know that deep in my soul, but unfortunately, this time, I've gotta take my girl's back."

My jaw aches from holding back a curse. Ben Ritter has been my second father since the moment I took Madison to homecoming our freshman year of high school. Our lives are so damn entwined they can't be untangled. He's always been there, rooting me on. Hell, he was always louder than my own parents when he sat in the stands, freezing his ass off, years on end.

It's been over a month since Madison told me she was leaving to spend the holidays with her family in Minnesota. Three weeks since I was served divorce papers, papers I still haven't returned even though the deadline is coming up. I have at least called a lawyer and have a meeting with him later this week.

A part of me wants to give her so much more than she asked for. The other part of me wants to shake some damn sense into her and beg her to come home.

Which is pretty damn impossible considering she won't answer a single phone call. Hence why I've called her dad as soon as our plane landed back from a ten-day-long stretch of away games.

I figured calling in the big guns and talking to her dad would get me somewhere.

"Ben—"

"I can't do it, Sebastian. And it kills me. Kills me seeing you two going through this hell, hiding it, not telling us what's going on, but Maddie, she's a mess."

"Because she's not with me." My eyes burn and fuck. I can't stand this. "If she's in pain, it's because she knows she's doing wrong, here, Ben. Come on." I don't give two shits at how I'm begging. The quiet pain in Ben's voice is worse. He's torn up, torn between the two of us.

I'd feel bad about that if this wasn't my last shot.

"Yeah, but right now, she just wants her mom and dad and as much I think what she's doing isn't right, I also want to do right by her and give her what she thinks she needs."

I scan the hangar to make sure no one can hear me, but fortunately, everyone else on the team is still getting their bags.

"She's my wife," I grit out.

For the first time, that word seems to mean a whole hell of a lot less than it once did. We're supposed to lean on each other during hard times. She's supposed to let me give her strength. She's supposed to love me, damn it. Better or worse. All of that shit. Marriages survive worse than the hand we've been dealt. Quite possibly, it's talking to Ben, finally getting able to take out my anger on someone other than my punching bag in my workout room that I realize how absolutely, completely fucked up this all is.

Tears burn my eyes and piss me off even more. My fucking wife ran back home to mom and dad instead of turning to *me*.

Through the phone, Ben coughs and clears his throat. "Son…"

Not really. Not anymore. I'm too pissed off, too emotional, to call him on it. None of this is Ben's fault.

"Yeah." I sniff away my tears and pinch the bridge of my nose before someone sees. Jason's been giving me pretty consistent strange looks considering I've been in a piss poor mood off the ice and more aggressive than usual on the ice. I don't need to hear questions I'm not prepared to answer. "Tell her I called at least, would you? Tell her I just want to talk to her."

And that I love her. It burns, claws at my throat to say but they get stuck, lodged somewhere deep. Because damn it. I do love her. But is what she's doing loving me? It's so screwed up I don't even know what's right side up anymore.

"I'll tell her. Encourage her to call you back, but I can't make promises. She's in a state."

"Yeah. Aren't we fuckin' all? Bye Ben. Take care."

"You too, Sebastian."

I end the call. I'm not sure I've ever sworn while talking to Ben Ritter and I don't quite care now, either. Before I can take a second to think about what I'm doing, I pull back my arm and let loose as hard as I can.

My phone goes flying through the hangar, slams against the cement wall at the far end and falls to the floor. Damn case I have on it is so good the thing doesn't even look broken. At least there's that.

Saves me a trip to the store.

"George's."

I jump at the demand and glare at my teammate over my shoulder. "Not now, Klaus."

"Oh, yeah, fuck now. We're all going. Blow off steam tonight before heading home. We've earned this night and by the looks of that phone you just sent sailing, you need it more than most."

"I'm good." I go to take off, but his hand lands on my shoulder and clamps down.

"No, you're not. And even if we all have to carry you out of here and throw you in the back of Jude's truck, you're coming."

Klaus Newman and I are the same age, although he was only traded to our team a few years ago. Originally from Sweden, he's usually a pretty quiet guy. Looks like he's been working on his bossiness.

I keep glaring at him. There's a fire burning so hot in my chest it's amazing I don't self-combust.

Movement behind him catches my attention.

Shit. Jason and Jude and Sawyer and Byron are all standing there, arms crossed over their chests. Slow growing beards taking shape and hiding their pursed lips. They're scowling at me, all but Jason who looks more worried.

"I said I'm fine." I shake off his grip and go to grab my phone and when I get back, Jason has my bag.

"You're coming. Not kidding around. And you're not fine."

"Playing fine, aren't I?"

In reality, my game is better than ever. All the frustration and anger I've had the last month is getting taken out on the ice, in my speed, and abusing my body working out. I've scored more goals in the last away stretch than I did the first two months of the season. I'm also spending more time than ever in the sin bin but even Coach can't get too pissed when I helped the team to four wins out of the last five games. We're still up in the league by three games. I could not show up for a week and we'd still be in first.

"For now. You keep going balls to the wall like you've been doing though and you're setting yourself up for an injury, and that pisses me off. Hell, you even eating?"

My hands curl into fists. I might not be able to take Jason, but we could go a few rounds before we wear ourselves out. Although that would risk the injury he's pissed about. I'm also not sure I care much about that, either.

"Back down, Taylor." He might be one of my best friends. He also might be the only guy on the team who has a *hint* of why I'm in such a shitty mood off the ice.

Doesn't mean I won't take a swing at him, though.

He leans in and lowers his voice. "Come with us. Have a few beers. We're *worried* about you, Hendrix, because we give a shit."

"This whole night out planned for me?"

"Wouldn't be the first time we've done it. I seem to remember you hauling my ass out, too."

"Yeah, because you were a dick on the ice."

"And that swing you took at Thomas today wasn't you being a dick?"

He has a point. The winger for St. Louis probably didn't deserve that, but he'd been playing almost as physically as me.

"I show up for a drink, will it get you off my back?"

"Only if you stay for at least two."

"Seriously not in the mood for this," I warn him.

Jason grins. Now that he's happy with Tessa and they're shacking up together and he's getting laid on the regular with a woman he loves, he wants that goodness for everyone.

Problem is, when my personal life is imploding around me, I don't exactly want to be around happy people.

At least Gigi will be there. She'll let me drink whatever I want at the bar and help me ignore the guys if I want. I'm sure of it.

"Fine. I'll go."

The bigger problem is now I'm not sure if I'm agreeing to go to get the guys off my back...

Or if it's to see Gigi again.

BY THE TIME I get to George's, I'm of half a mind to turn back on Providence Road and keep heading south to my own home. It's only the reminder that the house is empty and my live-in housekeeper has already taken care of Bruiser for the night that has me triple-guessing myself in the parking lot of George's, hands wrapped around the steering wheel of my Maserati, glaring at the wooden sign with the faded paint of George's Bar in bright red.

My team is a great group of guys. After years of most of us playing together, our team is successful in part because there's been very few changes with trades, only welcoming new players during drafts and time to prove themselves. They're more like brothers. Their wives and girlfriends immediately welcomed as sisters. All except Madison, even though she was in the beginning.

The problem is the sadder she became, the more upset

about our lack of starting our own family, she withdrew when what she needed was support. And since she refused to allow me to help, allow me to tell anyone what we were going through because she was so embarrassed and upset about it, she continued to withdraw, began refusing to go to team functions with me. I'd had to practically beg her to allow us to throw a New Year's Party at our home last year, thinking maybe she'd remember how good these people were, how much they cared about us and how much they'd want to help us.

But even that night she barely kissed me when the ball dropped and then disappeared off to our bedroom. She went to bed and the party continued on.

Maybe everything would have been easier had I let them know more earlier. At least then they would have understood. Madison didn't want the pity and false hope in the beginning. So I tried to keep her away. I tried to keep her happy. I tried to ignore the looks from the team when she started being bitchy and bitter they were all having their own kids and we weren't. I tried to be accepting when the medicine she took made her hormones fly out of whack. Or when I had the flu and she was ovulating, and she still insisted we had to have sex.

Let me tell you—

Fucking your wife with a hundred and two temperature while trying not to puke and doing it only to get your sperm inside of her was not fun. Or enjoyable. For either of us.

I'm not even sure when the last time was we had sex for fun. I don't know the last time either of us woke up on a Sunday morning, even during the off-season when I had nowhere to be and reached for the other. When we spent a weekend tangled in sheets only pausing to shower and order pizza, which we ate in bed so we could get re-tangled in the sheets again.

Our intimacy became tied to a doctor's appointment or a line on an ovulation stick. But even with all of that I tried...

Damn it. I am so damn tired of trying so hard.

A pound on my window makes me jolt. I turn to see Duke's ugly mug grinning back at me. I slap my hand to the window to piss him off and shut off my car.

He steps back and as soon as he hears the doors unlock, opens my door.

"Get the hell out of here. Time to stop moping."

"I'm not moping." I wouldn't call what I've been doing moping. I've been angry. Confused. Extremely pissed off. Worried. Moping? I haven't had the time for that.

"Sure you are." He throws his arm over my shoulders and shoves me toward the bar with him like I'd run if he didn't force me inside.

Not entirely inaccurate, but I shove him off.

"You smell, Fletch."

He shoves up his arm and sniffs his armpit. "Nah. That's good old-fashioned Old Spice right there." At twenty-five, Duke reminds me a lot of myself. He's also married to his high school sweetheart, Regan, who's a total doll and possible half-angel for putting up with this guy. He's off the wall bonkers. He's the guy you want at all the parties. He's the fun guy, the loudmouth, the beer drinking, down to earth, rabble-rouser as my grandpa would call him.

Tonight, he's the last person I want to be around.

He throws the door open to George's and for a moment I don't immediately realize my eyes have gone straight to the bar.

Where a tiny little thing in a tight black shirt and her hair in pigtails is busy pouring drinks. Black towel tucked into the back of her jeans, I notice when she turns away.

Shit.

I shouldn't be here.

CHAPTER SIX

Gigi

I TENSE UP AS SOON AS Jude and Jason saunter into the bar, grinning happily due to their win earlier. They lift their hands in a hello gesture to me, request three pitchers of a wheat ale and as many clean glasses as I have before taking up a few tables on the far side of the bar near our pool table.

Steve and Tim are in their usual spots at the bar, sipping their drinks, talking about the game. They tell the guys good game before looking back at the television screens above the bar.

I grab what Jason and Jude request, bringing a pitcher and a few glasses to start with over to where they've made themselves comfortable in a booth by the pool table.

"Saw that y'all had a great win tonight."

"Can't complain," Jude says. His dark hair flops over his forehead and he shoves it back. "How's it been here lately?"

"Quiet. Dad and I do somethin' to offend our favorite

customers? Y'all haven't been in much." I haven't seen anyone on the team since New Year's when Sebastian was here.

"Just got done with a long away stretch. Figured we could blow off some steam before heading back out again in a few days."

"Saw the game. You're playing great."

"That's because I'm the best," Jude says, grinning and filling his glass.

"She meant the team, dumbass. Besides, we all know I'm better."

Brothers. These guys are a trip.

"Two hundred bucks says I'm better than you at pool."

Jason grabs his wallet from his pocket and thumbs through a thick stack of cash before slapping down two one-hundred-dollar bills. "You're on, dipshit."

"The team coming in too?" I ask as they slide out of the booth, grinning at each other in that way I know there's bound to be some serious shit-talking coming soon.

"Yeah. Most of the rest will be here soon."

"Good. I'll bring out the rest of the pitchers when they get here."

"Thanks, Gigi," Jason says. "Your dad on tonight, too?"

"He's in the back office right now. Need him?"

"Nope. Just making sure you're not here alone. It might get busy."

"We'll get you handled."

"Always do. That's why we like it here so much." He grabs for his wallet again and hands me another hundred dollars. "This is for a bottle of your best bourbon. Bring that to the table with a few shot glasses, too okay? On me."

"Maker's Mark?" I ask before I can stop myself. I

haven't been able to pour a glass of bourbon without thinking of Sebastian and wondering how he's doing.

"You know Sebastian's favorite drink?"

Unfortunately. I slide the cash into my pocket and shrug.

I attempt an innocent expression. "Is it for him?"

Based on the narrowing of Jason's blue eyes, I fail. "Right."

"Hey old man!" Jude shouts. We both turn to him where he's chalking up the tip of his cue. "You get so old you need a cane to get your ass moving or what?"

"Brothers," Jason mumbles, winking at me. "Little brothers are a pain in the ass." He grabs his beer and heads toward the table.

I trudge back to the bar and try to shake off the sudden, strange tingling sensation in my fingertips.

Sebastian and I have done nothing wrong. So why does it feel like I lied to Jason for no reason?

If he's surprised I know what Sebastian drinks he either doesn't realize I'm a bartender and that's my job, or Sebastian hasn't told anyone of his night getting skunk drunk at my bar.

I'm back where I belong, filling pitchers and setting up more glasses on a tray to take when my dad makes his appearance, first going over to where Jude and Jason are and shakes their hands.

He's moving slower these days. He gets mad at me when I ask him about his health, but he isn't losing the weight the doctors have told him he needs to. Fortunately, when he was hospitalized and I got the phone call from my aunt, it wasn't anything serious and the doctor said he was overworked and needed to slow down. Not that he's done much of that, either.

"When it's my time, it's my time," he always mumbles when I try to get him to do something different.

The problem is, when it's his time... it leaves me alone. And I'm not ready to think about that yet.

For now, I smile as he clasps Jason and Jude on the back, watch as he jokes with them and hangs out while they shoot pool, and I slowly brace myself for the arrival of Sebastian. If another bottle of bourbon has been ordered, means he's most likely not in any better of a mood than he was the last time I saw him.

I'm aware of the exact moment he walks into the bar. I'm serving Sawyer a fresh bottle of beer, and I'm not facing the door at all, but I still know it's him. Partly because Sawyer turns in that direction and he tenses. The bottle of Maker's Mark Jason paid for earlier is still sitting untouched, unopened, like he's not letting anyone touch the thing until Sebastian arrives.

"Thanks, Gigi," Sawyer says, shoving a ten-dollar bill into the tip jar.

When I turn back toward the door, I catch Sebastian. Another of their defenseman, Duke Fletcher, is at his back, and he's pushing Sebastian toward the table, pointing.

Sebastian's features are tight and he looks worn down. It's one glance I give him, a moment, where I watch him but as I catch him turning to look at me, I quickly glance away.

I'm here to work, not worry about how a guy I barely know is doing.

"Hey Steve, Tom. Need anything?"

Steve lifts his almost empty glass. "One more round, I think, butterfly, then it might be time for Tom and me here to take off."

"You got it," I say, but my dad's hand on my shoulder stops me.

"I've got Steve and Tom. You go see if Duke and Sebastian need anything."

"I think they're covered." They're already at the table where Jason and Jude have full pitchers of beer and the bourbon.

Sebastian is untwisting the bottle while Jason says something to him, and then he stops. Scowls at Jason. The bottle.

He turns and faces me, one brow arched.

I have no idea what he's trying to silently communicate but I give a quick shake of my head. *No. I didn't tell them anything. Promise.*

He dips his chin, opens the bottle and takes a long pull straight from it while Jason watches him.

Worry is stamped all over his handsome, but not nearly as sexy as Sebastian's, face.

"Damn," I whisper, more to myself than anyone.

This isn't good. It's also none of my business so I check my inappropriate curiosity, shove it into a box in the far corners of my mind and make my way across the bar, grabbing a few emptied bottles on my way and stopping to say hello to the guys.

By the time I reach Sebastian's table, he's at least two shots in, sitting back on his bench across from Jason. Both are scowling at each other.

Odd how it wasn't that many months ago I saw these two men in a similar position, except that night, Sebastian had been smirking and doing most of the talking while it was Jason who was scowling.

Now, you couldn't smash the tension between these two by dropping an anvil on the table.

I power through the thick fog of fury wafting between

them and put on my happy smile. "Anything else I can get for either of you?"

"Nope." Sebastian doesn't look at me as he talks, but he slams another shot and clunks it back to the table.

He's no longer slouched, but ramrod straight on his bench. The stupid part of me wishes he grew tense from me or is at least reacting to my presence.

The smart girl inside me kicks that girl in the butt and turns to Jason.

"Jason?"

He graces me with a smile I'm sure sends his girlfriend Tessa into fits of lust right before she jumps him, but fortunately, does nothing for me. "No, Gigi. I'm good."

"You sure?"

I scan both of them. Sebastian hasn't once looked at me and that hurts.

It's not like I expect him to be besties with me after spending a night in my bed—*alone*—but to all out ignore me?

Whatever.

"Fine," I grumble. "Enjoy your night."

THE STUPID, insignificant moment has cast a pall on my mood through the night. The guys didn't show up until eleven, and it's growing closer to last call. Some of them have left, but it appears that the Taylor brothers are in absolutely no rush to leave without Sebastian, so the three of them along with Klaus and Duke have still been piled around a table. I can tell from where I've planted myself behind the bar that none of them are exactly having a blast.

There's been no more pool playing, no more brotherly teasing.

As far as Sebastian, his rigid posture and steely gaze directed at the men across from him have given me enough of a clue as to how his night is going. Fortunately, the bottle is only half-gone, so at least he's not getting smashed out of his mind again.

I also hate I've been paying attention, looking for any indication of that smile I like so much, or the hungover, but slightly amused expression he gave me that morning in my apartment.

"Hey Dad?"

"Yeah, butterfly?"

His back is to the bar and his eyes are glued to a basketball game. Since I don't give a flying fig about basketball, I'm busying myself with cleaning up the bar, putting away the clean glasses, Kollin, our dishwasher, completed before he clocked out an hour ago.

"Go home." He has dark circles under his eyes and I hate how the late nights here have seemed to make him more rundown in the last few months. We're not rolling in it enough to hire a large staff, but we have enough set aside to at least hire another bartender. We have Dom, but since he's a college student in Charlotte, his schedule is erratic and he's unable to work a lot during the school year.

"I'm closing down."

Stubborn old fool. "No. You're not." As I scold him, he hides a yawn behind his fist and shakes his head. "Go home, Dad. You're tired. I've got this."

"Hate this for you," he says and turns, finally facing me.

"What?"

"This." He swings out an arm. "Hate this for you. This was the bar I wanted because I always wanted a bar. This isn't you. You're here because you're worried about me and you should be scaling Mt. Everest or something equally crazy."

"Dad. We've talked about this." He scowls at me and to erase it, I quickly add, "I hate the mountains."

His responding eye roll couldn't be any more exaggerated. "If I wouldn't have had that scare last year, would you be here?"

I'm not sure what's brought on this argument we've had a half-dozen times since I've been back, but between the already difficult night and this, I'm raring for a fight.

"Maybe. Maybe not. But I *am* here, and I like being here. I like being with you. If I didn't want to be here, I wouldn't."

"You say that, but—"

"No buts."

He sighs, thick shoulders heave with the weight of it. "Your momma. You're so much like your momma. Stubborn to the core, beautiful to the soul. Don't know what I'd do without you, butterfly."

My eyes burn, like they do every time my dad mentions my mom. Linda Barnes was beautiful. Taller than me, but I have most of her looks. Sometimes my dad gets a sad smile on his face when he looks at me, and I know as much as he loves me, he still misses her a thousand times more.

"I like being here. And I don't want to have this conversation again. If, or when, I decide to take off again, or go find something different, I promise you I won't hesitate."

"You haven't seen old friends since you been back."

That's mostly because I've been busy working. With very little staff, I do most of the late shifts, kicking my dad home before it gets too late and he gets too tired. Tonight's one of the rare ones where he's stayed.

"Evan got the friends in the divorce." I flip my towel in his direction. "Now go home. Stop worrying about me and start worrying about your health. I'm good. Promise."

His mouth opens like he wants to say something but then his gaze goes to something behind me.

"All right, butterfly," he says, finally looking at me again. "I'll take off. Be safe, though, okay?"

"Always." I kiss his cheek and turn to the person who caught his attention.

Hotshot. Of course it is.

"What can I get for you?" I ask Sebastian. His gaze follows my father and slowly comes back to the bar. To me. It takes effort to force myself not to react to the quizzical way he's looking at me, but I manage.

"You're divorced?"

"Yep."

I have no problems telling people of my time or my marriage to Evan. We were young. Made the wrong choice. Fixed it when we realized, and to this day, we're friendly and amicable when we see each other. He's now engaged again to a woman who teaches pre-school, someone much more suited to his conservative and simple ways.

I could go on and on with Sebastian, telling him all of it, because I haven't forgotten that his wife has recently left him, but I'm still pissed and hurt at his earlier behavior.

"Need another drink?"

His tongue slips out, sliding along his bottom lip as those beautiful green eyes narrow. Damn him for being so darn good-looking when I'm irritated with him. I have a feeling the look he's giving me right now has gotten him out of a lot of trouble in his days. Hard to be mad at someone who looks like the world's cutest and maybe saddest puppy.

"Gigi—"

"Drink, Sebastian. It's late. Last round. What do you need?"

That cute lip of his curls before it disappears into a thin line.

"One more pitcher for the guys," he relents, sounding unhappy with me, but whatever.

I need to remember these guys, Sebastian specifically, aren't my friends. Just because I see them every few weeks doesn't mean we're buddies. They're customers. Good tipping ones.

While I pour up the pitcher for them, I work at plastering on my professional, polite face. I'm feeling pretty good I have it back in place when I face him again.

"Here you go. Enjoy your night."

"Gigi. I didn't mean to be a jerk earlier."

"Okay." I take the twenty-dollar bill he's slid onto the counter even though the pitcher's only ten. "Need change?"

"No. And would you talk to me?"

"About what?" It comes out as a snap and I inwardly cringe. This is silly.

He jerks back, stunned and then he shrugs. I wonder if he's always been this sheepish or if it's something new. I've tried not to pay too much attention to him since he's married and all.

"Well, how have you been?"

This guy. A laugh bursts from me at the inane questions. "How have I been? Good, Sebastian. I've been just fine, same ol' same ol' over here. But shouldn't I be the one asking you that question?"

"Yeah." He scrubs his jaw, the beard on his cheek, and shrugs. "About that."

"How are you doing with Madison gone? You guys talk yet?"

"No. She won't have anything to do with me. Even called her dad today and he wouldn't put her on the phone either."

"Her dad?"

"Yeah. Ever since she left me, she's been staying with her family."

"Madison *left* you?"

The outburst comes from a newcomer. Sebastian's lips press into that line again, and his shoulders tighten before he turns to Jason, the new arrival. Behind him is Klaus, I think. Cute and blond, I know he was born in Sweden but has lived in Canada and then the States for most of his life.

He does not look cute right now, though.

Both guys look like smoke might plume from their ears at any second.

"Madison fucking left you and you didn't tell us?" Klaus sounds shocked. Pissed.

Jason looks like someone stole his most beloved possession.

"Maybe I shouldn't have brought her up." I take a step back, away from the sudden surge of male anger pulsing along the other side of the bar.

"No," Sebastian snarls at me. "You shouldn't have. But maybe I shouldn't have told you in the first place." He shoves the pitcher in Jason's direction, tosses another glare at me like this is somehow *my freaking fault* and grabs his keys from his pocket. "I'm out of here. You guys can have this."

"Hendrix—" Klaus calls out but Sebastian doesn't stop. Instead, the door flies open and he disappears out of it. The slam of it hitting the hinges causes a silence to fall over the whole bar.

Which is mostly his teammates.

"Shit," I mutter, staring at the door.

"Well fuck," Jason says. "Now I know why he's been in such a shitty place lately." He says it, speaking toward the door as well, and then his head swivels in my direction. "My question is... how in the hell did *you* know?"

I'm pretty certain I've said enough tonight. "Talk to your friend. I'm just the bartender."

And I've most definitely been reminded of my place.

CHAPTER SEVEN

Sebastian

IT OCCURS to me as I wake up from a night with little sleep, head thumping but not nearly as bad as the last time I went to George's, and replay the events of the night before... that I *might* have overreacted and been a massive dick to Jason. Not only to him, but all of my teammates, and worse, I was an absolute ass to Gigi.

She's been nothing but kind to me except for her attitude when I went to the bar and overheard her talking to her dad. Considering my earlier behavior, her bluntness wasn't unwarranted.

Worse, I only went to the bar because I couldn't stop trying to catch a glance of her all night. I tracked her around the bar, knew her every movement and yet every time she turned to look our way, I scowled at my drink.

It makes no sense. Why would I care where she was? Why would I like watching her pour drinks, kiss her dad, laugh with the other regulars at the bar?

Why did it make my jaw tic when she went and stood by the pool table when Klaus and Duke were playing, giving them crap, laughing along with them.

Why did I care about any of that when I was trying to hide my face from her? And worse... what difference does it fucking make anyway?

None of it does, but I'm not this guy. I'm not a jerk to my friends. I don't fly off the handle and storm out of a bar. I don't avoid hard conversations. Hell, the last two years of my marriage were filled with nothing but hard conversations. I should be a professional with them by now.

Sighing, I shove off my bed and hit the bathroom where I take a few minutes and get cleaned up. It's early, only eight in the morning and we have the day off since we have to hop on the plane again tomorrow. I have all day and nothing to do with myself.

Stupidly, a woman who *isn't* my wife is the only thing on my mind.

I might not have a chance in hell of making things okay with Madison, or save my marriage, but I can make things right with Gigi.

At the very least, I can apologize for my asinine behavior. I'm not ready to talk to the team yet. I don't want their pity-filled looks or slaps on the back. It's become such second nature to hide my struggles over the last few years, it feels much too difficult to begin explaining now.

Starting with Gigi will be easier. Then I might grow a set of balls and get the courage to return one of Jason's phone calls and texts he fired off last night as soon as I took off.

I used the excuse I was driving for not answering him when I was in the car. Once I got home and spent a few minutes playing with Bruiser before allowing him into my bed—somewhere he was never allowed *before*—then I used the excuse it was too late to call Jason. He'd be home with Tessa, his girlfriend and sister to teammate Sawyer. No way was I interrupting their late night.

But now it's morning, I hate feeling like a dick.

And if I don't get out of my house, the walls will start to close in on me despite the five thousand square feet of space I have here.

"Hey Bruiser." I pick him up and scratch his head.

When I mentioned getting a dog to Madison years back, I was thinking something big, loud, and scary looking. Like a mastiff. Or pitbull. Or a Rottweiler. I wanted a dog who would protect her when I was on the road.

She insisted on a Maltese.

So a Maltese it was.

When I'm on the road, I feel like shit leaving him alone so much. Even though Cara practically lives here now while I'm gone, he still goes batshit crazy for attention from me when I'm here.

I swear he misses Madison. When he sleeps, he curls up onto the spot on her couch where she always sat when he used to have to stay on the floor. I didn't even bother telling him to get off the couch the first time I saw him there, looking so pitiful.

Probably a lot like myself lately.

"Aren't we a matching pair?" I say, setting him on the floor where he does his standard three-circle spin before taking off down the hallway, barking at nothing.

After grabbing a shower, dressing in casual black athletic pants and a tight athletic top that zips from the collar to mid-chest, I slide into my running shoes and grab some coffee on my way out the door.

Bruiser, who hates car rides and almost always pukes

during them, is tucked away in his doggie room since I won't be gone long. I've fed him, scratched his ears a few more times and promised to give him lots of attention as soon as I get home. Probably outside in the pool because he loves to swim despite the mess it makes of his fur. He's one of the reasons why I keep it heated and ready to use all year.

Not that he cares about that, but I do.

I'm pulling up to the alley of George's Bar where there are very few parking spots. Most are marked for deliveries but since I'm only coming to apologize and not stay long, I take my chances. I close my door, push my sunglasses to the top of my head when the door to the second-floor apartment where Gigi lives opens and she steps out.

She hasn't seen me and for some reason I can't fathom, I don't call out to her to grab her attention. Instead, I take in the thin, black nylon bag strapped to her back like a backpack, the larger, black bag draped over one shoulder. Her skintight leggings match the black bags and cling to her short legs. On top, she's wearing a sweatshirt and on her feet are lime green sneakers. A groan bubbles in my throat as I watch her maneuver her way down the rickety metal stairs.

Something stirs inside me, in my groin, and I quickly pinch my eyes closed.

I should *not* be having this reaction to her. To any woman.

You're a married man, for Christ's sake. Get it together.

But am I?

Yes.

Or not really.

The internal argument makes me cringe. I open my eyes to see Gigi nearing the bottom steps, one hand on the railing like she's about to swing my way.

I have to end this. Perhaps for my own sanity than anything.

"Gigi," I call out.

Her shoulders tighten before she slowly turns in my direction. Her hair is up like it was last night, but instead of two ponytails from behind her ears she's rolled them into little buns on her head. Little puffs of purple are knotted tightly behind her ears.

"What are you doing here?"

Her eyes are hidden behind sunglasses so I can't see exactly how upset she is, but her expression says enough. She's *pissed*.

"I came to talk to you."

"No thanks. I've got places to be."

She hops off the last step. Unfortunately, she doesn't head my direction but away from me.

Fortunately, I have long legs, strength, and some damn good speed on my side so I catch up to her in several quick strides while she hurries away.

"Please. I want to apologize about last night."

"Seems to me," she says, flipping up her glasses and peering at me as the harsh sun shines directly on her, "that lately all you've been doing is apologizing to me and, no offense, Sebastian, but you're a customer. You want to be rude to the woman who serves you drinks, that's no big deal to me. I'll still take your money."

Ouch. I take the well-deserved shot.

"I'm really sorry, though. I was a dick."

"Mm-hmm."

She slides down her glasses and keeps hustling. Since I'm so much taller, my legs so much longer, it's more of a brisk walk for me. I can't help but smile at how small she is.

Pocket-sized. So petite I could throw her easily onto a bed.

Woah. The thought slams into me so hard I jerk back.

"What?" Gigi says, looking back at my sudden stop.

My mouth is gaping. Where in the hell did that come from?

I shake my head to clear it and unfortunately when I focus on her again, her head is tilted in a curious way. I swear there's a faint blush on her cheeks before she blinks and looks away.

Doesn't matter. I shouldn't be noticing any of that anyway.

"I'm really sorry, Gigi. It's not your fault my wife has left me and is still refusing all of my calls. It's not your fault I'm pissed about it, pissed about my marriage ending this way. And it's definitely not your fault I haven't told the guys on my team yet." I shove a hand through my hair, forgetting about my sunglasses, and they go flying to the cement. Before I can bend down to reach them, Gigi does, handing them to me as we both stand.

"I was a dick to you, upset with Jason for trying to get that information out of me and now he's pissed and hurt because I didn't talk to him. None of that should have been taken out on you last night."

Her eyes narrow, sparkling blue pools that are so bright they remind me of the ocean. For a moment, I'm lost in them until she smiles. It's so blindingly bright it almost steals my breath away.

Goddamn. I should go home and jerk off, get that out of my system so I stop gawking at this woman.

"Forgiven," she finally says and shrugs.

"That easy?"

She sighs, squints at the sky like she needs to think

about it, and my chest grows tight at the thought of her not meaning it.

Now is *not* the time to wonder why her forgiveness means so much to me. Something tells me if I think too hard about it, I might not like the reason. Mostly because I'm in no place to do anything about it.

"You're having a hard time, Sebastian. I get it, to an extent. And you owe me nothing. Yeah, you were a jerk last night but to be honest, I was more upset you ignored me earlier. I wasn't expecting that, so when you came at me with the other, it made me angrier than it should have. But we're good. Okay?"

She adjusts a black strap on her shoulder, bouncing as she does.

"Is that a camera?"

A deep line divides her eyebrows. "Yes."

"You going somewhere with it?"

"I plan on spending the day hiking, taking pictures out at Crowder's Mountain."

Crowder's Mountains State Park is less than an hour from us. Beautiful views especially on a cloudless day like this and warm for the last week of January.

"Mind if I go with you?"

"What?"

I shrug. I can blame my need for fresh air. The absolute sudden hatred I have of being in my house all alone.

Or, it's something far baser—I'm attracted to this woman despite it being the worst thing for me.

"Yeah. I like hiking and I don't have anything to do until we fly out tomorrow." I say it with as much nonchalance as I can to hide my desperation for her to not say no.

"Sure," she drawls slowly. "You can come, but I'm driving."

She points to her Jeep Wrangler, bright blue in color that doesn't surprise me one bit given her love of bright colors in her apartment and hair.

"Lead the way, captain," I say, teasing. "Will my car be okay there?"

"It's fine. I'll text Dad and let him know it's there so when he gets in, he doesn't have it towed, but we don't have deliveries planned."

"Okay then. Let's roll out."

She grins at me, that blinding smile again showing bright white teeth and a gleam in her eye before she lowers her sunglasses and they disappear.

"All right, hotshot."

CHAPTER EIGHT

Gigi

MAN. What a strange turn of events I was not expecting this morning. Sebastian's attitude last night kept me awake, tossing and turning more than it rationally should have.

So I have a crush on a guy I can't have. It's not the first time. Won't be the last. So he hurt my feelings.

Big freaking deal. It's life. It happens.

The only thing it reminded me of is that Sebastian Hendrix is a man who needs to be kept at a far distance from me. I'm way too susceptible to his sexy hair and beard, the sadness in his eyes, the strength of his body's frame. Every time I'm around him, I want to brush my finger along his cheek and tease him until he smiles a real smile.

Stupid.

I'm in no position to *heal* anyone, and the last person I should be trying to heal is someone who makes my heart skip a beat at the mere sight of him.

So why did I allow him to come with me, sitting close to

me in my Jeep, his hand tapping his knee to the beat of my country music playlist?

Because I'm an idiot. And glutton for self-inflicted punishment.

We've barely spoken since we reached the highway, both of us probably having no idea what to say, so I jump when for the first time in twenty minutes, Sebastian speaks.

"So, you're divorced?"

"Yep."

"Sorry."

"I'm not." I grip the stick shift to my Jeep harder than necessary. Next to me, his gaze is a heavy thing, barreling down on me.

"Don't want to talk about it? I get that."

"It's not that. Evan and I... he's a good guy. We still get along when we run into each other." I sigh. Sometimes, the reasons why we divorced seem so trivial. "We were young. Dated in college. I think he proposed and I agreed because our friends were getting married and it was the next step after college. Then we moved in together and realized outside of partying with friends and tailgating at football games, we didn't have a single thing in common. So we admitted our mistake, divorced, and moved on."

"And you took off to see the world?"

"Yeah." I grin at the windshield in front of me as we zip down 485.

"It was that easy? Ending your marriage?"

I peer at him quickly and am stunned by the tightness in his jaw.

"I think my situation is incredibly different than yours. They're incomparable. And no, it wasn't easy. It was sad. But Evan and I... I don't know how to explain it best because he's a good guy. He's kind. He's stable. He's the first one willing to help someone in need. He volunteers at homeless shelters. He's great. He's just... he's not at all what I want outside of that."

I watch as Sebastian shoves his hands down the tops of his legs. Veins bulge along the backs of his hands as he flexes his fists.

Before he can speak, because I'm not at all certain what'd he have to say if anything, I continue.

"Listen, we graduated when we were twenty-two. We'd dated for two years before then. He was an accounting major to my art major. He wanted to set up a townhome, start having babies and have me stay home and join the PTA. He wanted a simple life. I wanted to explore. See the world. I have things I want to do in my life. He wanted beige and brown all over our home because it was classic. I wanted to paint walls purple and he was concerned about the resale value. They were all small things, but they were incompatible long-term things. We realized it. We both recognized it, and then we corrected our young mistake. He's now engaged to a pre-school teacher who's absolutely perfect for him and I'm happy for him. What we had, that's a lot different from you and Madison I feel like. Don't compare my dissolved marriage to yours. No two marriages or reasons for ending them are the same."

I take the exit to head out west of Charlotte and it's miles before he speaks again.

"Madison and I, we both come from large families. She's one of four sisters. I have two as well. All of us are married, and all of them except us have kids."

He trails off, and I notice him bite his bottom lip between his teeth, staring out the side window. His chest heaves and I give him a second before asking, "Was that... is that something you want?"

"We tried for three years," he finally says, and God...the pain in his voice is brutal as he says it. "We've been trying. Doctors. Medicines. She's had surgeries for things she'd kill me if I repeated to anyone. We tried the natural way, the medical way... nothing."

"I'm so sorry."

He shrugs, but it's tense. I'm pretty sure the sadness growing inside my Jeep weighs as much as the vehicle itself. "She wants kids and the chances of us having them together are pretty much zero. That's why she left."

Together? The way he phrases it makes me frown, and I focus my attention on the road and not on the pain wafting off him in palpable waves.

"I'm sorry."

"Me too," he whispers.

It sounds ripped from his throat and my own clogs for him.

Every part of me wants to reach for him. To comfort him. My grip on my steering wheel tightens so I don't do something that stupid.

"A part of me thinks I should let this go. I get it. I get why she left. I get why she's hurting. And it pisses me off to know she can so easily cut off contact with me, end things and walk away without talking to me. I told you last night she's back in Minnesota, where we're from?"

I didn't know he was from there, but I nod. "Yeah."

"I called her dad to get her on the phone. Even he won't let me talk to her. Fifteen years I've loved her, almost half my life, and now she won't let me be there for her. Fucking kills. Deep down in my gut, it kills. And yet, if this is what she wants... if this is what will make her finally happy... shouldn't I want that for her?"

He groans, shoves his hands through his hair again and

plops his head to the back of the headrest. "I'm sorry, Gigi. You don't need this bullshit. You didn't even ask for this when we left."

"Curse of the bartender," I try to joke. Based on his lack of a smile, it doesn't work. "In all seriousness, I'm sorry. That has to be hard for you. Fortunately, you just spilled all that to someone who's happy to listen to you, happy to let you get that off your chest if you want and need it, but I have no advice. No sage wisdom for what you're going through."

He turns to me and licks his lips. "I think you've given me exactly what I need today. Thanks for listening."

My lips twitch. "Anytime, hotshot."

The last thing I notice before he turns to face the road and I do the same is his lips lifting at the corners.

Almost a smile.

Which makes me smile harder. I gave him that small grin.

I'M SO glad I took advantage of the warmer weather and cloudless sky to get out and do some hiking instead of walking around the city like I usually do this time of year. It's beautiful. With the temperature in the mid-fifties, I have a small line of sweat beading across my hairline and down my spine, and we're barely halfway up the trail.

Next to me, Sebastian is keeping pace easily, making my workout seem like a daily stroll for him. I'd be angry about it if he didn't look so good, if I couldn't almost feel his stress and sadness evaporate with every quarter mile we walk, and if he wasn't such good company.

The beauty of it is we've been quiet for the most part

except for me telling him to pause when I stop to take pictures, or when he warns me of something in my way as I hide behind my camera lens. As soon as I took my camera out of my black bag, he offered to take the vinyl backpack that holds some water and snacks, my car keys, and wallet. Since it's a pain to have that and the camera bag slapping my back and hip as I walk both bags are now slung over his shoulders giving me more freedom to pause whenever something catches my attention—whether it's the birds, trees or our view when we reach areas that allow us to see for miles.

We're close to the top when Sebastian finally shows signs this has been a workout for him. Meanwhile, I've been huffing and puffing for the last mile. I grit my teeth so I don't outright groan at one point. I can blame my shaking muscles. It's most like the view I get when he takes off his shirt and tucks it into his waistband.

Dear sweet heaven... wowzers.

"You were an art major?" Sebastian asks, turning to me. He lifts one hand over his eyes to block the sun shining on us.

I glance at him and almost lose my footing. It should be a criminal offense to be so good-looking, so out of my league. All wrapped up in one forbidden and most likely, uninterested package.

"Yep. Before I took off to Europe, I worked at an interior design firm, but I always wanted to be a travel photographer." I shove my eye to the camera and focus on the view.

"Is that what you liked working with the best?"

I hold up my camera and wiggle it. "Obviously, but I enjoyed all mediums. Watercolor paints were probably my best talent, though."

"Did you have any of those in your apartment?"

"No. Pretty sure those are all in Dad's attic in storage somewhere. I haven't done much since I came back home."

"But you like to go out and take photos? Just for the fun of it?"

I can't tell if he's teasing or genuine, so I lower my camera and risk stealing another breathtaking glance at him. When I do, Sebastian is at the peak of the path with me, hands on his hips. His gaze is out toward the horizon and I can't help myself.

I turn and snap a photo of him.

He turns to me and grins. "What was that for?"

I glance at the screen. To his jawline. The turn of his lips I can barely pick out from the edges of his beard.

"You look sad. But peaceful."

"Hmm." He turns back to his view and rolls his shoulders. "Thanks for letting me come with you today. For forgiving me about last night."

"I have an Instagram account."

"Don't most people?" His head falls to one side, along with his thick mop of hair.

What I wouldn't give to be able to run my fingers through it. They itch to move, to twist a wayward curl behind his ear.

I focus on his question, still unsure if he's teasing me or not. Hard to tell with all that solemnness he carries.

"I get out and take pictures around Charlotte and surrounding areas. Whatever I feel like, wherever I end up. I like showing people what they might be missing in their own back yards. I feel like people tend to get comfortable in their own areas, their own favorites. I want people to see the beauty in exploration, even if it's simply a different neighborhood."

He's silent for a beat before he asks, "And you're following?"

"Over forty-thousand." I grin. It's been less than a year and that's pretty impressive. I don't tell him some of my pics have been used in local travel brochures. Or that restaurants have asked to share photos to their website when I've tagged them. I don't tell him about the freelance job offers that have come my way. It used to be all I ever wanted, to get paid to take photos, but I'm not sure I want my muse to come from someone else's need to make a buck or two anymore.

"Is that still what you want to do? Professionally?"

"The only thing I used to want to be is a travel photographer. To get paid to see the world and take pictures of exotic locations."

"And now?"

I let go of my camera so it hangs from its strap around my neck and step closer to him. Sometimes I need to remind myself to see and experience my own images out from behind the camera lens and screen. "Now, I don't know. I loved the traveling I did. It was so thrilling. Exciting. Maybe partly scary since I was on my own. I learned so much about myself, about people and humanity in general. Then Dad had that scare..."

I can feel his interest on me, see the way his shadow is turned, paying attention to me, and I quickly blink away the emotion that threatens.

"I like being home too. I missed my dad when I was gone and until I can trust his health, I'm not sure I can leave again. He's all I have."

I shrug like the pain of losing my mom isn't still as piercing as a knife to the chest. All these years later and I still wish I could hug her and run to her for advice. She probably would have cautioned me about marrying Evan in the first place. But then I wouldn't be here. Enjoying this view with a guy who is easy to talk to, seemingly interested with his questions and not just along for the ride or being courteous.

"You're very interesting, Gigi. I'm not sure I've ever met anyone like you before."

And just like that, my heart trips all over itself. A bud of hope is planted before I can uproot it and toss it out.

Because Sebastian Hendrix is looking at me, smiling softly and sweetly. And I've done that for him.

"Is that a compliment?" I ask, teasing.

He laughs and shakes his head before swiping a hand through his hair. "Very much so."

CHAPTER NINE

Sebastian

IT'S BEEN two days since I phoned Ben. Thirty-six hours since I spent the day with Gigi, the first woman I've spent time alone with in my life who isn't either related to me or my wife.

I'm unsettled. Beneath my skin there's an incessant, needling itchy sensation I haven't been able to ignore.

I *like* Gigi.

And I'm still married.

What kind of man does that make me?

Regardless of how much I've tried, I can't forget Gigi's easy manner on our hike. How I spent six hours with her, hiking up that mountain, back down. We stopped and grabbed dinner on the drive back to her apartment where she left me in that alley.

It'd taken restraint not to follow her inside and take a seat at the bar while she worked.

It was that desire that forced me to thank her for the

day, hoping I ended it much less awkward than the other times I've walked away from her and get back into my car where I went home and fed Bruiser.

I took him out to the backyard pool area, tossed the ball around and afterward, blow-dried him so he wasn't soaking wet when I brought him to my bed. He then proceeded to do his three-circle spin move before plopping down on Madison's pillow.

Now I'm in the hallway at Pittsburgh's ice arena, head-phones in my ears, pacing the hallway and trying to ignore the clatter of pre-game rituals going on around me.

As soon as we got on the plane, Jason glared at me. He's pissed. Probably hurt. I never returned his call. I have to deal with that before the puck drops. There's no way we can beat Pittsburgh if we're not playing together as a team.

I need more time. A few more minutes to get my head on straight. Jason can't help me with that.

Only Madison can.

Which means, I need to do something I should have done weeks ago.

I have to go to her. I deserve an in-person answer if she's walking away from our marriage or to give it one last chance to see if there's anything worth salvaging.

Ripping off my headphones, I head back to the visitor locker room where all of our gear is stored. Jerseys are neatly hung, pads ready to go and skates tucked in the bins below. Our sticks are already out by the entrance to our bench on the ice, multiple extras in case we break one or two.

As soon as I'm about to open the door, it comes slam-ming toward me, making me jump back and out of the way. Jason's in the doorway, dressed in shorts and a T-shirt with sweat clinging to his chest which means he's spent the last half an hour since we arrived running the bleachers to warm up like he usually does.

"We need to talk."

"I know." I respond immediately, ignoring his glare. "Come with me while I go talk to Coach."

"Coach?"

"Yeah. Is Tessa on the trip with us, or is it Sylvia this week?"

We're starting a four-game away stretch. Sylvia is our regular travel director and earlier in the season she hired Tessa to be her assistant. One or both of them travel to most of our away games, especially when we have stops in multiple cities. They take care of everything for us, so all we have to do is take care of ourselves and focus on the game.

"Tessa is, but that's not telling me anything—"

"I need to make a flight plan."

"For what?"

I'm almost to Coach Wood's office, so I don't answer. Instead, I rap my fist on the window where I can see him scribbling down notes on a notepad he always has with him. Our assistant coaches tap wildly on their iPads, nodding and listening.

At my knock on the window, he looks up, waves me in before ushering the other coaches out.

"Hendrix. Taylor. What's going on?"

"No clue," Jason says. He wears a scowl well. He's getting impatient with me and I get it. But I'm only going to say this once.

"I need a few days off after this game, Coach."

"What the hell'd you say to me?"

"A few days. Maybe only two. I have a personal matter I need to look into."

"We just had two days off," he says. "And do you have any idea what this means for the team without you?"

"I know, and I wouldn't ask if it wasn't important."

"Someone dying?" he asks, and he doesn't say it to be an ass, he's just blunt. Coach cares for us which is why I know he'll give this to me, why I know the team will support me.

We're family, and I've forgotten that recently.

"My marriage." Coach's eyes widen. I push on even though vomit pools in my throat. It fucking hurts to admit it. "Madison left me and went back to Minnesota. Won't talk to me. I just... I need to get focused and in order to do that, I have to go talk to her. She just left, over the holidays. Didn't give me any warning and then served me divorce papers. She won't take my calls... I need this," I say after a pause.

Anger and embarrassment clog my throat. The looks they're giving me are only part of the reason why I haven't wanted to say anything.

"Damn, son. Hendrix, I get that, but..."

Next to me, Jason has gone strung tight too. They deserve to know everything. "Please, Coach. I'm hanging on by a thread. We, well, Madison and I, we've been trying to have a baby, and it hasn't worked. For years. News got worse back in December and she left. Now she won't respond to anything I do, calls or texts, and the other night I tried her dad, and he's holding up to what she wants."

"Hendrix—"

I can see the pain in his eyes. Feel it coming from Jason. Probably mixed with anger, too, but at this point, I'm done hiding what's going on because of Madison's wishes. I shouldn't have let it go on this long.

"She's struggled, sir. Struggled a lot. I'm worried about her... emotionally. Mentally. I have to see her. See how she is, see if there's a way to fix this or repair this. She runs from getting help from doctors to see about helping her cope with all this and now I'm just fucking scared for her."

It's not the first time she's shut me out like this. The problem is the last time she did it she cried for three days and then turned into a walking zombie where I was so damn concerned I called a doctor for her. She refused the help. I hid the knives and any strong pain meds I was that worried.

Madison not being somewhere where I can see she still has a damn pulse is eating a hole in my gut.

"You know you have my love, son," Coach says, and I almost smile despite the fear and pain I've only allowed others to have a glimpse of. Of how bad it's truly, really been lately. "You always have my love. How long you talking?"

And like that, I have his approval.

"Couple days. Minimum. I won't know for sure until I see her, tomorrow if I leave after the game tonight. I can meet you at the game in Dallas."

That's four days away. Missing our second game here in Philly before we head south.

"You okay to play tonight?"

"Yeah." Now that I have a plan. Now that I have *something* to do instead of sitting around waiting and worried. "Yeah, I can play tonight."

"Good. Then see that you do it and keep a check on the penalties."

That easily, I gulp in a deep breath. It feels like I can breathe for the first time since New Year's. "Thank you, Coach."

Jason's hand settles on my shoulder and squeezes. I close my eyes for a minute to fight back showing them more than I want them to see. When I have a lock on it, I open my eyes and meet Coach's gaze.

"You take all the time you need, son. We got this. Just make sure you come back ready to get us where we want to be."

"Yes, sir." I reach out, clasp my hand in his and he yanks me forward until I'm in a half hug, half back slap with him.

"You're good people, Sebastian. So is Madison. Beautiful too. Hope this trip gives you what you need."

I nod and squeeze his hand tighter but can't find the words to express how much this means to me. I've got a game to play. A schedule to change with Tessa, and a wife to go see.

When I pull back, I head out of the office with Jason who's already on his phone. "I'll call Tessa. Tell her what you need. You go do what you need to get ready."

"Thanks, Jason."

"You'd do the same for me."

He eyes me with all seriousness and that burn I felt earlier returns.

"I know. I would. Still, thanks."

"Nothing at all, brother. Nothing at all."

He takes off, phone to his ear, out of the locker room so he can have privacy, and I follow until I run into Newman and Conan and Chauncy out in the hall in a circle, juggling a soccer ball between the three of them. As soon as it catches air, I jump in, tap it to Newman and for the rest of our warm-up time, I hang with my guys.

My brothers.

My family outside my blood. For the first time in weeks, I actually believe everything might be okay, even if Madison and I aren't.

"I WAS WONDERING when we'd see you."

My mom's hug is warm and tough, and I fall into it easily. I might be almost thirty years old, but there never has been and never will be, anything better than my mom's hug.

"Thanks, Mom. Dad sleeping?"

It's practically the middle of the night, and he's always been an early to bed early to rise kind of man. I'm not surprised Mom waited up for me when I called her after the game to let her know I was headed home. It's way too late to see Madison, so I'll do it first thing tomorrow.

"He is." She pulls back from the hug and places her palms at my cheeks. At barely five foot four, she has to tilt her head back to look at me. "You doing okay? Saw Madison's parents at church a few weeks ago. Said she was home for a bit."

"Yeah. She's home. Been here since before Christmas."

"And you didn't tell me?"

"I was thinking she'd come back at some point." How utterly stupid of me.

"Oh honey." She pats my cheek with one hand and steps back so I can finally enter my childhood home. When I made it in professional hockey, I tried to get Mom and Dad to let me buy them a new home. Somewhere with space for all of us when we come back and for my sister's kids. When we're all home, it's a crush to be in their modest split-level home, but they always resisted.

Now, groggy and exhausted and thinking of only tomorrow and what in the hell I'll say to Madison, there's comfort in seeing my childhood school pictures lining the short stairway down to my room and their rec room. Upstairs is the kitchen, living room, and three bedrooms. Downstairs has always been mine with my own bedroom, full bath, and a room that had been large enough for me to run around and be a boy. All my youth and high school hockey trophies still fill the shelves.

"I'm beat, Mom. We'll talk in the morning, k?"

"You bet. It's good to see you, though. Despite everything. And Dad wanted me to tell you good game tonight."

"Thanks." Somehow, I'd been able to focus. Scored a goal and stole a few passes from Pittsburgh in our win, we didn't clinch until the last few minutes of the third period. "Tell Dad I'll see him before he heads to work in the morning."

He's been a high school history teacher and soccer coach his entire career. Thirty-five years he's taught and he still always, every morning, gets up early and goes for a run unless it's too cold to be outside. Minnesota hasn't had snow in the last few days and it's only a hitting a low of single digits overnight. As long as the brutal winds don't hit, he'll be out and back before I wake up.

"You don't have to."

"Doubt I'll get much sleep anyway." My mom's lips press together into a frown and I kiss the top of her head. "Don't worry about me, Mom. We'll figure this out."

"She's a lovely girl," Mom says, and I almost laugh. She's called Madison a girl since she was eight, even though she's grown now. "You know we love her."

"I know."

"But I also hope you know we love you *more* and just like we always have, we're here to support you and love you with whatever happens."

I swallow the lump in my throat. This is so damn embarrassing. I'm not even sure how much my own mom knows. How much Madison has confessed to her parents over the years because she always said she didn't want anyone to know. With the way Mom's looking at me now, something tells me she understands more than maybe even I do.

"Night." I lean down and kiss her cheek, grab the bag I dropped in the small entryway as soon as I entered. "Love you."

"You too, honey."

CHAPTER TEN

Sebastian

THIS MOMENT IS such a stark reminder of the phone call I had with Ben Ritter only days ago it makes me wonder if I'm experiencing some kind of funky déjà vu.

Except that's not possible because instead of refusing to put Madison on the phone, he's currently on his front porch, small enough we both barely fit, blocking my view of the closed door behind him.

"Ben."

His arms are crossed. Pain slashes his face every time I call him that. I've called him dad since I was eighteen. I'm not feeling very familial with him or the rest of the Ritter clan at the moment.

"You should be in Philadelphia."

I don't exactly like knowing he's been following my games. Are they all sitting around, cheering me on while my *wife* refuses to see me? Or are they bashing me on the ice in solidarity of their daughter?

My hands ball into fists. "I need to see her."

Behind him, the door opens and through the glass storm door, I get a glimpse of the fiery red head of hair I'd recognize anywhere. I step to Ben's side and my jaw falls open.

"Madison." Without thought, I reach for the door only to have my forearm gripped by Ben's hand.

"Son..."

"I'm not your son. Not anymore." I glare at Ben and quickly revert my attention to Madison.

She looks horrific. Sunken eyes with dark purple rings below them. She looks like she's lost at least twenty pounds on a frame that didn't have an ounce to lose. Her red hair is messy and wild, pulled into a mess at the top of her head with small pieces frizzed out along her temples and behind her ears.

"It's okay, Dad," she says, and I realize she hasn't once looked at me. "I can handle this."

Her voice is scratchy, sounding as wrecked as she looks and when Ben drops my arm, I yank the storm door open, take the one step into a house that has always felt like my own home and pull her into my arms.

Pale, thin, and cold even though she's wrapped in layers of clothes and a chunky black sweater.

"Madison," I say again on a breath.

Her arms are at her sides. Her entire body tenses. I hold her for a moment more, hoping she'll relax into my hold.

My eyes burn and tears I've kept at bay for so long beckon and come forth. She smells the same, flowery and sweet, but she feels so much different.

Small hands come up to my chest, I barely feel them through the wool pea coat I grabbed before heading over.

"Sebastian." She says my name with a small amount of

pressure on my chest, pushing me back. "You shouldn't be here. You have a game."

"This is more important."

"Madison, it's cold outside," Ben says, and I glare at him again.

He shakes his head and lifts his arm. "You kids go on in. I'll go warm up my car to get to work."

He turns and hurries down his driveway, hands shoved into his suit coat, head down and shoulders hunched to block the biting chill of the wind.

"You going to let me in?" I ask, turning back to Madison.

She shivers from a quick burst of arctic wind and good Lord, as much as I love Minnesota, I do not miss the miserable winters.

"There's nothing to say I haven't already said," she says, but she still steps back farther into their split-level entry. It's so similar to my own home with a smaller landing and my thigh hits the door handle to the door leading to the garage. I flinch from it but brush it off.

"I think there's a lot to say, Mads."

She shrugs and curls the sweater tightly around her, nodding toward the downstairs. "Let's go down there. Emma's here and she and Archer are still sleeping upstairs."

"Archer's here?" For a moment, I'm thrilled at the idea of seeing my eight-month-old nephew. Then I realize I'm not exactly welcome. Wanted. Desired. Hell, I'm not even sure I can still consider the little guy my nephew anymore.

Madison's face scrunches and I grind my teeth together, but I wait until we're down the short flight of stairs and she closes the door behind me.

"Have you told them? Does your sister know how much it hurts you to see him?"

"She's trying to help me and be there for me." Her voice is monotone and I hate it.

There was a time, over a decade ago, when Madison was one of the liveliest people I've ever met. She'd stand on her feet and shout so loud during my games her voice would be almost this hoarse by the time I was done.

She was always studious, had a serious introspective side, but when she was ready to play, she did it hard, without remorse or regret.

Until infertility happened.

"So you haven't told them?" I'm aghast. "How can you... Madison... why do you do this to yourself? She has to know she's not *helping* you by shoving her baby in your face. Hell, she's staying here?"

Goddamn it. The need to defend her is so damn strong and this is what I've always hated. Madison the martyr. She doesn't want to upset anyone, doesn't want to make anyone else feel bad so she internalizes all of it until she can't handle it. Then she turns inward.

"This was a mistake," she says. "You shouldn't be here and there's nothing left to say. I said everything I needed to."

"In a letter—" I grind out. "And with divorce papers without talking to me. Did you really think I would just walk away?"

"And I did all that because you're not *listening*. I can't do this anymore. I can't want this and fail to give you what you want and now we know it'll never be possible."

"There are options—"

"I don't want those!" She cringes at her raised voice and squeezes her eyes closed. "Damn it, Sebastian. It's over."

"We're *married*," I stress. "Committed. Better or worse. Or have you forgotten that?"

"Well maybe I'm tired of living the worse all the time."

She snaps the words out and they lash at me like a whip. Painfully slicing open my skin and ripping open my heart.

"The worse?"

Her chin trembles and her gorgeous blue eyes have no more beauty in them. Only dullness and pain. I've spent fifteen years being there for her. Fifteen years where I've comforted her and encouraged her and tried to support her in following her own dreams so she wasn't all tangled in my demanding career. I've done everything, damn it. Not perfectly, I admit. But this? It was the *worst?*

Logically, I get it. The last few years have been the worst. But things could always be worse than not being able to have our own child.

"What about... we talked once... a while ago, about having one of your sisters carry the baby."

We'd hated the idea. What if Grace or Sarah, her older two sisters who both have their own children as well grew too attached? How would that complicate things? I didn't like thinking of possibly having to fertilize her sister's egg.

Madison blinks. "And whose sperm would we use?"

She says it with a drawl heavy with sarcasm, almost disgust.

And damn her. I've never thrown this in her face. Ever. I've never intentionally made her feel less like a woman because she can't do this.

I know this side of Madison though and as much as it hurts, I know when I've reached our impasse. Hell, I should have already known what condition she's in. She's not in the mental place to think clearly.

"I can give you time—"

"No. I want you to sign the papers. I didn't ask for much."

The force of her words throws me back a step.

I'm speechless. I've known she thinks it's over. But this isn't the first time she's been so upset with disheartening news she turns on me. We've always worked it out. That's why when she left for Minnesota, I figured we'd talk after the holidays. But I never expected it'd turn to this.

"Face it, Sebastian. It's over." She unwraps and rewraps her sweater, tying the belt at her waist tightly.

Damn. She's so damn skinny.

How can her family not *see* this? Or push for the real reason?

I can only imagine what she's said. *"Sebastian's gone all the time. I'm lonely. It's too hard."*

Sure, that's all true. I have absolutely no doubt about it. But that's not *why* she's doing this.

"Madison—"

"I've already made up my mind." Her voice is cold. Almost as arctic as the cheek-burning wind outside.

She means this. Down to her soul, she means this and standing here, unwelcome in a home that's been as much mine as hers for so many years... I feel it.

The emptiness in her.

Her love for me.

It's gone.

All of it's gone.

Perhaps it's shock. I must be in shock. But this hurts so much less than I imagined it would. Maybe it's because I've had so much time of her being gone to imagine this actually happening, even if I still doubted it.

Why am I fighting so hard to save something that's already been destroyed?

"It ends this way?"

She shrugs. Bites her bottom lip. My chest constricts from how unhealthy she seems.

Madison is elegance and refinement. She's always showered and dressed and looking like she could be ready for the occasional gala we do for the team at a moment's notice.

She's never disheveled. Un-showered. Wrapped in leggings and oversized cardigans without makeup.

She's a mess.

I might be a bigger one as I stand here watching my wife put the final stake in our marriage. There's not a damn thing I can do about it this time.

"You're sure," I say and it's more of a statement than a question.

She nibbles her bottom lip. "Yup."

We stare at each other for a moment. I expect her to apologize. To cry. To fall into my arms and weep and say she doesn't mean any of it, she just *hurts* so damn much and doesn't know how to fix it.

When I realize I have nothing to say because I know there's nothing I can, and she doesn't either, I nod once.

"I hope you know I'll always love you. And I hope you get the help you need."

I'm not just talking about her infertility. I'm pretty sure us not being able to have children caused her to have depression. Or exacerbated it. Something. I don't even know because whenever I bring it up she glares at me with narrowed slits for eyes and lips that could spit fire if she were to open them... much like she's doing now.

That's it then.

If she won't seek the help she needs, there's not a whole lot I can do to help either of us.

I turn, unable to say goodbye to her, knowing if I lean in and kiss her she'll push me away.

Perhaps that's why she left the note in the first place. It would make it easier because this sure as hell didn't help anything.

By the time I'm outside, I'm thankful for the chilling whip of wind and that Ben is outside, smoking a cigarette at the driver's side of my mom's SUV I drove over. He rarely smokes, only when drinking or stressed.

I bet he's been smoking more lately.

I make a split-second decision because I know he's out here waiting for me, probably trying to tell me some fatherly advice that's no longer his to give. I don't want to hear any of it.

He can't be filled with wisdom when he doesn't know the real problem.

With my keys in my hand, I beep the locks on Mom's Toyota 4-Runner and meet Ben.

"We can't have kids," I say without preamble or politeness. His brows shoot sky high. "Tried for years. It messes with her head and she doesn't want you all knowing. That's only part of what this is. My suggestion... get Emma and Asher out of the house. The baby being around Madison is *killing her*, and then get her some damn help. Mentally. Professionally. She needs it, and she's never been willing to take that truth from me when I've tried to get it for her."

I walk to my door, forcing him to take a step back and swing myself up into the driver's seat. Before I close the door, I look at the man who's been my father-in-law, my supporter, a great man and provider with four incredible girls, other sons by marriage, five grandbabies. He's a man who wants to help everyone, and I know he'll do right by Madison.

I'm done hiding the truth for her. She needs the help and clearly it can no longer come from me.

He glances at his house, back to me, face paling in a way that has nothing to do with the weather. "We... we didn't know."

I already knew that.

"Take care, Ben. Of Madison and yourself. You're a good man."

Before he can answer, I pull my door closed and back out of their driveway.

By the time I'm at the street, he's thrown one cigarette into the snow and is digging a fresh one out of the pack.

Three days later, after a loss our second night in Pittsburgh, we win against Dallas.

I don't score but I block the hell out of the goal for Maddox.

But I play well enough for Coach to lose the concerned look he gave me when I showed up at the arena.

We're getting ready to board the plane to Charlotte where I'll head back to my empty home and it's the last place I want to be.

Somehow, seeing Madison gave me a little bit of what I wanted. Closure, in a form I don't particularly like and am pissed off about, but there's a sense of freedom that's been lifted.

I'm no longer holding her dirty, dark secret as she calls it. Now, hopefully, she can get what she really needs from her family instead of internalizing everything.

I turn to Jason once we're seated on the plane. "Listen, I know you've been gone a while, but—"

"George's?" he asks and this is why he's such a damn good friend.

"Yeah. If that's all right. I could use a night."

To get it all off my chest. To go home so tired and slightly drunk I fall asleep as soon as I get home.

"I'm here, man. Anytime."

I hold up my fist and he hits his against mine. "Thanks, man."

CHAPTER ELEVEN

Gigi

I'M worried and it's stupid. It makes me stupid for being worried, and yet I've bitten off more fingernails from nerves in the last few days than I have in years.

Sebastian wasn't at their game in Philadelphia a few nights ago. Announcers said it was a personal decision made by him and the coach, and that's all he'd give.

He's back tonight in Dallas, playing well, and while announcers are speculating during the game on his strange absence considering he's having one of the best seasons of his career and he doesn't appear injured, I'm still worried.

Which is what makes me stupid. Also, because I went for a hike yesterday back to Crowder's Mountain. As if hiking to the top of the peak would make me understand what's going on with him.

It's none of my business, but I can't help it.

I'm crushing on a guy whose marriage is going through a

really serious time... I feel as small and icky as a cockroach I squashed outside earlier just thinking about it.

He needs a friend, not a girl who'd strip him down and take advantage of him if given the opportunity.

Not that I'd *do* that, but I definitely have spent some time imagining it since the hike we went on and he opened up to me.

Still, I'm foolish, being distracted by my libido and his sexy beard when I should be focused on enjoying one of my rare nights off. And this is how silly I am because I'm spending my night off work, at the bar, sitting on the opposite side of where I serve drinks. I've watched the game down here because I don't have a television upstairs and now I'm chomping on some seriously awesome nachos, kicking it with my dad and Steve and surprisingly, there is a rather large crowd of guys about my age near the pool table who look like they're having their own celebration.

Based on the wrinkled and rolled up dress shirts and collars that have lost their ties and the fact they're all wearing black suit pants, I've placed a bet of fifty dollars one of them just got a promotion... and that they're all lawyers.

Who else would come here and be uptight, few looking like they've had a pool cue shoved up their ass with the way they silently judge the bar's appearance.

Hell, one or two, curled their lips at my newly dyed hair... platinum blonde with teal streaks.

It's not my favorite, but it gave me something to do yesterday for a few hours so I didn't spend more time alone, thinking of Sebastian. It worked, mostly because Mark, my hairstylist at The Color Bar Salon, is hilarious and keeps me laughing when I'm in his chair.

It stopped working when I realized my teal hair matches the Ice Kings team colors.

I changed out my nose ring to a little gold hoop and since it's my day off and I'm not caring about dressing to impress anyone or help with tips, I have on a pair of peach-colored sweat shorts and an oversized black sweatshirt. I cut off the collar, so it drapes off one shoulder and shows my white bra strap.

Next to me, Steve and Dad are talking about the upcoming election and since we rarely agree on most matters outside believing everyone we meet should be treated with kindness and respect, I've left them to it and zoned out to St. Louis playing Minnesota in Minnesota...

Which is where Sebastian is from.

Where his wife ran off to when she left him.

Yeah. I need another drink.

"Dad!" I call out and when he turns to me, I swing my empty glass back and forth. "Any chance I can get another?"

"Better check her ID, George. Girl looks pretty damn young."

"Shut it, Steve," I tease the old jerk and stick out my tongue at him.

My dad slides the dirty martini in front of me, laughing. "You're not driving, are you? I'd have to ask for your keys."

I slide the glass and coaster close to me and take a sip. "The only driving going on here is you two driving me crazy."

"It's a two-drink night," Dad says, losing his smile. "Everything all right?"

Just trying to forget a man who I have no business liking. Outside the cheap beer I drank a lot of in college because that was all we had, I've never acquired a taste for much alcohol. And when I do have some, Dad knows I rarely have more than one. I'm not surprised he's noticed or that he asks.

"Kicking back and enjoying my night. Leave me alone with your fatherly concern."

"Never," he promises and leans forward to kiss my cheek. "Who's winning?"

"St. Louis, heading into third period, up by one though, and Minnesota just had a great run right before. It'll be close."

"Look at you, sounding like you actually care about this stuff now."

My dad's teasing smile is laced with concern and I shrug. He knows me well. Better than I know myself, I'm sure of it, but that doesn't mean I'm going to assuage his fears right now. Not when I'm already so confused by my own feelings.

"Nothing else on the screens down here and I'm pretty sure if you turn off sports so I can watch that dating reality show I like, the boys in the back will revolt."

My dad slides his glance their way, where all six are standing around the pool table, talking and drinking. I don't know why he bothers. He's been keeping an eye on them all night.

"Point taken," he says. "You going to stay down here much longer?"

"Probably until the end of the game. Why? Need to go do something in the back?"

"Nope. It's your night off anyway."

"All right, old man."

Steve scoffs at the name calling, and Dad tosses the towel at him.

"Mind your own business," he calls out, lifting a hand toward me as he heads toward the guys at the tables to clean their empties and see if they want another round.

I turn back to the game and a mindless game on my

phone, keeping an eye as Minnesota pulls out the win with one more goal and keeping St. Louis from scoring again.

After it's done, I switch to a glass of decaffeinated soda, pull up a photo editing app I have on my phone for when I take pictures and don't have my SLR camera on me, and I get lost in the comfort of the familiar atmosphere and editing photos of my recent walk through Uptown.

***

IT'S GETTING LATE, which means I'm still wide awake. The curse of a bartender and my usual night not ending until almost three in the morning. The lawyers... which I end up confirming right before one of them paid their tab and took the fifty bucks from Steve happily... are throwing on suit coats and draining the dredges of their last beers when the door opens.

"It's late, boys," my dad calls out which grabs my attention to the newcomers.

A quick glance at my phone tells me it's after midnight, which means it is really late. Usually that's cause for concern. No one starts drinking that late... typically, they come from other places where they've either been kicked out or ran out of their own alcohol and too drunk to drive far.

"Never too late for us, is it?"

I recognize that voice. It's booming, loud and friendly. My dad's friendly opener to them should have been my giveaway.

I crane my neck around two of the guys in suits who are sloppily trying to fix their collars and sleeves and see the guys who have walked in.

Sebastian. Jason.

They're here.

Why are they here?

I'm still leaning back in the stool, both hands gripping the bar when they both spot me and for the first time I inwardly cringe at what I'm wearing.

I look like I'm in my pajamas and they're dressed in fancy suits.

Of course they are. They probably just hopped off a plane... but why are they *here?*

"Hey George, Steve." Jason lifts a hand and says something to Sebastian who nods.

He heads my way and lifts his hand and says my name in passing as he heads toward the back.

"Hey," I say to Sebastian. For some strange reason, my arms are trembling. I rub them quickly and he follows my movements.

"Cold?"

"Oh. Um. No."

Warming by the moment with him standing close to me, waiting at the bar while Dad finishes the tabs. "How are you?"

"All right." One side of his lips curl beneath his beard that's longer now than it was weeks ago but still nicely groomed. "No. That's a lie. I'm pretty shitty."

"Saw your game tonight."

"Yeah?" I swear that lip curl turns into a smirk. "You watched?"

I point at the television behind the bar that's now running hockey highlights of all the night's games. "It's what Dad had on when I got here."

"Hmm." Dad comes over and Sebastian orders a couple of drinks, two local brews from Dream Chasers Brewery in a nearby suburb. As he takes one, he turns so he's facing me and then that smile I swear I saw behind his beard grows more noticeable behind his thick hair.

"Nice hair," he says, and gives my bun a quick tug. "I like the new color. Teal matches my jersey."

Had I been drinking my soda, I would have sprayed it all over his dress shirt. A furious heat rushes to my throat, up to my cheeks. "I wasn't aware when I did it."

That smile falters and his head cocks to the side. "Not a fan of the Ice Kings?"

He's teasing me. Wow. I haven't seen the side of him before. My body is still flushed with a strange, unsettling heat that feels like needle pricks deep in my pores.

Sebastian Hendrix is *teasing* me. Not scowling. Not being rude.

My mind cannot compute with this.

"Not really," I tease back. "Although I think maybe one or two don't completely suck."

He shakes his head as soft laughter falls from him. It's so deep, so beautiful with a bit of gravel to it I almost fall right off my stool.

This is what Sebastian sounds like when he laughs and I want to hear it every day.

"You played well tonight."

His laugh dims and whatever spark was in his eyes evaporates when he sips his beer.

"Wasn't my best, but it's been a hard week."

I don't ask why he missed the game. It's none of my business. Reminding myself of that doesn't help. The question is burning the tip of my tongue so badly I take a sip of my soda to wash it away.

"Hey Gigi!" Jason calls, sliding up next to Sebastian and grabbing his drink. He gives him a quick *thanks, man* before tugging on my hair like Sebastian did. "Nice hair. I like it. You working tonight?"

In ripped-up sweats looking like I just pulled them from a balled-up corner of my floor? Which, let's be honest, that's definitely where they came from.

"Night off, just came down to hang with Dad."

"And watch our game," Sebastian cuts in. "She likes us."

"Only one or two of you," I repeat.

"Which one is it outside me?" Jason asks, nudging my shoulder.

I lift my glass to my lips and hide my smile. "How do you know you make the cut?"

"Because I'm awesome." He clinks his beer bottle to my glass and nods at Sebastian. "Talk. Now. Before I'm too tired to listen."

"Right." Sebastian's lips press out and then roll together. He gives me a look that makes my heart squeeze painfully tight in my chest. "See you later?"

It sounds more like a question than a statement that I'm thrown. So I'm laughing pretty stupidly, trying not to hyperventilate at his nearness and his smile and his *everything*, that I end up choking out, "You know where I live."

He smiles, shakes his head and follows Jason to a booth table on the other side and I turn back to the bar, dropping my forehead into my hand.

You know where I live? What kind of response was that? Stupid, Gigi. Stupid.

CHAPTER TWELVE

Sebastian

YOU KNOW WHERE I LIVE.

Was that a tease? A taunt? An invitation?

A year ago, hell, months ago, I probably wouldn't be questioning Gigi's remark as I follow Jason to the booth. A month ago, I probably wouldn't have thought anything of it.

And yet, now, I'm remembering that tie-dyed psychedelic blanket thing hanging on her walls. The haphazardly stacked books all over the place. The canvases she'd started telling me about and the floors so covered in clothes I'm still unsure what color the wood is on her bedroom floor.

The bedroom... where I slept.

Passed out.

Whatever.

"So," Jason says. "Tell me what happened."

With Gigi? How does he know? It takes me a second to

catch up and realize he's talking about the trip to Minnesota and not what happened with the bartender.

Which is *nothing*... outside of passing out at her place and going on a hike with her. Totally innocuous activities.

I take a sip of my drink and kick out how cute her ass looked in those leggings she wore. "I didn't really want to talk about it, I just didn't want to go home."

"Tough shit. I'm not missing out on another night with Tessa only to get drunk."

Fine. He wants to hear the humiliation of what my marriage... or lack thereof, has become? I'll tell him.

"Madison left before the holidays. I got served divorce papers on New Year's. I just — before it's *done* done, I needed to try. To make sure it couldn't be saved. Or something. Maybe I just needed to say goodbye." I take a drink of my beer to rinse away the vile taste in my throat. "You know I told you last fall we were having a hard time? That we were trying to get pregnant and it wasn't working?"

"I remember."

"Well in December we did more tests, and we found out the problem isn't only Madison, but us together were going to make it pretty much impossible." His brows furrow and God, I hate this. I'd rather choke on someone else's spit than admit my guys don't work right. "Doctor said I have issues, too, which would make getting pregnant pretty difficult even if everything was working correctly with Madison."

"Shit." He takes his own drink and grimaces. "That, that sucks, and I'm not blaming you. I get how that'd be hard to manage, but you didn't have to hide it all, either. Not from all of us."

"I know, but how do I walk into practice and announce, *hey everyone, I'm sterile.*" I laugh, but it's cold and falls flat.

Frankly, I could happily live the rest of my life and never have to talk sperm count. "Even with all that, I'm glad I went. She needs help and I hope her family can get it for her."

"Help?"

This is the one thing I've always held back. From everyone until I briefly alluded to it in the locker room last week. No one can possibly understand what it's like to watch your wife spiral downward, for days, weeks at a time sometimes, refusing to see someone for it. And every time I mentioned it, she grew angry.

I'm unsure if the infertility caused her depression or possibly exasperated something she never sought help for previously but either way, I'm hoping the parting words I shot to Ben the other night stuck.

I explain it all to Jason, through more beers George delivers when our first ones grow close to empty.

Jason responds with surprise, end-capped by curse words. He shakes his head at the appropriate moments. It feels good to get it off my chest. To finally share. Talking to Coach and him the other night was barely the tip of the iceberg. Seeing Madison looking so completely distraught and destroyed was the worst.

I have no doubt she means what she says about us being over.

Now, I'm not sure how to proceed with that. How do you let go of the only woman you've ever loved, who truly, disappeared before your eyes years ago? I meant what I said to her. Marriage was a commitment. Through the worst of times. And we certainly had our unfair share of those.

But don't I also deserve to have the best?

Even if it's without the woman I thought and wanted to be my forever?

It's not something I've ever pictured, ever imagined, but it's not like I can truthfully admit our marriage was a good one for years.

"I wish you would have said something earlier," Jason says when I take a break, but really, I'm done.

What else is there to say?

"Why? So the whole team would have hated her less?"

"We didn't—"

I lift a hand to stop him. I don't have the energy for any more lies. Intentional or otherwise.

"You did. At least some of you did, and I get it. She changed. I changed. It's just such a huge goddamn mess I can't describe, and she wanted it to stay private... but it's over. The divorce papers say sixty days."

I met with the attorney, and since there wasn't anything to fight because she asked for nothing, it could end faster. I just have to sign everything.

Another lingering taste of vomit pools in my throat and I drain the last of my second beer.

"I'm sorry, man. It sucks all around. I just wish we could have had all been there for y'all. Or at least known so we could protect Madison from all the babies and shit. I mean, now I feel like a dick."

"You weren't. And I got it. Just didn't make it easier."

Another set of drinks arrive at our table, served by a pair of small hands, with a tiny little broken heart tattoo on a ring finger and dark purple nail polish.

"Thanks, Gigi," I say, lifting my head and grinning at her.

She smirks at me. "No problem, hotshot. Dad wanted me to give you these but says it's last call."

"Damn," Jason groans. "I didn't realize it was so late."

"You can take off. I'm good."

"You sure?"

"Yeah."

He turns to Gigi who's taken our empties and is starting to walk away.

I try. I try really hard to not let my gaze drop to her short, cut-off sweat shorts, to the length of her legs beneath them. The shape of her calves or to notice the dark red polish on her toenails.

I fail.

Miserably.

There's something so damn attractive about her petite size.

I grip my new beer bottle harder and take a healthy swig.

"Hey Gigi," Jason calls out. "Keep this loser company for me so he doesn't get shit-faced before practice tomorrow?"

"Me?" She's turned, gaze bouncing from me to Jason and she frowns. "You need my help?"

"No—"

"Yes—" Jason says at the exact time I disagree.

She smirks at Jason. "Seems to me he doesn't need it."

"Sometimes this asshole doesn't know what he needs." He slaps the table and slides out, holding out his arm in a gesture for Gigi to take his spot.

"Jason—"

He shrugs and holds out his fist. "I'll pay the tab. You get home safely, yeah?"

"Yeah," I grumble and return his fist pump.

"And you'll thank me for this someday, too."

I watch him go, frowning.

What the fuck does that mean?

"I can pretend to sit here until he leaves if you want to be alone."

Her voice *does* something to me. Like a bug is happily leaping in my gut when she looks down at me, all that teal hair and new nose ring and tattoo peeking out from the wide collar of her sweatshirt.

It's the collar I'm noticing. And the tattoo.

Not the thin, white strap of her bra.

Shit.

"You can sit. Please. You want Jason's last beer?"

"Nah." Her nose crinkles and the soft light above the bar flints on her nose ring. I quickly look away as she slides in. "I've never acquired the taste for beer. No matter what kind it is, it always tastes like wet cardboard."

"You know what cardboard tastes like?"

"Yeah. Like beer." She grins.

I grin back.

This girl is funny. Well-traveled.

Divorced. Cute. And *fun.*

The exact kind of temptation I do *not need* in my life right now. Yet as I sit across from her, taking in every little nuance about her like the freckle on the back of her hand, that broken heart tattoo... I can't for the life of me think of an excuse to leave.

THIS IS, quite possibly, the most absolute asinine thing I've ever done in my life.

I met Madison at school. When it came time to ask her out on our first date, we'd already been "going together" for weeks so of course I asked her to our school's homecoming dance.

That was the last time I've officially asked someone on a date.

This is not a date.

Right. It's not a date... not exactly.

I'll ignore my sweaty palms making the cardboard coffee cups in my hand in danger of falling from my grip. And I can definitely not feel my pulse going slightly erratic. And I'm not hot.

It's the weather. Sixties in February isn't unheard of, but it feels freaking hot with the early morning sun rising while I stand on the metal, rickety landing at the top of Gigi's apartment.

Because I'm back here.

Like an idiot.

Although this time, Bruiser is with me.

It's been two weeks since I saw her last and I've realized a few things since then. I like the way I feel when I'm around Gigi.

I can't stop thinking about her.

We have a week of home games ahead of us, but I don't have to be at the arena until three.

Which means I'm here, hoping Gigi plans on going somewhere to take pictures today.

It's logical. I don't like being at home and I like being outside.

So does Gigi.

There's no harm in asking a newly made friend if I can spend the day with her again, right?

Right. So, it's not a date. It's a guy asking a friend to hang out.

"Man up and knock on the door, asshole."

It takes a hot minute to juggle the coffee due to the hotness of the cups and the sweat on my palms but when I finally grow the balls to knock, the door swings open almost immediately and Gigi is there, smirk on her face.

"I was wondering how long it was going to take you to knock or if you were going to disappear."

"Wha... what?" I stumble.

She *saw* me practically doing a toddler "have to go pee and have to go pee *now*" dance and *let me.*

"Want to come in?" Both of the cups are pulled from my hands and she steps back, her ass holding open the door.

Still wearing that damn smile.

Her hair is crazy wild, pulled back from her face and it's one of the few times I remember it not being in a ponytail or in those buns at the sides of her head.

I didn't realize how long it was.

Or thick.

Or beautiful with the stripes of colors.

And... hell. I like it.

"So, I brought you coffee," I say, further stumbling over my words.

"I gathered," she says, happily sipping from one of the cups, still wearing that grin and looking like she's fighting a back a laugh. "Any reason why you're here today? I don't think you need to apologize for anything?"

Funny woman.

"No, no apologies. It's just that..." I got home from Nashville last night only to realize I was thinking about heading to the bar. Because I kept thinking about her and the last time we were together. I didn't stay there long after Jason left, but in the time we spent together, I spent a lot of time laughing.

And I swear every time I smiled or laughed, she grinned like she'd won something.

Fuck if that didn't feel good.

We'd sat and talked long after the bar was closed. She shooed everyone out, and while she did that, I took a seat at the bar. Somehow, it felt natural. Like I was meant to talk to her for hours. It wasn't until I gathered my keys to leave, I realized I'd be headed back to my house, alone.

For a moment, I'd wanted to see if I could crash at her place, but that wasn't the right thing to do.

Although, hell... I'm not sure what is *the right* thing to do anymore. I've been doing that for fifteen years and look where it got me.

Here. Which, oddly enough, feels like a pretty damn good place to be.

"There are bugs outside. And if you're dropping off the coffees and taking off, I'm keeping both of them."

Her head tilts toward inside and yeah... I should probably stop acting like an asshole any minute now.

"I stopped by today to see if you were going anywhere before your shift. Thought I could go with you again?"

"You did?"

"I like being outside. Seemed fun. Plus, I promised Bruiser I'd spend the morning with him and while he hates car rides, he loves walks. And hikes. And swimming which is strange for his breed."

And... I'm still sounding like an asshole, except this time a socially inept nervous asshole, and yeah... I'm going to be quiet now.

"So... walk? Pictures? You headed anywhere?"

"I wasn't, but if you want company, I can come with you."

"I'd like that," I say, on a rush so fast I think I surprise us both. I *know* I've surprised myself, but Gigi smiles again at me, shaking her head like she thinks I'm adorable as my dog who she hasn't even met yet.

"Let me do something with this mop" —she points to her head— "and grab some shoes."

She all but shoves a coffee into my hand and I grip it before the top can fly off and splash us both.

CHAPTER THIRTEEN

Gigi

I HAVE no idea how I seem to find myself in the strangest situations when it comes to Sebastian, but when I saw him headed up my staircase this morning, the metal rattling beneath his heavy steps, I'm pretty sure I had a mini heart attack.

He's here to hang out? With me?

And his dog? Who's the cutest little ball of white fluffy fur. Bruiser, which made me snicker at his name, hopped up into my lap and declared my lap his before I could buckle my seat belt in Sebastian's Maserati.

And holy crap, I'm sitting in a Maserati.

I'm not even letting my mind wander to how much this luxurious German chunk of steel with buttery soft leather costs. Although I'm certain I'll Google it later.

"So, where'd we leave off last time?" Sebastian asks.

My cheeks heat. From what I can remember from a couple of weeks ago, before he said goodnight, I left off wanting to run my fingertips down his beard. Prickly? Soft? I'm dying to know. Then I wanted to flip a curl of his long hair behind his ear. He has one stubborn curl. It doesn't matter how many times he runs his hand through his hair, there's always one chunk on his right side that flips outward, curling opposite of everything else.

I want to tame it. About as much as I want to see Sebastian untamed.

Probably not what he's looking for.

"Uh... what?"

"With your travels." He gives me a quick glance before returning to the road. "You were telling me about your time in Turkey."

"Oh. right." See? Foolish. I need to figure out a way to stop my runaway thoughts when it comes to Sebastian. "Turkey." I laugh softly and shake my head at my naivety back then.

"What is it?"

If I'm not mistaken, he has a small smile twitching behind his beard and it momentarily distracts me. He's just so... potent with his masculinity, but it's understated, not macho manly, just confident.

"Turkey," I say, getting back on point. "Probably not my greatest idea for my first stop."

"Dangerous?"

"Yep." I pop the 'p' and fight a shiver at the glare he gives me. Before he can ask, I carry on. "More in theory than anything I saw, but life is so different in much of it. It was my first glance at a really eye-opening different way of living. I did a lot of reading before I left, so I was prepared, but nothing really could have prepared me for the concern of terrorism in Ankara. It wasn't, well, it wasn't safe for me alone at night, which I tried to avoid in most places anyway,

but there was the way I had to dress, as well. It was just..."
There's really no way to describe Turkey with its traditions
and history and beautiful hot springs in areas I was able to
tour with a group on camels. Or vibrant colors in the shopping districts which made the cities come alive and yet the
women were mostly still dressed in long sleeves, bodies fully
covered. I'd packed for those scenarios and made sure I had
a headscarf to visit a mosque, but even then, there was an
eerie feeling that followed me there.

"It was gorgeous," I say, on a sigh, thinking of everything
I experienced. "I rode a camel. Visited a mosque. Saw more
beautiful landmarks and historical sites I can still so vividly
see in my dreams. And then there were the Hammam.
Incredible."

"The what?"

"Oh. Turkish bathhouses. So cool."

His hand makes a squeaking sound on the steering
wheel as he makes the turn into a park area near Freedom
Park. "The bathhouse?"

"Yeah. Public bathhouses. Steam rooms where you
would also get massages."

"Right." He clears his throat. "Ready for that walk?"

If only I could understand what brought on this sudden
rigidness in his posture.

"Sure," I drawl out, handing over Bruiser. He leaps into
my face and kisses my cheek, paws flail in the air when
Sebastian takes him.

The vision of him curling the little ball of fluff in his
strong arms makes me snort.

"What?"

"Nothing," I say, covering my laughter.

"That's not a nothing sound," Sebastian says. He slides
on Bruiser's harness and clips the leash, which seems like an

impossible task given Bruiser's constant flailing and bouncing around. If I didn't know the dog was real, I'd think it was fake, stuffed with springs and long-lasting batteries.

"It's just... you... you're all... that..." I flip my hand in a circle at his face and point to Bruiser. What am I doing?! "And Bruiser is all tiny and sweet."

"Are you suggesting I'm not sweet?"

"Um. Kind of... prickly?"

He huffs a laugh and shakes his head as he reaches for the door, he looks at me over his shoulder and that look, I swear, it has a direct connection to the tops of my thighs. "You say the oddest things."

I shrug and open my door, grabbing my small backpack where I stowed my camera and snacks. Hiking and walking make me hungry. "I'll take that as a compliment."

"You should."

I meet him at the driver's door and even with the thin layer of hazy clouds and my sunglasses, it's still bright so I place my hand over my eyes to shield the sun and tilt my head back. "So, where are we headed?"

"Greenway Creek. Thought you might be able to get pics on it."

"Lead the way, then." I've been here frequently, but like with hiking, I have a feeling Sebastian and I approach our walks differently. It'd taken him a while to slow to my pace, and it's not because I'm out of shape, but because I'm constantly scanning the trees and areas for anything inter-esting and photo op worthy. He approached our first hike together as a man on a mission, to reach the peak in the shortest time possible. That was, until he kept losing me every time I stopped to snap a photo.

As if he remembers, he slows to my pace as we hit the trail, Bruiser on his right side, me on his left and for as spastic as the dog was in my lap in the car, he's completely calm on the walk, sniffing happily and little pink tongue lolling out of his mouth.

"So, after Turkey," Sebastian says, "where'd you go next?"

"I went to Greece first, down to Athens. I was there about five days, maybe? Although I could have stayed for a month and not gotten bored. The people. The history... and dear Lord, the food was incredible. Then I traveled up through Macedonia, stayed for a few days to travel to the Millennium Cross, which was one of the most breathtaking sights I saw."

"What is it?"

"The cross?" I elbow him in the side. "It's a cross."

He laughs softly and I tally up another win for me. In truth, I'm not paying attention to our walk or anything photo-worthy. I'm next to Sebastian who unlike the last time I was talking about my photographs, of which is one of the Cross I'm currently talking about, this time he's hanging on every word. Interested.

In what I have to say.

Just remember that he's not interested in you.

Right. I'm a diversion. I'm not an idiot. He might enjoy my company, but I suspect that the only reason he's here with me is because then he's not alone.

I'll take what I can get, even if I understand it more than he does, but I need to be careful.

"Where'd you go?" he asks, and he takes a couple steps in front of me, turns and looks down at me. The shade cover is so thick he has his sunglasses shoved to the top of his head and that hair.... Man, I want to run my fingers through it.

"What?"

"You just stopped talking."

"Sorry." Right, because my mind went down a rabbit trail of warning. "Anyway, Macedonia has this Cross that's over two hundred feet high. It's at the top of the mountain near the capital city and I had to take a gondola ride to get there. Scary as heck, but once I was there, I stayed for hours, sitting, thinking, seeing the land from such a high viewpoint. I didn't want to leave."

"You like the quiet." He turns and keeps walking.

It sounds like a reprimand. "You don't?"

I have to hurry up to him, his strides are so long. Someone should tell him he has a pretty quick triggered attitude problem. He can go from smiling and kind to that prickly attitude I accused him of earlier faster than I can snap my fingers.

It's not going to be me, though.

Even irritated, I like his company too much.

Which is a red flag I should be heeding.

Unfortunately, I've always enjoyed the thrill of danger.

"I think I'm too active to be quiet," he says finally, brows furrowed like maybe this upsets him.

I shouldn't spend so much time trying to figure him out.

"But on your days off, what do you usually do? Don't you ever rest? Chill out and watch a movie?"

"A movie is your idea of quiet?" He peers down at me and I swear behind that beard a corner of his lips has kicked up.

"Well no, I'm a book girl. But we all have our ways of self-care. If movies and video games are your thing, I'm not one to judge."

"Music." His nose wrinkles like he hates it. "Madison always had music on. Even when we were out of town or out to dinner, she'd set the house system so it was always playing music when we walked in. I don't know if my house was ever quiet."

"And now you hate it." It doesn't take a genius to figure this out.

It also confirms my suspicions.

Something heavy and ugly settles in my throat. I swallow it down right as he takes a fist and jabs it into my gut.

"I hate the quiet. It's a good thing you're around to keep my thoughts off it."

I stop. He keeps walking and I'm still standing there, blinking stupidly at his retreating figure.

My hands curl into fists when in slow-motion, he slows and drops his head.

It took him that long to figure out why that would hurt so much.

It's not intentional. Not even surprising, but damn... that hurts.

He has the actual power to hurt me, and if I'd driven myself, I'd walk away right now.

"I think that came out incredibly wrong," Sebastian says.

At least he's self-aware. I peer down at my phone. My finger is shaking. I have the Uber app. There is no reason to put myself in this position.

Besides, he's *married* for cripe's sake.

"Gigi." His voice is soft. Carries a hint of pain in it. I'm still staring at my phone and I can see the tip of his running shoes in my vision. At his feet, Bruiser is sitting patiently, little white fluffy tail whipping back and forth on the cement. "I didn't mean it like that. I should have said thank you for being willing to spend the day with me. Even though we barely know each other, I like being with you."

He likes being with me isn't the same as liking me.

"Yeah, well, I'm a barrel of laughs."

Since I'm still being stupid, and staring at my phone, I jolt when a warm hand curls around my shoulder and his thumb slides to my neck.

And oh dear sweet gracious. That thumb on my neck sends a spark straight to my lower stomach.

He's *touching* me. I'm not sure he's done that. Ever.

"Can you look at me? Please?"

There's a slight pressure on my shoulder, where he's curling his hand over it, fingertips in the back, and that thumb... it grazes my pulse and makes it skitter out of control.

Looking at him now would be a mistake.

He'll see too much.

"Sebastian."

"Please."

And oh my. The man should never beg. It makes knees tremble. Hearts leap. The hairs at the back of my neck stand at attention.

I do as he requests and then blink when I meet his face.

Because he's looking at me with so much the same look I'm currently experiencing I'm not sure I know what to do with this.

"Sebastian—"

"I'm sorry. Again. Someday, I swear I'll get to a place where I'm not constantly putting my foot in my mouth around you. I like being with you. It confuses me, and I like it. Can we... can we leave it that for now?"

At our feet, Bruiser barks and I grin down at the dog who's distracted by a fly. He yanks on the leash and bounds off for it, jerking back when Sebastian doesn't move with him.

"Okay," I say, because I'm a glutton for punishment. I enjoy things that are bad for me, adrenaline rushes and the unknown.

I have a feeling for the first time with Sebastian, it just might be my downfall.

He brushes against my neck one more time. Emerald green eyes watching and flaring when I can't hide my shiver from his touch. And then it's gone, his hand shoved into his pocket.

He clears his throat. "Walk with me?"

I try to resettle my racing heart. "Sure."

I fall in step next to him and it feels like a step toward my doom, but I'm too enamored to fall back to safety.

We walk for a while, mostly in silence, the patter of Bruiser keeping our attention. I'm not sure how upset I should be, if anything.

He likes being with me. Isn't that enough? He's made no promises. Heck, as far as I know, he may have already put me in the friend zone.

But that look when he said, *it confuses me.*

Yeah... that wasn't exactly friendly. Still, I need to be careful. He's a mess.

I prefer the only messes of mine to be my clothes in my apartment.

Kicking a small rock in our path out of our way, I watch it clatter to the weeds to the side. The silence is killing me. Odd, consider I've confessed how much I like being alone with thoughts.

Just not these particular ones.

"So, you have a game tomorrow?"

"Home. You working?"

"Always," I confirm. My eyes squint against the bright sound despite wearing sunglasses. "Will you... well..."

I'm not sure if I should ask, but I'm dying of curiosity.

"Will I what? Play?"

"Yeah. I saw you didn't last week."

"Ahh." His hand scrubs his hair and he tilts his face to the sun. His beard, while growing longer every time I see him, is still neatly shaven at beneath his jaw leaving me a view of his corded throat, the muscles at his shoulders. And hell, I mean, he's muscled everywhere, obvious beneath his shirt.

"I went to Minnesota to see Madison."

"Oh." I'm not expecting that, and I trip over a small stick in my path before righting myself.

I can offer him nothing, not even real understanding because my divorce was my idea and it was mutual. Not painful like the ripples of his hurt rolling off him.

"I'm sorry."

He huffs and rolls his shoulders as if the mere mention of Madison bunches his muscles to the point of pain. "It sucks. A lot, but I guess, I think more than anything, I needed our goodbye to happen in person. I needed to hear it from her."

My fingertips burn to squeeze his arm. Wrap my small arms around his waist and place my cheek to his chest to hold him, to promise it will be okay, but I do nothing.

I say nothing. My role in his life is uncertain and I don't know what moves of comfort would be welcome.

"Did it help? Seeing her?"

His jaw falls forward and tightens before he shrugs. "In some ways. She... I don't know how to explain it. I think the pain over the years, of not getting what she wanted, of all the help we had, I think it made her depressed. Or made it worse. I'm not really sure how that works, and there were medicines she took. The hormones she took were hard for her. We've had years of it being hard, I'm not sure I remember now what it was like when we had fun."

I kick another pebble. At my side, I can almost sense his defeat. He's given up. But on what? His wife? His marriage?

"She was beautiful and crazy and wild. Always the one planning our social calendar and God, she could make me laugh. All of that... I don't know how to describe what happened and I can promise you it wasn't all her fault, it wasn't all the medicine. I think I started getting upset when we stopped having sex for fun. You know what it's like to be told no because it's 'not the right time?' Or because I had to wait forty-eight hours? It sucked, and I can't say I was always nice about it, even if I understood."

His sex life with his wife is the *last possible thing* I want to hear about, but I'm trapped, and yet fascinated. Especially while he seems to be focusing on nothing and talking more to himself than me. Perhaps this is what he needs—to work this out verbally instead of bottling it all in.

"Did you... were you ever able to figure out what was making things difficult?"

"Yeah, and when we learned it was her body not working the way most women's do, that was tough for her. She felt broken. No longer a woman. But then we learned it was me too, I think that was the tipping point."

He hangs his head in such sadness I can no longer stop my instinct to comfort. I reach out and wrap my hand around his wrist, squeezing. "You?"

"Turns out my swimmers aren't the manliest either."

Another huff, that disgusted, hard rough sound that sounds like it's torn from razor blades and sandpaper.

"You...?"

"Can't help her make kids even medically. Not anymore."

"I'm so sorry, Sebastian."

"Not exactly something I planned on talking about," he admits slowly. "Or ever, but yeah... after we learned that, it was her final reason for leaving. Together, we can never have what she so desperately desires."

I drop my hand.

There's nothing I can do for him. No way I can comfort him. He's just confessed it himself.

I have more questions, about adoption. Or surrogacy. Maybe one of her sisters. Or a company. Yet it's not the right time and if I'm being honest with myself even though it makes me feel like there are ugly bugs crawling inside my stomach at the thought... I don't want to hear any more about Madison.

I can though, switch the topic to something I'm hoping is more pleasant.

"How'd you get started in hockey?"

CHAPTER FOURTEEN

Sebastian

I'VE HAD ABSOLUTELY no intention of telling Gigi any of this. And yet I'm learning that's part of my draw as well as concern with Gigi.

She's too easy to open up to. She's too easy to talk to.

And when she reaches out and touches me?

My blood sizzles and sparks so deep in my veins it's possible she electrocutes me.

None of these things are what I should be thinking. Or *why* I'm so drawn to being around her, and yeah, I might have royally screwed up earlier, but everything I said is true.

I like being around her.

I like her.

It's confusing.

For fifteen years I haven't looked at a single woman and yet now, even on this stupid path, my lame excuse to be able to spend time with her, my muscles are feeling the strain of forcing myself to *not* stare at her.

Ask her about her tattoos. Her hair. Her piercings. Good Lord. I want to trace all of her visible tattoos with parts of me that shouldn't be anywhere near her. I want to discover if she has any that aren't visible, ones she keeps hiding.

More intimate ones with deeper meanings in more intimate places.

And piercings? She has several in her ears, one in her nose. Does she have her belly button done like Madison and her sisters got in their rare rebellious act as teenagers? When their parents freaked out and made them all remove it.

If Gigi does, I bet there's a brightly colored jewel dangling from a ring.

She's too intentional with everything else she does to have a simple hoop, that much I'm certain.

The thing I'm not certain of is *why* I'm so damn curious outside the fact I haven't had sex in months.

I'm too smart to know it has anything to do with simple horniness though.

No, it's Gigi. The way I'm drawn to her.

The way I *want* her even knowing it's the dumbest thing I could do right now.

I blow out a sharp breath, clearing my head.

In front of us, Bruiser is slowing down. He's not used to these kinds of long walks but I'm not ready to turn it around. And since I've slowed to Gigi's smaller steps, this hasn't even been a workout for me.

I take the out she's giving me, not surprised in the least she's changed the subject. Sometimes I think she can read my moods better than I can.

"Hockey?"

"Yes. I imagine you were one of those kids strapped to

skates before they can walk, put in all the fancy camps. I bet you were a rock star from the time you could tie your own shoes. Or skates, I guess."

Her nose wrinkles at her joke and I chuckle.

"That's not it at all."

"No?"

I scoff. "Hardly. I started when I was six."

"Oh. That's late, isn't it?"

She's not wrong. Not entirely. I'm also enjoying the way she's teasing me.

"For us Minnesota boys? You betcha." I throw in the heavy accent and earn a laugh from her which makes me feel all kinds of good about myself. "Truthfully, I sucked when I was a kid. Thought about hanging up my skates quite a bit but my mom knew I liked it, even if I wasn't the greatest, so she kept encouraging me."

"Really?" The shock in her tone is adorable.

"Swear it. I didn't even make the varsity team the first time I tried out."

"Noooo..."

Her hip bounces into me. She's so small I barely feel it.

"You're a pain in the ass, you know?"

She gives me a smile full of teeth. "I try."

Shaking my head, I smile back at her. Adorable isn't the word for her, but all the words I can think of to describe Gigi don't fit. She's so much *more* than any of them.

"Anyway, I begged my parents to put me in training camps that year in the off-season. I worked out in gyms with a personal trainer, did everything I could think of. We didn't have a lot of money. My parents are both teachers, so I had to get a job to cover all the expenses. It wasn't even until I was in high school and made the school team, I had brand new equipment for the first time."

"Really?" Her voice softens and shoots straight to my chest.

"Yeah, I mean, we didn't have a lot and when I was young, my equipment always came from a secondhand store. Most kids on the team had sticks that cost hundreds of dollars, skates that were batshit crazy in price, and there I was, going through four to five used skates a season, getting them sharpened all the time. I wanted this and I worked for it. I owe my parents a lot for sacrificing so I could have it."

It's been a long time since I've thought back to those earlier years. Amazing how once you get millions, you can lose sight of some of that, some of what made me who I was, what helped me get to the pros in the first place. It was all that grit Dad said was ingrained in me. I was too stubborn to give up. Too stubborn to quit.

Which makes me wonder if I've lost that somehow with Madison. When did I give in? Or did I? Or did she?

The thought makes my heart squeeze and I blow out a breath.

No, she's the one who walked away. And with all the hard times we've been through, that hurts maybe more than anything.

"Hey. Where'd you go?" Gigi asks, and her lips are pressed together. I don't even notice her hand is on my arm until I look down and see that little broken heart on her knuckle.

"Mind wandered," I admit. "There's a picnic stop up here. I need to get Bruiser some water."

Gigi's tattoo on her ring finger has piqued my curiosity. Odd for her to get a broken heart on her left hand's ring finger if she claims she wasn't all that cut up about her marriage ending.

I wait until we find the picnic area, moving slow while

she stops and starts a few times to take pictures. There's nothing interesting outside trees and leaves and sticks and the ground, but she chooses all different angles. I make a mental note to check her Instagram feed later to see her photos. What is she seeing that I'm not?

Once we find a picnic table, I dig out a collapsible bowl I brought for Bruiser and pour a bottled water into it. He slurps it up happily while Gigi wanders the small area, phone in hand, thumb pressing away on her photo app.

"Can I ask you a question?"

She peers at me over her shoulder, that soft smile on her face. Her cheeks have pinkened from our walk and are almost as bright as her lips. "Of course."

"What's with the heart tattoo on your finger?"

"Oh." She laughs, shakes her head and her teal hair bobbles back and forth. "Stupid, drunk night shortly after I left Evan and wondered if we did the wrong thing. It was a few weeks before I went traveling."

"Did you? Make a mistake?"

"No." She drops her phone to her side and climbs up on the other side of the table top, putting her back to mine but she scoots back onto the table and leans back on her hands so I can see her face tilted up to the sunshine. She has another tiny semicolon behind her ear I've never noticed before and I want to ask her about that too.

And her mermaid. And the butterfly.

All of them.

Good Lord... I want to know so much about this woman it's unsettling.

"I think, when Evan and I decided to part ways, I was more upset I'd failed at something. Or that I hadn't taken our vows seriously enough or worked hard enough. I mean, the final straw in my marriage for me was a paint color on the walls on the surface. I was out with some friends, who all knew us, who loved Evan too, and I just... had a moment of fear. Or sadness for what I'd lost."

She shrugs and her thumb swipes over her tattooed knuckle. "I was sad, and I was drunk, so I went and got the tattoo to remind myself to be smarter about choices I made in the future. I'm not sure why I chose the broken heart outside the fact that night, it felt like it was broken. Live and learn, I guess." She smiles up at me and shrugs. The winter sun hits her face so perfectly and brightly I'm almost blinded by her beauty. "Not all the tattoos I have are ones I wish I would have gotten, but they're all part of me. Of who I was... who I'm becoming."

I've never considered tattoos anything more than artwork. Not as deep as Gigi explains it, anyway. My interest in her—in her ink—piques so much deeper. Who was she? Where has she come from? What has she conquered or lost that she's memorialized on her skin with ink and permanency?

I shake my head and then let it fall back so we're both looking at the sun.

"If I were to get a tattoo," I ask. "What should I get?"

Her lips press together in a teasing smile and that blinding spark in her eyes dims to a glimmer. "A wolf. Surrounded by daisies."

"What?" I bark out a laugh. I'm already shaking my head. "Daisies. Really?"

Her shoulder bumps mine and she turns her head toward me. "Yeah. You're all gruff and growly and so serious, but I think beneath that, you're one of the good ones, Sebastian Hendrix."

Gruff and growly. My lips pucker. I'm not... but perhaps that's who I've become? I'm not sure I like her first part of her impression of me but I'll take the latter. "A wolf, huh?"

"Yeah. And since you're from Minnesota, that's probably rather cliché but it suits you."

Several Minnesota professional sports teams have logos with wolves, so she's not wrong.

"I like wolves. They're fiercely loyal, strong, and pretty badass. Just like me."

Gigi snorts. "Don't let it go to your head, hotshot."

I can feel my smile stretch my cheeks wide. This woman. Everything about her makes me feel *good*. And with the way she's looking at me?

Something inside me stirs.

I push off my sunglasses, wanting to see her without the barrier. The way she grins at me and when I do, her lips part.

She sees it. She sees everything she's making me feel, and I'm not hiding it.

Not anymore.

"Sebastian," she whispers as if afraid of breaking the moment.

I whisper her name back even quieter and move in a fraction. The pull she has on me is indescribable. My tongue slides along my bottom lip on instinct.

Because she's close to me. And no longer smiling. I can see her eyes behind her own lenses drop to watch my movement and I swear she pulls up so she's closer.

And then she clears her throat, cheeks flushed, and she pushes up to sitting, jumping off the bench.

"I should probably get going."

I turn and watch the way she brushes her hands down the thighs of her leggings, avoiding me.

Maybe I've read that wrong.

Maybe I shouldn't be doing this.

Not with her or with anyone, but I don't want anyone.

I like *her*.

"Yeah." My voice is gruff. Scratchy.

I clear my throat and slide off the picnic table, packing up the travel bowl and water bottles before tugging on Bruiser's leash, who's panting beneath the table in the shade.

"I should get back too. I have a workout later."

We head back to the car in near silence. Her clicking away at photos randomly. I feel like I should apologize.

Although I've done nothing wrong except make her uncomfortable.

But I'm not sorry, so I don't.

I like this woman. I'm interested in her, in everything she says.

It's too damn bad I have no clue what to do next.

CHAPTER FIFTEEN

Sebastian

I'M KICKING back on the bus, Klaus next to me. The bus is silent, all of us pissed we lost to New York. It took us too long to find our rhythm and our skates. Our passes were sloppy and we moved too damn slow out of the gate when New York came out barrels blazing. They were on fire and after two quick goals in the first period that had Maddox letting loose his helmet and curse words that would make a sailor proud during the first intermission, we got our shit together but we spent the rest of the game playing catch up.

It was an embarrassing two to five loss playing a team that has no hope of making the playoffs.

"You coming to the bar tonight?" Klaus asks, pulling out his phone and tucking his headphones behind his neck.

"Probably. Think we could all use it."

"No shit. I don't think I've played that bad since I was twelve."

"I hear you. Tonight was ugly."

"Coach is going to have our balls in a tight grip this week."

As gross as the visual is, he's not wrong. You know you've done shitty when Coach stares at you in the locker room post-game and then leaves without saying a word. It's more powerful than if he'd come in cursing as mad as Maddox.

For me, even with my goal, I have an excuse for playing like crap. Twenty minutes before I took to the ice my lawyer sent me a text.

Papers are signed and filed. Divorce final.

I pull up the text again and re-read it. It's final. I gave Madison everything she asked for after she declined my one attempt to give her more money. She made it so damn easy and months ago I would have been devastated.

As it is, now, I just feel numb. I've joined the ranks of the other forty percent of people who have their first marriages end in divorce. Not exactly a statistic I'm proud of and there's definitely no textbook for how you're supposed to feel when the woman you loved forever leaves you but sitting here on the bus, letting it set in...

Maybe it's possible I've already started moving and accepting it.

My phone buzzes in my palm, making me almost drop it.

And then I grin when I see the name.

Maybe I don't feel all that upset about my divorce because there's another woman who makes me smile.

Gigi.

Nice goal tonight, hotshot. Sorry about your loss and that shitty penalty call.

I was sent to the sin bin for hooking and it didn't even freaking happen. She's not wrong at all and before I got off the bus and stepped foot into the hotel, it was the thing I was most upset about today. The stupid power play because I was off the ice allowed New York to score the goal that put them in the lead after we'd skated our asses off to tie it up in the second.

I don't want to talk about the game anymore. I'll get enough of that tomorrow when we're watching film.

Instead, I grin at that stupid nickname she insists on calling me, and type back,

Can't win them all, even when you're the best. Like me.

"What's got you happy?" Klaus asks. "I don't think I've seen you smile like this in weeks."

Yeah. Something tells me I'm moving on. The only question is am I moving on to someone else? Or just acceptance?

"Gigi texted," I tell him and press my lips together as his eyes widen.

I've kept my friendship with her relatively quiet. We haven't been to the bar a whole lot but we've gone and when we're there, she treats me like every other player so I assume she's been taking her cues from me.

There's no longer the awkwardness about our last walk or what I confessed and I haven't done anything about it because I'm still confused.

And because I'm married... or was. But I'm not anymore, am I?

"Gigi the bartender?"

"Yeah. We've become... friends, I guess."

"You guess?"

"What?" I shoot him a look. "I can't have friends?"

"Friends that are that fiery and sexy? I wouldn't keep her just as a friend if it were me."

The idea of Klaus, or *any* other man calling Gigi sexy or thinking of her that way has me gritting my teeth before I can stop it.

Klaus laughs, slaps my leg. "Yeah. Friends, my ass."

Hell. If he's going there, I know one way to get him to shut up. "Friends," I repeat. "Like you and Jillian."

She works for a marketing company that produces all of our gear for signings. They met at least two years ago and became fast friends. He was dating someone, she was out of a relationship and they've been friends ever since. But I'm not a moron. Just like with Jason I can see when one of my friends is panting after someone and not acting on it. Now they're both single and he's still not doing anything.

Sort of maybe... it might possibly be the same way I'm acting with Gigi.

He scowls at me. "Fuck off." He tugs his headphones over his head and smirks. "Hotshot."

That little fucker. He read my damn text. I punch him in the thigh, relishing when he bends over and grabs it. Serves him right.

I return to my text and Gigi and yeah... I'm smiling.

Not because of the shit talk with Klaus, because of Gigi.

You think you're the best? At what exactly?

And shit.

Oh. The ideas and visions that suddenly pop into my brain are not respectable, especially with nosey Newman sitting next to me.

It takes me a minute to respond. No flirting. Straight to the point.

I want to see you. Saturday.

I turn my phone off. I'll look at her response later. Tonight I want to kick back with the team. Bond. We need to get over our loss so we can win the next one in two days.

And I need to take a few days to figure out exactly what it is I want from Gigi Barnes, the petite little vixen who makes me think sometimes, getting divorced might not be so bad after all.

I HAVEN'T MADE love to a woman in longer than I can remember. I have not *fucked* a woman in longer. That I've been married for so long, only had one woman, does not mean those two things happened.

We were schedules and rituals. In the last three years, there was not a single time that I came home, smiled at Madison and she smiled and dropped to her knees in our kitchen like she'd done so many countless times before.

A blow job? A wasted effort when our sole focus was procreation.

Fun? When in the hell did that end?

I had sex with fevers while trying not to puke. I had sex with bruised ribs and black eyes and bloody lips because games fell during optimum ovulation timing.

I was woken at six in the morning with Madison's hand on my dick, getting it hard and sliding on top of me.

Sounds sexy, right?

Only until the first words she said were, "I'm ovulating. I need you before you leave town."

She didn't need *me*. She needed what I could give her. And unfortunately, now we both knew even that was wasted effort.

Our sex life might have started off fun when we started trying to have kids... practicing is fun, right? Two years into it when she finally talked to her doctor, all of that ended. So for the last three years, I felt more like a milking cow than a partner or lover.

At the time, I didn't much mind. I wanted a family as much as she did and I wanted to give her everything she wanted. Everyone goes through sacrifice and everyone goes through hard times.

All this means it's been a really long time since sex has been fun, or the mere *thought* of sex has been fun. So when I wake up in the morning, for the umpteenth day in a row with my hand wrapped around my hard length after having another sex dream about Gigi, I groan... in both pain and pleasure.

In part because I can't stop thinking about her. Logically, my head and heart are a mess.

Also, the last game in New York earned me a check into the boards, so I have a lovely bruise in that soft area above my hip.

Pleasure because... holy crap. If the thought of Gigi makes me feel this damn good, what in the world will it be like if I can actually have her?

It's that thought that has my hips bucking fiercely up into my fist, abs coiling. Hot, blinding heat spikes down my spine. I finish all over my stomach and my chest on a groan so damn loud Bruiser starts yipping outside my door.

Gigi hasn't responded to my text about getting together, but I'm all out of fucks to give.

Waking up this morning, multiple mornings over the last couple weeks have already cemented the decision I've been waffling on.

Tomorrow...

Tomorrow, Gigi becomes mine.

CHAPTER SIXTEEN

Gigi

I'VE ALWAYS ASSUMED QUITTING my job and taking off for Europe by myself in my early twenties would be one of the most radical, outrageous things I could ever do.

Boy, was I wrong.

Turns out, not setting fire to my growing and simmering crush on Sebastian is riskier.

I can't stop thinking about him. It's been a week since the day he showed up at my apartment, sweet little grin twisting his lips, beard cleanly shaven, hair hidden beneath a ball cap and tucked behind his ears while holding two coffees before so sweetly asking me to hang out with him.

What's a girl supposed to do? How could I have possibly stopped my attraction to him when he looks at me the way he does?

And that moment when he leaned in and licked his lips? The promise of what a kiss from him would be like radiated down deep between my thighs. For a moment, I was tempted.

Then reality slammed into my brain.

This is a guy who's *married*. Or is he? Sort of though, right? Because even if his wife says she wants a divorce, things can change.

So when he pulled back up to my bar and building, handed me his phone and asked for my number, the smartest decision would have been to say no thanks.

I'm learning when it comes to dealing with my feelings for Sebastian, I'm not all that smart.

"You want my number?"

"Yeah…"

My hand shakes as I slide his phone into mine. Sebastian Hendrix wants my phone number. "What for?"

I glance at him as I start tapping in my phone number. "Because I like talking to you."

"Right."

Such a simple statement shouldn't make me warm all over. I can't even blame the heat or the sun, it's February for crap's sake and we've been in his air-conditioned car for a half hour.

My thumbs tremble, causing it to take me three tries to get my number right. Thanks a lot, fat thumbs. Before I can stop myself, I send myself a text that he'll see. Hotshot's digits.

Handing his phone back to him, he takes it, sliding his hand beneath mine holding his phone and squeezing.

"Gigi."

My other hand is already wrapped around the door handle. Is it hot in here? It has to be. Perhaps his AC is on the fritz and the temp just rose thirty degrees.

I'm still remembering the way he licked his lips, gazing at me with such warmth in those green eyes my body still feels it.

"Yeah?" *I have to force myself to look at him.*

His hand squeezes mine so sweetly. He's warm and strong. Calloused palms scrape the back of my knuckles. Man. That scrape would feel delicious in other places.

"Look at me."

It takes effort but I finally manage and when I do, his expression is inscrutable. My lips part in response. This is not a friendly look. It's most definitely not a happy one, although I've rarely seen them on Sebastian so I'm not altogether certain what that looks like him. It's definitely not anger.

It is, however, intense. Extremely so.

"If I were in a better place, a different place, I think I'd end this walk and our time together today very differently."

"What?"

He drops my hand slowly, sliding his phone out of my palm and smirking. "You heard me." *He waves his phone back and forth.* "We'll talk soon, okay?"

I don't think talking anymore to Sebastian is good for my health. My heart is currently palpitating at unusual speeds.

"Okay," *I croak out and climb out of his car. It takes a second to gather my balance, although the cement beneath my feet is firm and flat. It's my knees that are wobbling like a newborn foal.* "Bye, hotshot."

My first text from Sebastian came later that evening.

Someday you're going to tell me why you insist on calling me that.

He was referencing his nickname. I smiled, so surprised at the buzz of my phone in my pocket while I worked behind the bar that night on a slower than normal evening that when another buzz came while I tried to think of a reply, his next text made me roll my eyes.

I'd prefer the lone wolf.

No way, I'd typed back. **You need a team behind you. A pack. Like the Ice Kings.**

I hadn't even thought of my response, and it wasn't very playful, but I wasn't going to ignore him despite the alarm bells blaring in my brain while I remembered one of the last things he'd said to me earlier that day.

How would it have ended differently?

What different place does he need to be in?

Would that different place slash different ending come with those full, dark pink lips pressed to mine? Perhaps parting my own before he tasted me fully?

Ridiculous.

Yet what else could he have meant?

That was a week ago. Since then, he's texted almost every day.

Good morning texts. *Do anything fun today?* texts. Even more mundane texts follow, like, *Favorite food. Favorite color. Favorite movie and favorite show to binge-watch.*

Uh. The Last Kingdom. Obviously. No one should have to ask that question. Ragnar... le sigh.

If he's been offended I've rarely asked the same back of him, he hasn't shown it, but if I'm not mistaken, I think he's trying to get to know me. Slowly. Platonically. And I'm not quite sure what to do with that.

I've sent him texts after games, congratulating the team on their winning streak, the fact they're now ahead by five games in their division is huge with six weeks left before playoffs begin.

And maybe I shouldn't have teased him about being the best the other night, but I couldn't stop myself. I expected something stupid back. Maybe a hidden talent like juggling, or that he's a yo-yo master.

When I received his text back saying he wanted to see me, I froze. I stared at the phone.

Then I had no clue what to do. I really like this guy. He's confused about his marriage. He's absolutely the last person I should be spending time with or luring into conversations with flirtatious texts. I ignored it until I had a better response.

I haven't heard from him since.

I do know that tomorrow is Saturday so I have got to get my shit together and fast.

"Georgia."

My dad is standing across from the bar, brown envelope in hand several inches thick, a deep line digging into his forehead between his bushy brows.

I finish drying a glass and toss the towel onto the bar, wiping my hands down my hips. "What's up?"

"We been talking about you liking working at the bar or if you want to do something different, right?"

"Not this again."

"It's not. Not exactly anyway."

Based on his expression, this doesn't sound good. "Okay..."

"I've been thinking about something for a while. Started thinking about it while you were gone, actually, but my heart and head couldn't connect."

"Spit it out, Dad," I tease and flash him a smile, but it wobbles. It's rare I see my dad uncertain or so serious.

"Thinking of retiring. Selling the bar."

"What?"

My hands go to the towel on the bar and twist it in my fist. "But—"

"I want you to have it. If you want it."

"Dad—"

"You don't have to. And if you want, I can keep it but frankly, I'm getting too old for this crap and the late nights and the wondering if we'll keep making it. And I don't really like the idea of putting that pressure on your shoulders either, but I also can't stomach the idea of it going to someone else. Or a business who wants to tear this place down. It might not be much, but it's been mine for over thirty-five years, so I figure it should go to someone who'll care for it. But if that's not you—"

"It is."

I grab the envelope he has without further thought. No way am I letting George's go. There's a table in the corner that has multiplication facts scratched into it from when I used to sit and do my homework for goodness' sake. This is my home as much as it's a bar.

My fingers tremble as I undo the clasp and slide out a thick stack of legal paperwork and I scan the top page which doesn't say much except for the name of my dad's law firm.

"You want me to buy George's? I don't have—"

"For one dollar. It's easier that way. So if you want it, it's yours."

"Dad. Why so sudden?"

A rock sinks to my stomach. He's been on me about this for months, and he's been more tired lately. "Are you...?"

"Healthy as a horse, butterfly. I promise you."

A weight falls from my shoulders and yet I'm still shaky, grin wobbling as I inspect him. He seems sad. Older. "Dad, if there's something you're hiding from me—"

"There's not, I promise. I'm just old. Getting older.

Slower. Want George's to go to someone who will love it, but if it's not you, I'm okay with that, too. Not asking you to decide tonight, but if you're interested, take your time deciding if it's right for you. You know I don't like the idea of saddling you with something that might make you feel trapped someday but if you're happy here, think you could be happy here, then there's no one else I'd want more running George's than you."

"Thanks, Dad. It means a lot you'd trust me with this."

"I'd trust you with anything, butterfly. Now come give your old man a kiss before I take off."

He doesn't even have to ask. I round the bar and plant a kiss on his cheeks, squeezing him tight. "Love you, Dad."

"Always love you."

He unwraps my arms from his waist, because somehow they've cemented themselves to him. Thinking of my dad getting old and slowing down makes my heart hurt.

He's all I have.

When he pulls away, he brushes my forehead with his lips and tugs on one of my braids. "You good for the night?"

"Yeah. Go home. I've got this."

I wait until he's gone, grabbing his coat from the back office and doing another scan of the bar on his way toward the front door before I reach for the papers again.

Run George's Bar? Alone?

I've never considered, but like my dad said, who else would love it as much as he and I do?

It's hours later when the bar is closed, I'm exhausted and smelly, curled up on my couch in my apartment with the stack of papers in my hand when my phone dings. My eyelids are heavy and yet I perk right up.

There's only one person who would text me this late. Or early, depending on your sleep schedule.

Odd how a simple chime of a text tone can make me think of Sebastian.

It's probably a sign I'm in far deeper than I should be with him.

Taking a chance here since it seems like you've blown me off but hoping it's been a busy week for you. Still thinking about you. Plans tomorrow?

And just like that, I'm rattled all over again. I've been able to forget thinking of Sebastian ever since my dad's announcement.

Now? At three o'clock in the morning and he's still awake? Thinking of *me*. My heart does some wild, rapid flutter as the realization settles.

Goodness. I think this guy *likes* me.

My thumb hovers over the screen. I've always been a risk-taker. I tend to act first, think of consequences after... my marriage to Evan the perfect example of leaping before I look. Yet now, I have responsibility.

I have a potential plan for my future that I can see myself loving and I'm not sure where Sebastian fits in.

But screw it.

He's a pro hockey player. He'll surely be destined for something more.

I'm probably a rebound for him.

A walk on the "wild" side.

I'm not sure if that excites me or hurts me, but before I can think too much about it, I type out a text.

I'll be working. But I'd like to see you.

I turn my phone off, toss it onto the coffee table littered with books, and I shove my dad's papers back into the envelope.

I have time to consider all of this insanity swirling around me.

What I need is sleep and a clear head so I can decide what to do with it.

CHAPTER SEVENTEEN

Gigi

GEORGE'S IS HOPPING TONIGHT, busier than it usually is. I've been running on my feet all night. The only break I took was to run upstairs to change out of my jeans and into denim cut-off shorts. I'm a freaking hot mess but thankfully I've got Dom behind the bar working with me. He doesn't work much due to his classes at the University in Charlotte, and our generally slow evenings, but when he's here, he's a lifesaver.

I don't know what in the world it is about the place the last few weeks but we've been busier than normal almost every night. While it's not like me to look a gift horse in the mouth, I'm still wondering why.

Especially when most of our customers tonight are sporting dress shirts and ties, all of which are haphazardly undone and loosened. Perhaps there was a nearby wedding or something.

Most of the tables are full. There's been a crowd around

the pool table and dartboard and I've already had to change the toilet paper in the women's bathroom a couple of times, something much different when we can normally go several days.

All that to say, I'm exhausted. I'm sweaty. I've totally forgotten about my text sent to Sebastian last night about working and being willing to see him tonight until I'm pouring two gin and tonics for a pair of younger looking women near the pool table and a hand I'd now recognize anywhere settles itself on the bar across from me.

"Hey you." I'm already grinning, raising my head to look at Sebastian while I place the drinks on the tray. The expression I see on his face wipes the still forming smile right off my face. "What is it? Are you okay?"

"Can we talk a minute in private?"

I scan the bar on instinct. "I'm kind of busy. Can it wait a little while?" Or tomorrow, with the way this crowd is going.

"Not really."

I swear, beneath his beard his jaw is clenched. "One minute. Won't take long."

"I've got this," Dom says, grabbing the tray from the bar. "Take your minute." His dark brown eyes flicker between the two of us. I know he recognizes Sebastian. Hard not to when I've had the televisions constantly on hockey games.

"You sure?"

With Sebastian looking all growly, I'm not sure I want to be alone with him. I glance at him, and he seems to understand my hesitancy because he makes a face that makes his features loosen. "Please, Gigi."

"Okay. Sure." I turn to Dom who already has the tray in his hands and has now loaded it with six different beer bottles. "Thanks Dom."

"No problem, Georgia."

I huff a laugh as he walks toward the bar back. I hold the lift for him before following him out. Very few people call me my given name so much so that sometimes it surprises me it's my actual name.

Sebastian has pushed his way through the small crowd at the bar and meets me at the end where I take off down the hall. The office is small and messy, smells usually like stale popcorn for some strange reason because we don't sell popcorn. My dad has a habit of leaving piles all over his desk and the small leather loveseat is so old there's barely any padding left in the cushions. There's a tear on one side of the back that I think has been there longer than I've been alive.

Embarrassment floods my cheeks at how old and junky it looks. I turn to Sebastian to say something, ask him what he wants, apologize for the lack of space or do *something* when I realize he's so close to me, I can make out all the tiny lines on his upper lip.

"What is it?"

His hands fist at his sides and he flexes them. "I want to see how something feels."

"What?" I jerk back, but I'm stopped by those large palms of his. One at the side of my neck, one on my cheek.

"Sebastian—"

"This," he mutters, still growling, right before he slides his lips to mine and presses.

And oh my... he's *kissing* me. Sebastian Hendrix, my crazy year-long crush has his hands on my face and his mouth pressed to mine and what in the world is going on?

My head spins, all the thoughts and I'm so confused I'm still tense when he tilts my chin and changes the angle. I gasp, shocked from everything that's happening which means my lips part and then his tongue slides inside mine along with a groan that seems to shoot straight from his gut.

It's that sound, the rumble of his chest pressed so firmly against mine that snaps me back to the present with the sting of a rubber band.

My hands find their way to his chest and I shove.

"Don't ever use me like that again."

My chest is heaving. The taste of him is on me, inside my mouth, and I wipe my lips to brush it away. "Don't ever do that again," I repeat.

"I'm not—"

"Please. I won't be your experiment to see if you can enjoy kissing women when you're still strung up about Madison."

He jerks back. Eyes widening in a swirl of emotions. He gapes at me, closes his mouth. His nose scrunched and lips curl and he takes a step forward.

I step back, bumping my backside to my dad's desk. Papers go flying and I'm pretty sure I'm sitting on an uncapped pen due to the poking sensation in my left ass cheek.

"That's not what this was and if you think back to all our interactions in the last few weeks, you'd know that."

I refuse to believe this. He's not even divorced yet. Technically, he's still married and while this wouldn't make me a homewrecker, it doesn't feel right.

"Madison—"

"My divorce is finalized. And I've spent the last week thinking of what you'll taste like and you *know* that because you know what I said the last time you got out of my car. And as for kissing?"

He smirks.

I swear it makes my lady parts tingle. Especially when

he leans in closer and that tingle turns to a full-on torment deep in the apex of my thighs. His cologne is woodsy with a light hint of citrus. Edibly scrumptious.

"We'll be doing that a whole hell of a lot more."

I still can't catch my breath. I can't move. I can only stare at this magnificent, beautiful specimen of a man that I'm pretty sure was hand carved from stone.

"What is happening here?"

My hands curl into the edges of my dad's thirty-year-old Formica topped and metal desk. There's a part that's ripped and torn, and it digs into my palms. Pretty sure I'll be dripping blood from my hands with an ink stain on my ass by the time I get out of here. None of that is anything compared to the rioting inside my chest.

"I like being with you. I like it when I *think* about you. I like laughing with you. None of that has anything to do with experimenting with women like I'm gonna start leaving a string of puck bunnies in my wake. That's not who I am. I kissed you because I've been thinking of kissing you since I woke up at your apartment and I wanted to see what kissing you would be like."

He's been thinking of this since then? Woah. "And?"

"I want more."

He's no longer married. He wants me. He's single and he wants me. Which means there's really nothing to do except do what I've wanted to do since the first time he sauntered into the bar.

I launch myself at him, hands going straight to the back of his head so I can tangle them in his hair. His beard scrapes against my cheeks and my lips as I kiss him. He doesn't tense like I did. He doesn't wait or pause. He opens my mouth with his and he takes over in such a way that I have a very firm and very realistic preview of what this man will be like in bed. Confident.

Dominating.

Freaking incredible and powerful.

He spins us so quickly I lose my footing but his hands are clenched to my waist, digging into the waistband of my jean shorts and then I'm practically thrown against the wall. The door handle digs into my back causing me to mewl in pain but it's nothing compared to the pleasured whimpers already sliding out of my mouth.

Yes. This. This has been worth a year-long abstinence lull due to not finding anyone interesting besides Sebastian since I've been home. Already my core is clenching. Needing.

This is… this is not what I thought he meant when he texted if he could see me today.

Wowzers.

He yanks back, his breath coming in ragged spurts and he presses his forehead to mine. "We should stop. I think this has gone well past the minute I promised."

"Dom can handle it." Now that I have him, now that I've tasted him, I don't want to let him go. "Do you have a game tomorrow?"

"Day off."

"You could…" I slide my hand out of his hair, to his shoulders, down the curves of his chest and lose my train of thought.

His hands cover mine, stopping their exploration. Pity. "I could what?"

"You could wait for me to be done here. We could finish this later?"

My lip finds its way to my teeth. I don't usually lack confidence. I have no problems asking for what I want, but

Sebastian makes me nervous. Him recently out of a marriage to a woman he loves makes me more so. Being a rebound isn't my thing. And I don't want to start it with him. Not when my heart's already involved.

"You want that?"

When I look up at him, he's grinning down at me. Eyes shining with anticipation. Excitement. I do this to him, and man, is it thrilling.

"If you want."

"I want. And I want one more kiss before we leave here."

A knock pounds on the door behind me, making me jump. "Need you, Georgia. Getting slammed out here!"

"Be right there, Dom!"

"Georgia?"

I grin up at Sebastian and giggle. "It *is* my name."

He shakes his head, laughing in a way I've never seen him before. Unguarded. That's the way he looks right now. "I had no clue."

"Then I suppose if you wait around tonight, we'll have lots more to learn about each other."

His gaze dips and scans. He pauses at my exposed skin between my shirt and shorts. His inspection is so intense even my covered skin flushes and heats beneath him. "Yeah, we do."

He kisses me again without warning, without tongue, but still hot and heavy and when he pulls back, he has one eyebrow arched.

"That wasn't so bad, was it?"

I lick my lips and shrug. Reaching for the door handle behind me, I tease him. "Passable as decent."

"Ouch." His hand goes to his chest.

"Maybe you need more practice, hotshot." I wink and

flush with happy thoughts as his smile widens. "I'll see you later?"

"I'll be the guy at the bar waiting for closing time. Go. If you don't mind, I need a minute."

I peek down. I can't help myself. Not with that innuendo. When I do, he adjusts himself and well, hey there... it looks like there's a lot to adjust.

"Nice," I say, flashing another wink before I hurry out the door. "Take your time!"

CHAPTER EIGHTEEN

Sebastian

I'VE SPENT hours sitting here, drumming my thumbs on the bar top. I've only had a few drinks. The last thing I need to do tonight is be too drunk for whatever comes next. The problem is I've had hours to figure out exactly what that next step is and I'm uncertain how to proceed.

I've had sex with one woman in my entire life.

Before tonight, I've kissed one woman—unless you count Macy Johnston in the sixth grade at a pool party during a not-so-innocent pre-teen game of Truth or Dare.

I skipped right over the wild "sowing your oats" phase when the guys in college and early years making pros were plowing through women like they plowed through their millions. It's never once interested me. And it's not only because I had Madison.

When I was eleven, I made a girl cry getting off the school bus because I told her I didn't like her and didn't want to be her friend. My father found out, sat me down and told me that a woman's heart is her most precious possession. Her body is the second. As a man, you treat the latter with absolute respect and the first with absolute tenderness.

I was young, but my dad's a man of a few words, few times of seriousness. It was our first serious, man-to-man conversation, and it stuck.

Which means, I should probably figure out exactly what I want out of this night with Gigi before I charge forward and for the first time, ignore that advice from my dad.

The only thing I'm certain of is that my body wants her. Her lips were softer than I could have possibly imagined. She tasted like fresh life and sweetness.

She felt better than a warm towel wrapped around you right out of the shower when it's thirty degrees below zero in a Minnesota winter.

It's closing time and while I offered to help Gigi and Dom clean up and take care of empties, she insisted I sit down, enjoy my glass of water and it'd go faster with me sitting there than it would if I helped.

Not exactly the best compliment I've ever received, but I listen and soon, she's waving goodbye to Dom who leaves through the front door. She stands next to it while the guy who has several inches on me looms over Gigi and gives me a look before he leaves and she locks the door behind him.

"I'm almost done," she says, turning to me with a look of exhaustion stamped all over her face and weighing down her slumped shoulders.

"I'm more than capable of helping you wipe down tables."

"I'm sure you can, but I have a system." She comes to

me then and places her hand on my cheek like she's done it every hour, every day, for years.

It shoots warmth straight below my waist.

"I'm not trying to offend you."

She hides a yawn behind her other hand and shakes her head.

"Hey, if you're tired, I can take off."

"And if you want to do that, I won't try to talk you out of it, but since you were so honest earlier, maybe it's my turn. Since the night you passed out in my bed and woke up in it, I've been hoping I'd get another chance at that scenario without the hangover and hazy memories."

Shit. Damn. This girl. She's so petite she only has a couple inches on me. It's the perfect height for me to slide my arm to her lower back and pull her forward so she's between my legs.

"I want that too, Georgia." I kiss her quickly and when I pull back, it takes her a moment to open her eyes. When she does, her smile is lazy, and my dick is hardening.

Yeah. I want a night in her bed, whatever that means.

"No one actually calls me that," she says. She dips a towel on the bar into a bucket of cleaning solution and wrings it out. "It's why I go by Gigi."

"Yeah, but it's something I didn't know about you and now I like that I know it and I'm guessing not everyone you meet does."

"I like that you do." She rolls to her toes and gives me a kiss. "This won't take long. You need another drink?"

"If I do, I know how to get one. Go get cleaned up before I'm too tired to walk up those metal stairs and risk my life."

She gives me a funny look and then shakes her head. "All right, hotshot."

It's less than thirty minutes later when she has the tables and chairs cleaned, the bar wiped down, the cleaning stuff taken somewhere and left wherever she put it.

She comes back from the office, keys and phone in her hand, shaking them and grins.

"I have a feeling there was something else you forgot that night you came here and crashed upstairs."

There's a lot of things I blacked out about that night, none have anything to do with her.

"Like what?"

"Come on." She gestures with her head down the hallway. "And I'll show you my cupboard under the stairs."

She's laughing at she says it, and while I'm totally flummoxed, I have the startling realization that there are probably very few places where I won't follow this girl.

So a cupboard under the stairs it is.

"WHAT THE HELL IS THIS PLACE?"

She's taken me to the storage room. Not exactly where I expected. As the door to the bar behind us closes, she tugs on a string hanging from the ceiling, lighting up shelves of supplies. The room is tiny and for one brief moment, every horror movie I've ever watched sparks in my memory.

"Uh. Gigi?"

I turn to see her smiling at me, keys dangling from her hands. "You don't remember?"

"Being shoved into a cramped storage room full of paper products? No. Can't say I do."

"Come on." She slides behind a metal rack where packages of paper towels sway back and forth when she bumps into it. I follow her, swearing I hear the music to afore-mentioned thriller flicks.

"The hell?" I ask, when she pulls out a set of keys and pulls open a metal door. A horrific creaking noise squeals into the tiny room.

With her back to me, she laughs.

The door is barely taller than Gigi so I have to almost bend in half to see what she's laughing about.

"The cupboard under the stairs," she says gallantly, swinging an arm out. "This staircase leads to my apartment so I don't have to go outside to get in and out when the bar is open. But you made the drunken, and admittedly, cute, Harry Potter reference the night I dragged you up here."

I'd been wondering how in the hell she got me up those metal stairs.

"I like to read," I mutter.

She laughs harder, shoulders shaking. Dipping her head to make sure she clears the door, she grins at me over her shoulder. "You coming?"

I wouldn't miss this trip for the world. "After you."

I have to bend so far forward to get through the small door I'm practically kissing my knees but as soon as I'm through, she's turned on another light switch and we take the definitely more stable set of cement stairs to the top where she unlocks two different locks on the door before pushing it open. As soon as we're in her apartment, I give the place a quick scan, noticing not much is different from what I remember before.

Bright colors. Small tables covered with books and a few cameras placed on top. Shelves heave from the weight of more books and then there are the photos she'd been trying to explain to me when I'd rudely left that morning.

To my right is the arch that will take me to her bedroom

area and bathroom, and to my left is the door to outside along with her kitchen.

"You're staring at my place like you can't decide what to clean up first."

Gigi's still laughing and this time, I give her a full smile. "You are not tidy."

She shrugs and tosses her keys and purse onto her kitchen counter, possibly the only thing in this place that's been cleaned recently.

"Life's too short to waste it picking up every thirty seconds," she says. Her hair is pulled up into a bun on top of her head, stripes of teal and blonde mixed together.

I follow her movements as she unwraps a cloth band from her hair and it all falls to a few inches below her shoulders. She's watching me, cheeks flushed with slight purple marks beneath her eyes that shows she's either nervous, or turned on.

Either way, she's exhausted.

As she shakes out her hair, a quiet groan escapes her parted, pale lips and it's my undoing.

I go to her, two quick strides to erase the space between us, and she neither backs away or moves forward. Her hands stay in her hair, massaging her scalp until I reach her.

My hands find hers and I take over, brushing her hands away. "Let me do this."

I've dreamed of what her hair would feel like my hands. All that color. All her vibrancy shown in strands of hair shouldn't be so damn sexy but it's Gigi, so it is.

"I should shower," she says, moaning as I massage her scalp, her neck. If I could turn her around and do the same for her shoulders, I would but that would also mean removing her shirt. Thinking of her in her shower while she's fully dressed in front of me makes me bite back my own groan.

What is it about this girl? She's so damn different—

I squeeze my eyes closed and tamp down that train of thought. This isn't about Madison. Or me searching for different.

"You're tired."

She nods, her head collapsing against my chest. "And I reek like beer and a whole host of nasty things."

"You smell like apples."

It must be her shampoo because the more I play with her hair, the more the scent wafts into the air.

She laughs and warm breath skates across my chest through my shirt.

"Come on. Let's get you to bed. It's late."

"Early."

"Whatever." I slide my hands down her arms until I have both her hands in mine. She tips her head up, smiling sleepily up at me and blinks.

"You don't have to be the nice guy here, hotshot. In fact, I think I might prefer it if you weren't."

Challenge accepted. "How about the first time you see me not being a nice guy is a time when you're not about to collapse on your feet. Like in the morning, after a decent night's rest."

"Well when you put it that way. Follow me." She winks and a laugh bursts from my chest. She lets go of one of my hands and tugs on mine still holding hers until she's holding my hand and dragging me to her room. With her ass in front of me, the white threads dangling down from her frayed denim shorts are a beacon to my eyes.

God, she's sexy. I could palm her entire ass with one

hand and I have to bite down on my lip so I don't actually do what I want and maybe bite *her*.

Tiny but mighty. My guess, physically as much as internally.

"I have extra toothbrushes in the bathroom in a bucket by the sink. You can go first if you'd like while I clear off a spot for you on the bed."

"Thanks." Another laugh. Another smile. It feels like I haven't done it in years and around Gigi I can't stop.

She moves to pull away from me, but I yank her back to me. Surprise shows on her face right before I lower my mouth to hers and slip my tongue inside.

I keep the kiss slow and gentle despite the need inside me threatening to take her up on her offer to not be a nice guy. It's ingrained in me to be a gentleman, but in the bedroom, I like taking the lead.

She'll learn.

I release her, running my thumb beneath her bottom lip when her eyes slowly flutter open. Before she's fully back to the present, I head to the bathroom. It's a small room with a shower, possibly sized just for Gigi. The showerhead alone would only hit my shoulders. I dig through one of the bins she mentioned and come back with a hot pink toothbrush and a small tube of toothpaste. I splash cold water on my face and when I open the door, it takes me a second to realize I'm in the same apartment.

Or perhaps this is another magical porthole.

"You done?" Gigi asks. She comes around the corner wearing a tank top so thin I could tear it apart in two seconds and shorts so damn short she's leaving barely anything to the imagination. She might be petite, but her hips are fucking perfect.

"What'd you do, throw it all out the window?"

The room where I'd barely been able to see anything before is now almost spotless.

"You're going to have to stop giving me so much shit for my housecleaning habits. I'll find your weakness and won't let up either."

She pokes me in the chest, but I'm faster. I grab her finger and kiss the tip. "Deal. But seriously?"

"I do have dressers and a laundry basket. Most of it was dirty. Get in bed. I'll be right there."

"Yes, ma'am." No better words have been spoken to me in a long time.

CHAPTER NINETEEN

Gigi

I AM ABOUT to climb into bed with Sebastian Hendrix.

I'm still spinning from this wild and crazy turn of events, but dang... what a great life I'm currently leading.

In the bathroom, I make quick work of scrubbing off my makeup and moisturizing. I brush my teeth and forego flossing even though I'm pretty obsessive about clean teeth, odd considering I'm not obsessive about anything non-teeth related.

Although, I can always buy more clothes. My teeth are the only ones I have. Grinning like a maniac into the mirror, I make sure my teeth are pearly white clean.

There's a high possibility I'm about to turn out of my bathroom, catch sight of Sebastian in my bed, and then collapse onto the floor in the blink of an eye.

He's staying. And he's thought of me.

And he *kissed* me! Kisses that are absolutely delicious, make my body sing like I was at the Opera.

Oh dear. If I don't get out of the bathroom now, he's either going to come see if I passed out from sleep or worse, he might already be asleep.

I throw open the door so quick I have to jump back before it scrapes over my toes. It slams against the wall and I throw out my hand so it doesn't bounce back and smack me in the face.

"Everything okay?"

"Yup."

Not a freaking chance. Sebastian took to heart me telling him to climb into my bed.

Oh dear sweet baby Jesus in a manger, he's here. Sprawled out on top of the covers with nothing but a pair of skintight and short boxer briefs in sight except for the muscles. A beautiful light fan of hair over his pecs that thin to one trail down his belly and beyond. His arms are thrown behind his head giving me the best display possible of his arms and that beard of his. His whole face turned in my direction, one brow arched while I stand in my doorway like a freaking fool, totally checking him out.

"Nervous?"

"Nope." Hell yes. He's too much. Too kind. Too hot. Too sweet. Too grouchy.

His lips lift, top one disappears beneath his mustache and his teeth are just as white as mine. I'd happily bet some serious money some are fake, but they're still pretty.

"Georgia."

Him using my real name snaps me out of my lustful viewing and I glare at him. "Gigi. I'm coming, you just surprised me. I wasn't expecting to see... so much of you." I throw out my arm to gesture *all* that's him and earn a deep, throaty chuckle in response.

It makes my knees wobble. To prevent having my fear

come true and collapsing to the floor, I hurry to the bed, lift the sheets and dive under them. Like a complete idiot, I tuck them close to my sides and flap down my arms.

"Nothing's going to happen tonight," Sebastian says, and I can *feel* him moving on the bed and hear him getting closer.

I blink and then he's there, looming over me, propped up on one arm, his palm to his cheek, and that beard is so close.

I want to tug on it. Bring him closer. Throw inhibitions out the window.

It's not so easy. Over the last couple of months, Sebastian has become a good friend to me.

"Why not?"

He glances down at my mouth, smile turning up the edges of his lips. His free hand slides over my arm that's plastered to my bed like I've been poured in quick-set cement.

"Because you're lying here like you've been frozen and I told you, I want us well-rested. You seem nervous and I am too."

"You... you... *you're* nervous?"

He chuckles and leans down and that brush of his beard over my cheek does crazy things to the synapses in my brain. Pretty sure if I had an MRI I'd be lit up like a Christmas Tree extravaganza.

"Gigi. I started dating Madison when we were fifteen. She's the only woman I've ever been with and you might not like me saying her name or bringing her up, especially not now or here, in your bed, but yeah... as much as I've thought about doing things with you over the last couple of weeks, trust me, I'm nervous."

"I don't mind you bringing her up."

His eyes narrow and I press my hand to his cheek. My thumb brushes along his scruff and toward his mouth before I sweep it back. God. I love a man with a well-groomed beard.

"I don't," I repeat, because he's looking at me like he wants to argue. "She's part of you and you've known her forever. Yeah, in my bed isn't the greatest place, but that doesn't mean I don't want to hear. You've gone through a lot, and don't get me wrong, I'm freaking glad you're here, but I get it. I'm only nervous because you showing up tonight and all that's happened since then has totally surprised the hell out of me."

The lines around his beautiful green eyes loosen and he blinks. After adjusting so he's under the covers, he rolls toward me and opens his arms. "Come here, Georgia."

I huff and listen, tucking my forehead where his throat meets his shoulder. He's so warm and whatever cologne he wears smells so damn good, I settle in closer, pressing my hands to his chest.

"You feel good next to me," I murmur and earn a brief chuckle from him.

"I like being next to you."

And my heart melts into a puddle.

We talk about his games and the upcoming week while he plays with my hair. It's whispered words, brief touches and kisses, and yet this feels so much more intimate than a night of bodies pressed together. He tells me about his family back in Minnesota, about his sisters and their kids. I tell him about my mom, and as the sun begins to make its way to the horizon, I close my eyes and we fall asleep.

WARM LIPS FOLLOWED by the scruff of a beard along my jaw bring me to life the next morning. I don't have to open my eyes to know Sebastian is next to me, or what he's looking for. I lie still, allowing him to kiss and tease me with his mouth while his hand stays still at my hip. It appears we've barely moved at all in our sleep but instead of being on my side facing him like the last time I remember, I wake on my back, with his body pressed down the length of my side.

Sebastian's hand begins its own exploration and slides to my stomach while his mouth travels south to my shoulder and collarbone.

I shiver, unable to fight again any longer and feel the curve of my lips lifting.

"Mmm. Good morning." I turn my head away, giving him easier access.

"It's definitely a good morning."

My body responds to his words, his touch, the warmth of his mouth on my skin, teasing and warming me oh so slowly. His hand at my stomach slides across, down, beneath my tank and as his flesh presses to mine, expectation ignites down my spine.

"Sebastian."

"Stop me if I go too fast."

"There's no such thing. Trust me."

"Trust me, I'm afraid *I* could go too fast."

I laugh and turn my head so I'm facing him and slide my fingers into his hair. Giving his silky, messy locks a tug, I bring his face to mine. "We'll deal with it if that happens."

"Like hell, it will," he practically growls and presses his lips to mine. "I'll manage."

He kisses like he's been starved for me, like he's been

waiting for hours for me to awaken just so he can taste me and taste me he does. He leaves no part of me untouched as he takes my mouth and begins exploring my body in earnest.

Everything about him seems to be a puzzle, a missing piece here or there, a clue I have to dig for. And every time I find one, it feels like the smallest victory, watching him start to laugh, to smile... to admit he *wants* this.

There are so many layers to Sebastian I'm not sure how long it'll take me to uncover them all, but damn it all to hell I am up to the task of searching. We kiss fervently as he presses up my shirt. His thumb runs beneath my breast and I arch into him, desperate for more. His featherlight touch coupled with the roughness of his calloused fingertips and palms sends sensations rolling through me, making me crave more, or everything. My back arches, and I tug on my shirt, pushing and pulling until I can remove it completely.

"Beautiful," he murmurs right before he rolls on top of me.

My legs spread, taking his weight and making room for him, and I barely have time to latch my fingers into his hair before he sucks one of my nipples into his mouth.

And oh God. His hair, I've spent years dying to know how it feels. Now, his mouth is the only thing I can think of. And he doesn't stop there. He kisses everywhere, as if he's trying to sear the memory of my shape into his brain with his lips. By the time he reaches down to my shorts, I am so ready for him it's almost embarrassing.

He lifts his head, green, cloudy eyes meet mine and I nod. "Please. I want you."

A salacious grin is my reward and as he tugs down my shorts, me lifting my hips to help, he continues kissing me.

The calla lily tattoo at my hip which he pays more attention to before moving down, glancing up at me, but I arch into him, giving my consent. Showing him my need.

At the first slide of his tongue at my center, my hips thrust up and I cry out, digging fingers into the sheets beneath me. "Oh. Yes."

He hums against my sex, presses me into the bed with one large, firm hand and with the other, he presses a finger inside of me.

I become a mess of sounds as he discovers what I like, which is everything. For a man who claimed to be nervous hours ago, he's certainly gotten over that in a hurry. He's a master at playing my body, adding a finger. Taking me slowly while driving me crazy with his tongue until I'm wet, so close but I don't want to come yet.

"I want you." I gasp it out, my hand flinging to my night-stand where I keep my condoms. "Nightstand. Please."

I don't know if I've ever been so needy, but with another slow swipe of his tongue that dives straight inside me, making me quiver, I don't even care. I've waited for this. Wanted this for so long and now that Sebastian is here, moving on top of me, giving me a close-up view of is *insanely sexy and perfect* abs, I want to etch every second of this into the deepest recesses of my brain.

Someday I'll be in a nursing home, drooling into Jell-O and telling the twenty-something nurse about the best sex I ever had and it'll be this moment.

This guy.

Sebastian kisses me, and I taste myself on his lips, his beard, and I hold him to me, fingers pressing into his cheeks and jaw to hold him close.

"Now, Sebastian."

"I like hearing you beg for me."

"I'll do it every day if you just get inside of me *now*."

He laughs, so husky and deep. I grin up at him as he opens the drawer to my nightstand. While he fumbles for a condom, I hook my fingers into the waistband of his boxer briefs. He's so damn pretty I don't know where to focus first, until I reveal his dick. Wide, thick, perfect length with a pearly drop of liquid at the end of it. Yeah, it's as impressive as he was last night in the office.

I take him in hand, needing to feel the weight of him and at that first touch, his forehead drops to mine. His groan echoes along my skin along with his muted, "Yes. Shit."

We watch together as I slide my hand up and down his shaft and then he kisses my temple, goes back to the condom and barks out a laugh.

"What?"

I stall my movements, surprised by his outburst and then he's back, a red condom wrapper in his hand and a smirk making his eyes gleam. Embarrassment stings my cheeks as I realize what it is.

Cherry-flavored condom. A random item I grabbed on a rare girl's night out when I first got back and tried to reconnect with old friends. It was a bachelorette party and I went home with condoms in more flavors than I knew existed. Why I kept them, I have no idea.

"I've wanted this with you since that morning I spent the night and a cherry-flavored condom went flying from your purse."

"What?"

"That morning when you looked for eye drops. One flew out of your purse and I swear I got hard when I saw it."

"Oh," I drawl. My hand at his dick begins to move again.

"Trust me. I've thought about that condom a lot. And what it would be used for."

"Next time." I seal my promise with a kiss and soon he has a regular condom in his hand, tearing it open. I take it from him, impatient and not ashamed in the least.

"God, that's the best thing I've heard in a long time."

I laugh. He's ridiculous. And then his dick in my hand twitches and my laughing ceases.

The size of Sebastian's dick is absolutely no laughing matter.

Plus, I really want to roll it on him, play with his dick some more. Once he's sheathed, he slams his mouth to mine and finds my center. His thickness stays there while above me, his biceps strain with restraint.

"You sure you want this?" he asks.

For a second, his brows pull together and concern makes his gaze turn dark. I'm about to ask if he's sure, but he rocks against my tender bundle of nerves he's already primed and I arch into him.

"Yes."

"Good. Then hold on to the sheets for me, Gigi. I want to have some fun with you."

And play he does. He takes my body and slides deep inside of me, barely giving me time to adjust before we're tangled in sheets and kisses. His mouth, warm and wet and still lingering with the taste of me takes mine in a breath-stealing kiss as he begins to move.

We find our rhythm easily, like so much of the time we've already spent together, and I revel in two things.

Sebastian is an absolutely *God* in bed.

And my heart is dangerously close to taking a leap that will no doubt leave it smashed to smithereens.

I come so hard I scream his name, cling to his arms, to my headboard behind me. And when he follows right behind me, grunting my name, I keep my eyes wide open so I don't miss a single second of this moment I drive him over the cliff.

CHAPTER TWENTY

Sebastian

HOLY SHIT. I can hardly breathe. I'm pretty sure Gigi just sucked all my breath out of my lungs and straight through my dick.

She's incredible. Confident. Willing. She has no problems going for what she wants and holy crap it's sexy as hell even while she lets me lead because I'm no fool.

She's absolutely giving me permission to lead when she takes what I've given her and already I'm thinking of the next time.

There will be a next time. It'll be at my place, where there are dozens of rooms we can continue to explore whatever in the hell just exploded between us.

With that thought, I scrub a hand down my face, pinch my beard in my fist and groan. "I need to get home to Bruiser."

"Yeah?" Her smile is soft. Her lips are swollen. Her

beautiful eyes are glazed over like she still can't believe how good that was.

I know the feeling.

"Yeah. You want to come with me? Spend the day with me at my place?"

Two perfectly trimmed eyebrows arch and a smile makes the lines around her eyes crinkle. "Really?"

"Do you have to do anything here? For the bar?"

"Nothing that can't wait. You don't have anything to do?"

"Yeah. More of what we just did. In my swimming pool. Or maybe the shower afterward." I stop there before I spill *all* the places I've considered taking her, but her eyes are already shimmering with excitement. Anticipation. And something even better that's threatening to turn my dick hard before we even get out of this bed.

But I do need to let Bruiser out of his kennel. I've been a crappy doggy dad.

"So, my place? All you need is a swimsuit. I keep the pool heated even when it's cold out."

"Hotshot, I was going to say yes because you asked, but the pool sealed the deal."

I lean in and kiss her lips, smiling as I do it. "Why do you do that?"

"What?"

"Call me hotshot." I'm the only guy on the team she has a nickname for. She might call some by their last name but it's not the first time I've realized I'm the one who gets a different name altogether.

"Oh well, that's easy. The first time I saw you, I thought you were the hottest guy in the bar." Her nose crinkles and she pauses. "Then I saw your wedding ring."

She wanted me. That was over a year ago. My thumb finds my metal band and I cringe. Surely she's seen it. It's been a part of me for so long, only taking it off for games, I haven't even thought about removing it until this moment. Even over the last few weeks, after the divorce papers came, I've taken it off for games, slid it back on and never gave it a second thought.

Which is pretty fucked up now that I think about it. Especially with all the time I've spent with Gigi, starting to feel things for her, and I've still been wearing my loyalty to Madison shining bright for all to see.

"Gigi—"

She stops me by pressing her thumb to my lips. I kiss the tip playfully.

"This doesn't have to be serious, you know. I'm okay with fun, as long as it's safe fun and we keep our cards face up on the table."

She's read me totally wrong, and I inspect her gaze, I search for anything she's hiding, that she's lying. In truth, I like this woman, but I can't and won't lie to her and say my head is in the right place for something more than what she's offering. Even if I think I want it.

"I'm not sure I have anything serious to give. Not now. Not in the season either." We're close to playoffs. But that's not the only reason. I don't want to make promises I can't keep to Gigi.

I might not quite know what we're doing, but she's important to me and for that reason I don't want to hurt her.

"It's fine. I totally understand and if I wouldn't have been okay with it, I wouldn't have mentioned it." She smiles at me, kisses my mouth and pulls back. She reaches for her tank top and slides it on, her back curving as she wiggles it on and all I want to do is throw her back to the bed and make love to her again. "So, let's go get Bruiser before he starts hating me for keeping you from him, shall we?"

She saunters off, wearing only a tiny tank top and nothing else and I'm left staring after her, feeling like the world has decided to throw me on a wild journey I never could have predicted. How in the hell did I go from getting so drunk over my wife divorcing me to finding someone as beautiful as Gigi in the span of weeks?

"YOUR HOUSE IS SOMETHING ELSE, HOTSHOT."

Shaking my head, I bump my hip into her playfully. Bruiser, after freaking out when he saw Gigi and then ran in circles before running outside, is now nestled in her arms while she cradles him, following me through the house.

"It's pretty damn crazy some days to think it's mine. Can't lie."

From a two-thousand square foot split-level home that's forty years old to a five-thousand square foot two-story with a pool and enough yard space to build an indoor ice rink if I wanted, this home sometimes still takes my breath away.

Madison and I found it as soon as I was drafted here. The first few years I thought the expense on something so massive was absolutely the dumbest thing we could do. But then we talked about filling it with kids. Space for all our siblings and families to come visit. Then we planned to add an ice rink outside in its own barn. And a workout gym for both of us. With all the plans we had, most of them were done besides the rink I kept putting off.

But other than that, Madison and I spent five years

getting this monstrosity exactly how we wanted it... or at least how Madison wanted it. Some days I walk through and it feels almost cold and impersonal to me now that she's gone. There's a hell of a lot of white in my living room and now that I don't have her music or her distracting me, when I sit down and watch television at night, I'm still afraid of spilling something on the rug or couch knowing it'd earn me a tongue-lashing from Madison.

When did we become so damn grown-up or distant that a spill on a couch we can easily replace would send us into a week-long argument?

I think of all of this while I show Gigi the small movie room with eight theater-style chairs. Her jaw drops, turning to me. "Do you actually use this?"

"Yeah sometimes. When the guys are over or when family visits. My nieces and nephews think it's the coolest thing in the world."

"Man, I bet they do."

"My sister tells me that it's all they talk about. Coming to see Uncle Sebastian for his movies."

"Bet that knocks you down a peg or two, doesn't it?"

Admittedly, yeah. I mean, they all still live in the town I grew up. People know who they are. Anyone connected with hockey or a fan knows the story of the teacher's son who's made it big in the NHL. So yeah, hearing that my nephews only care about my projector screen and fancy chairs is a kick in the gut.

"Keeps me humble," I tell Gigi. "Besides, the oldest one is seven. He has a few years yet to redeem himself. But I do laugh when he watches my games on TV and then goes and tells his friends about my movie room and nothing about his uncle on TV."

Gigi pets Bruiser's back, sliding her hand through his white fur and he gives me a look of complete contentment.

"Is it bad," I say, getting her attention, "that right now I want to kick Bruiser out of this room and have you all to myself on those chairs?"

She slides me a look full of mischief and promise. "I think that's something I'll take you up on after you feed me and take me swimming."

"Right." I laugh. We left her house in such a hurry this morning so I could get home we haven't even had breakfast. "Come with me then. I'm sure I've got something I can cook."

We head back down the long hall that takes us almost straight to my kitchen and again, the stark whiteness of everything feels almost blinding as we reach the large, open space with the kitchen island in full view. There's a small stack of mail sitting there I haven't yet gone through outside tossing the divorce decree into my office.

I force myself to focus on the present, on Gigi walking through my house, bottom lip pulled in between her teeth mixed with her eyes wide with wonder and I wonder what she's thinking.

"Come on. My housekeeper and dog sitter usually stocks up the fridge when I'm gone. There should be plenty to choose from."

"I'm okay with anything. But I need something before the monster growling in my stomach bursts through. Then we're all in trouble."

"We'll get you taken care of. Bagel and cream cheese? Eggs and bacon? Yogurt? Name your poison."

I pull open the refrigerator door and scan the contents. I have everything I just mentioned. Rows of Greek yogurt in various flavors. I usually eat a few containers a day with some granola and eggs and even though I should be focused on my diet right now, getting my protein and fats on my day off so I have energy for tomorrow's game, I'm more focused on taking care of Gigi's needs.

"Yogurt and a bagel are good."

I step back and open the door. "You choose then."

"Your fridge looks like a grocery store," she says, and that sense of awe flickers in her gaze. "You're so... organized."

"Cara just stacks things and puts them away."

"Well my fridge looks like a mess compared to yours."

"I thought I wasn't going to get to tease you about your cleaning habits anymore."

"You're not." She shoves my chest and then grabs a yogurt cup, already peeling off the top before she turns back to me. "But I never said I wasn't going to tease you about yours."

"Spoons are in the drawer to the right side of the island. Help yourself. Need coffee?"

"Does a giraffe need a super long scarf?"

"What?" I laugh. It feels like I'm always laughing with Gigi and damn it feels good. "You are... you are something else, Georgia."

She sticks out her tongue at me and grins. "You've said that once or twice, you know."

"And I've meant it every time." I grab my own yogurt and container of eggs along with some spinach and cheese. An omelet won't take much work. When I reach for my own spoon in the island Gigi is at the corner, hip to the counter, one leg braced up and the bottom of her foot placed on her knee like she's in some yoga pose. "I also like you. Even when you stand like a flamingo."

She snorts and looks down, shrugging unashamedly. "I know. It's weird."

"It's cute. Like everything else about you."

I kiss the tip of her nose and then get to my breakfast. We need fuel for the plans I have for us today. Lots of fuel. Lots of plans.

CHAPTER TWENTY-ONE

Gigi

MY HAND IS PRESSED to the wet, white subway tile in front of me. It's all I can see. White tile. Water droplets. The tips of my teal-colored hair falling down.

None of it compares to the feel of the body behind me. Sebastian's hands on my shoulders, massaging them, following the massage with his mouth and his tongue as he kisses and playfully bites me.

"Please," I whimper against what his hand is doing to my front. My breasts are heavy and full, wanting, and my legs are shaking.

"Patience," he croons into my ear. He's been playing my body for what feels like hours. Bringing me to the edge. Pulling back. Taking me there again. The cliff of my orgasm is beyond my reach, but my insides are screaming for it.

This man, who was nervous thirty-six hours ago, has absolutely no reason to be nervous about anything, especially when it comes to his skills in the bedroom.

Between the day at his house yesterday, spending the night in his bed, and then this morning, I can't even believe I have any orgasms left in me.

He's a magician and every time he touches me he makes my body sing.

"Sebastian." I reach behind me and dig my nails into his hip, his ass. His thick erection prods my backside, sliding through my crease, eliciting so many sparks of pleasure and making me crave something I've never done. But not today.

"How many times do you think you can come for me today?" He presses two fingers deep inside me and twists. I scream out, throwing my head to his shoulder and biting down on my lip. My legs are trembling, but it's not the physicalness of all this. It's not even the fact I've decided I love a man who's bossy in bed.

What's the saying? A lady in the streets and a freak in the sheets.

They need something like that for guys. A gentleman in the streets, a bossy alpha jerk in the sheets.

Sign me up every time as long as the bossy jerk ends with the last name Hendrix.

"If you make me come again, you might break me," I huff out. He has one hand on my hip, the other deep inside me and every time I arch he pulls me back to him, holding me still, forcing me to *take* everything he's giving without being able to take it for my own.

Glorious.

I'm not sure I've ever had sex like this before.

"If I break you, I'll put you back together," he whispers at my throat, the sound so gravelly it scrapes across my skin and makes me shiver.

"Please, I need you." Definitely not just for sex, but I force myself to remember my promise.

This can stay easy and non-complicated.

"I like the way you beg." As he says it, he continues sliding his fingers inside of me, twisting, pulling, creating a maelstrom of physical effects that start at my center and spreads out until my spine feels like it's on fire and I bubble over, finally falling.

"Sebastian. Oh God," I cry out, my hand on the tiles slip. My arm bends until I collapse forward as he strings every wave from me with his fingers and before I'm done, a different part of him is right there, pressing in.

Filling me so completely whatever breath I have left in my lungs is thrust out.

"I can't wait," he says, gripping my hip, my shoulder, pulling me back against him as he takes me without pause. "Shit, you feel good. So tight. So hot."

He's so much taller than me his legs are bent, but I swear it only adds more power to his thrusts as he bends me forward and takes me to the cliff so fast, so powerfully, it's a beautiful pain mixed with extreme pleasure and it doesn't take long before I'm thrust over into another climax, or perhaps it's been the longest one of my life that might cause my heart to stop.

He slams into me, bends over and buries his face into my neck and growls through his own orgasm.

He's not even done before he curses. Apologizing.

Leaves me so abruptly I almost slip on the wet tiled floor.

"Oh, shit, Gigi. I'm so sorry. I wasn't wearing a condom."

Oh. *Oh.*

"It's okay. I'm on birth control." I make a mental note to ensure I'm not late in getting another shot and inhale a deep, trembling breath.

"Still. I'm so... I lost my mind with how good you feel. But I'm clean, I swear it. And well..." He makes a strange, almost choking like sound, and gently runs his hand down my side, over my hip. "Obviously you know I can't have children so... no worries there."

"Hey." I turn into his hold and his hand at my hip skims to my lower back. "It's okay. I'm not worried. I swear. It's fine. Really."

One brow quirks up along with a corner of his lip. "It was just fine?"

Laughing, I playfully smack his bare chest. "Better than fine. Incredible, but I'm pretty sure I haven't hidden how good you feel or how much I like what you do to me."

The tension in his eyes finally melts away and he bends down to brush his wet lips over mine. Reaching behind me, he turns off the water as he pulls back. "Let's get dried off and get something to eat. But I hope you know I feel the same way about you."

I didn't. I mean, men can enjoy a woman physically without a connection. It's easy for them to get off.

I didn't know how much I needed to hear I affect him so much until he says it.

"I do now."

"Good." He opens the door to his shower and comes back with a towel wrapped around his hips, one in his hands, and he wraps me in it before I take it from him and dry off.

This part after shower sex usually carries an awkwardness to it, especially with the way the sex between us just ended would make me think my natural reaction would be to hide myself from him.

He doesn't need to see the small lumps of my ass and thighs. The stretch marks at my hip or beneath my breasts.

But my instinct to cover myself, to hide the imperfect parts of me, doesn't rear its ugly head while I dry off my body and then wrap the towel around my hair.

We take turns at the sink, me naked, him mostly so, brushing our teeth, and I help myself to a bottle of lotion he has on the counter and lather my legs and arms.

Through it all, he watches me carefully, yet not sexually, just with the lingering haze of two people who have spent twenty-four hours having sex.

Really great sex.

When he's done, he heads to his closet and from inside of it, he says, "I have to be at the rink at three for the game tonight. I take it you're working?"

Yesterday, when he told me to grab a swimsuit, I went a step farther and packed a small overnight bag. I dig into it and pull on a fresh pair of panties as I answer.

"Yes. I should get there a few hours early since I didn't do the prep ordering yesterday."

He comes out of the closet, tugging on a pair of black dress pants with nothing on top yet.

For a moment, we both stand there, staring at each other.

"Wow. This is a sight I definitely like to see in my room."

I blush from the tips of my toes to the roots of my hair and since I'm wearing essentially nothing, there's no way to hide it. I grin and bend back down to my bag. "Same for you, hotshot."

He snorts and the soft padding of his footsteps tells me he's gone back to his closet.

"Do you like the bar?"

"Dad asked me to take it over the other night."

"Really?" He peeks his head out and by now I have a

long sleeve pink shirt on and I'm pulling my still wet hair out from beneath it. "Is that something you want?"

"I can't imagine selling it. I practically grew up there."

"But is running a bar something you *want* to do?"

"I thought so at first." I pull out a pair of jeans and begin pulling them on. My toes get stuck in one of the frayed areas so it takes me a moment and I'm sure I look ridiculous, hopping around and balancing on one foot to get them on. Sebastian smiles at me, like my fumbling amuses him.

I'll fumble all over the house in all manner of dress to see that smile.

"Let's get you fed and we can talk about it."

"I might do my best thinking on a full stomach while I think out loud."

"Then I'm glad I can help you instead of it being the other way around."

He laughs softly, kissing me again and then slides his hand from my back to my stomach, gently shoving me out of the closet.

I grab my bag and toiletries on my way out and once we're downstairs, I let Bruiser out of his doggie room while Sebastian heads to the kitchen.

Bruiser yips and spins and circles before gaining traction on the wood floor and runs toward the back door where I let him out.

"Does he always do that spinning thing?"

"Always. It's weird."

"It's cute."

"That too. An omelet okay for breakfast, or would you like yogurt again?"

"What are you having?"

"Oatmeal and another omelet."

"I'll have what you're having. Need help?"

"Not with cooking." He gestures with a knife to a pantry behind him. "You can feed Bruiser. His food is in there. One scoop."

I turn back to watch Bruiser chase a stray leaf blowing and tumbling across the yard, yipping madly at it and decide to leave him to his business. While Sebastian starts making our breakfast, I fill Bruiser's food bowl and let him in when he barks at the door and then fill two cups of coffee from Sebastian's Keurig machine on the counter.

"So the bar," he says, whisking an enormous bowl full of eggs. "You need to do some more thinking about it?"

"Probably. When Dad talked to me about it the other night I was so sure, but I guess since then I've been thinking. There were so many things I wanted to do with my life, so many grand dreams and whatnot. When I was traveling, I kept thinking about that. How I could make those dreams come true but then I came home and Dad was sick for a while. He didn't have a heart attack or anything, but he was told to take it easy for a few months and I started thinking that the simple life I was living, a job that I could do and do well and then leave behind me without a lot of stress plus getting to supplement that income with my Instagram stuff seemed pretty damn easy. But do I want it *forever*?"

"You make money off your Instagram feed?"

"I get sponsors and ads for photography things. I only promote what I actually like or use, but yeah. It's not a ton, but it's a decent amount of fun money."

"That's cool. And you know whatever decision you make doesn't have to be forever, right?"

I watch as he pours over half of the eggs into a frying pan and then the rest into another. I hope that smaller one is mine because that's more eggs than I eat in a month in the larger one. How much protein does this guy need?

"I grew up in the bar. His friends that are always there practically helped raise me. I did my homework in the booths and carved my math facts into one of the tables. Pretty sure the initials of me and my fourth grade crush are carved into a heart somewhere else, too."

At that, Sebastian grins, shaking his head at me. I'm pretty sure right now he'd call *me* cute.

At my feet, Bruiser yips and scratches my ankles, so I pick him up and settle him in my lap.

"After Mom died, the bar was the only place Dad and I hung for a long time. At home, he was quiet and grieving. But at the bar, he was always the same, like it brought him alive."

"You running it won't end that. But why *don't* you want it?"

I don't have a good answer for it. Except questioning the decision. "Perhaps I'm allergic to responsibility."

I am, after all, the girl with a failed marriage who skipped off to Europe.

"Are you?"

"When did you become a therapist?" I tease, winking at him over the rim of my coffee mug.

"Perhaps a cute little bartender is rubbing off on me."

"I think you're the one doing all the rubbing me off lately."

"Easy." He points a wood spoon at me with a gaze so hot it could melt his granite countertops. "That kind of talk will only get you bent over this counter."

"You make that sound like a bad thing."

"Drink your coffee. I need to stop thinking about how good it feels to fuck you or I'm going to be playing tonight's game distracted."

I preen under his warning. Personally, I like the idea of

him thinking of me while he's at work. But I also know how important his career is to him.

"I'll try to dial it down a notch," I say, taking another drink of my coffee.

"Only until I can see you again."

"Deal."

He's distracted me from bar talk with all his threats and sex talk and we move on to his game tonight, playing Nashville and after we eat breakfast, and when it's time to head out, I tuck a whining Bruiser into his doggie room with the promise I'll see him later and meet Sebastian in his garage and Maserati.

By the time I'm back home, I drop off my bag there, take a few minutes to change my clothes and head back down to the office to get work done before we open.

Surprisingly, my dad is behind his old metal desk, reading glasses perched on the end of his nose.

"Late night?"

"Dad." He hasn't acted like an overprotective dad giving me that disapproving look in way too long for me to back down to it now.

"He's not in the right headspace for what you need, Gigi."

"You don't know anything about his headspace." In all honesty, his headspace is murky. There are moments he looks at me when I know he's seeing me. Liking me. And then there are moments when I can see him thinking. Wondering if doing anything with me is the right decision.

After this weekend, the only thing I think we're both clear about is that we like each other.

And the sex is amazing.

Since I'm the one who brought up keeping it casual, I plan on sticking to it. For at least as long as my heart can handle keeping its distance. I can already feel the pull to him, but I'm the girl who's getting the boy after a year-long plus crush, so I've already been emotionally invested.

This is all new to him, and I understand what he's going through to an extent. I'm willing to be patient.

Staring down my dad and having *the talk* with him about choices in men is not going to happen.

"You're the one who's been worried I'm not out with friends anymore. Or anyone, you know. Now I've found someone I enjoy spending time with. Leave it at that."

The tension around his eyes softens and he taps the pen to the desk slowly. "You know I love you."

"I've never doubted it and I never will."

"And you know I want what's best for you."

"Dad—"

"That's it. That's all I'm sayin', all right, butterfly?"

I lean across the desk and kiss his cheek, making an obnoxiously loud smooching sound. "I know. Don't worry about me so much."

It's not until later in the night that I realize he never once brought up the bar, and I didn't have the guts to do it either.

As soon as I hesitate, I imagine my dad pulling the deal and selling it to the next bidder.

And I still can't decide if it's what I want or not.

CHAPTER TWENTY-TWO

Gigi

I'M DRYING my hair with a towel, shoulders shaking with laughter as I watch Sebastian in the mirror, twisting and bending his tall frame in my shower that's not sized for tall people.

"Stop laughing," he grumbles, glancing at me. "The things I do for you, woman."

He came to the bar last night like he's been doing a couple nights a week when he's in town for the few weeks. Every time he showers at my place before heading back to his, I'm entertained watching him contort his body to get clean.

No shower sex here, folks. It's in no way possible.

"Trust me. I love all the things you do to me."

My eyes widen at my reflection as I realize what I said. That pesky four-letter word came out of nowhere, or rather, all the places I've been trying not to admit to myself—and definitely not to Sebastian.

"Same here," he says, either unaffected by my usage or maybe he misheard it over the water running. "Especially when you use your mouth and hand to—"

"I get it!" I say it loudly, making sure he hears and hang up my towel. I'm already dressed for a stroll around Charlotte where I plan on grabbing coffee at one of my favorite little places near NoDa and spending the morning and most of the day taking pictures.

Sebastian and I have been spending almost all of our free time together for the last three weeks. I'm learning during the season and with my late schedule, it doesn't really leave a lot of time together. But, if I was forced to admit to anyone, I'd say the last three weeks have been three of the best weeks of my life. Better than the cooking classes I took in Italy. Better than strolling through the coastal streets of Saint Tropez in the French Riviera.

Better than all the times I spent in Europe, alone.

Sebastian and I, in some strange way I never expected or saw coming, fit. I've spent hours next to him, crammed on my tiny couch, books shoved to the side and flipped through photos I printed of my travels.

I've spent hours in front of his fireplace, hockey on the television, snuggled up next to him on his much larger, and much cozier couch, while he flips through scrapbooks his mom put together over the years of his hockey career from Pee Wee through college.

A pre-teen Sebastian Hendrix with his shaggy blond-ish hair and misty green eyes in full hockey gear.

It's a miracle my heart didn't explode from how absolutely adorable he was.

And when I called him that, he flung the book to the floor and took me on the couch, making me beg and plead for an orgasm and promise I would never use that word to describe him again.

Needless to say, my mission to keep my heart protected from a guy moving on from a marriage and a wife he loved has failed.

While I blow dry my hair, Sebastian finishes his shower and towels off, heading to my bedroom to get dressed due to the lack of space. Most nights we're together I spend at his house, but even though there's more space and he has a bed a thousand times more comfortable than my own, I like it more when he's here.

Possibly because it means I'm not having sex with a man on the same bed he shared with his recent ex-wife.

Possibly it's because I *really* like the smell of him all over my pillows and sheets on the weeks when he's traveling, and I can't see him. Although, he's made up for that, too with ample FaceTime calls late at night or before his games.

Which to me, says this is more than keeping it easy and casual because he seems to want to be around me as much as I want to be around him, and it's not like it's just for sex. We don't always have it, but I do always fall asleep wrapped in his arms... in a position he puts me in.

That has to mean something, right?

Stop getting ahead of yourself.

Right. I'm the one who offered to keep this easy. He agreed. He's even admitted he doesn't know what he has to give. And there's the chance I could still be a fun way to pass the time so he's not alone all the time.

All the logic in the world can't penetrate my heart that's falling for him. But the view of of him dropping a towel, standing several feet away, unashamed in every glorious inch of what God gave him, makes it totally worth the heartache that might be coming my way.

Gah. He's so... everything perfect in a male specimen.

Rippling muscles. Perfectly curved pecs. Arms that show his strength without being overly bulky. As for everything below the sexy as sin V-shaped muscle at his hips? Utter perfection.

He's also holding my phone, and it's clear he's said something I missed during my visual stalking behavior because he's grinning.

I turn off the hairdryer and drop both it and my brush. "What?"

"You were getting a call, from an unknown number." He hands me the phone. I glance at it and see they left a voicemail.

"I'll check it later. Probably some stupid robocall or something. Thanks, though."

I'm still staring at him. Can't help it. "You should get clothes on."

"I like the way you look at me when I don't."

To prove it, he puffs out his chest and places his hands on his hips. God. He's showing off for me.

Ridiculous.

He's also stolen my quick comebacks and sassy words. The sight of him like this in front of me leaves me speechless.

"Stare any harder at me and something of mine is going to demand its own attention."

"I can't help it. Your body is just... well... *wow*." I exaggerate for effect and in return, get the reaction I was hoping for.

A full-on belly laugh with rippling, naked abs, is the perfect way to start my day. Better, maybe, than coffee.

"You are definitely good for my confidence." He moves toward me too quick for me to jump out of his way, not that

I would, of course and grabs my hand pulling me to him. "You can always make me laugh."

"I like hearing it when you do." I tip my head back. "It's one of my favorite things about you."

"My laugh?"

"Yeah, because you don't do it often."

"Hmmm." There's humor lingering in those gorgeous green eyes of his that quickly turns heated in a different way. "What else do you like about me?"

"Your hair." To prove it, I run my fingers through his shaggy, almost shoulder-length long wavy locks and then drag my hand to his chest. "Your chest is a pretty nice thing about you. Along with your abs." My hand drifts along every body part I mention until it curls around something lower, something hard. Hot. Steel and silky. "This is one of my favorite parts, too."

"Is it?" he murmurs, eyes slowly closing. His hips press against my hand and a low groan tumbles from his beautiful lips. "God, I like it when you do that."

"I know," I tease, moving my hand back and forth, sliding it up and down his length.

His face falls forward, forehead hitting mine and he cringes. "I really, really want to see where this will lead, but I have to get the arena."

"Hmmm. Pity." I stroke him once then twice more and when I release him, a stuttered breath comes out.

"Damn it."

"At least now maybe you'll be thinking of me later." I wink and step back. Too much of us too close together with one of us wearing absolutely nothing is the perfect equation to equal trouble.

"I always do," he says, and I'm so shocked by the admission and the way his eyes darken, my lips are parted when he kisses me which means his tongue easily slides inside.

God. The way he can kiss. My toes sizzle as the fire he can quickly stoke inside me with the lash of his tongue and his scent and his mouth and the scrape of his scruff.

He pulls back, ending the kiss slowly but oh, much too quickly, and kisses my nose. "I should get going."

"I know. Good luck tonight." My hands squeeze the warmth of his hips. The man really needs to put some clothes on.

Like he can read my thoughts, especially the dirty ones, he steps back and reaches for his athletic pants.

I gape at him while he dresses. Watching him cover his body is almost as sexy as being the one to uncover it.

"You should come to the game tonight."

"What? Me?"

"Yes." He laughs. "You. And your dad. Or his friends. I'll like knowing you're there."

I want to cry out yes. It's the first time he's asked. This must mean something, right? Something beyond what we originally agreed to? He's looking at me so earnestly, but it fades as I don't answer.

"Sebastian, this isn't..."

He silences me with a scorching kiss. He's still hard and even though he's now dressed, he can't hide that from me.

He ends the kiss abruptly, leaving me wanting more.

And then shocking the hell out of me when he continues.

"This isn't just about having sex anymore, and I think we both know that. I'll have tickets for four at will-call. I want you there if you can make it or have someone cover the bar."

I'll close the bar down—business be damned—for a chance to see him play live.

This isn't just sex.

Does this mean it's more?

No way am I ruining this moment by asking.

"I'll be there," I say, ignoring the rest of what he's said. "I'd love to watch you in action."

"You see me in action plenty." He kisses me and grabs his keys. "See you later, Georgia."

A delightful shiver skates down my spine.

I love it when he calls me by my given name.

I love it even more that somehow, he seems to be liking me maybe as much as I already like him.

Hopefully?

IT'S WELL after lunchtime where I've spent hours at a coffee shop getting caught up on editing some of my more recent photos, responding to messages on Instagram and emails. I've had a few requests for sponsors, companies who want me to try their products. They usually include everything from sunscreen to outdoor clothing to food preparation delivery kits up to cameras and accessories or gear to carry it all on in. It usually takes me a while to research the product I'm being offered. I only agree to accepting their offer if they're willing to understand I will only share it on my feed if it's truly something I can promote without feeling like I'm selling myself to make a quick buck or two on the reward codes.

After Sebastian left, I spent the time doing a little bit of picking up and cleaning of my apartment. He's quit teasing me for my housekeeping skills and yet, for some stupid reason, I actually like making my place look nice now.

Odd.

Afterward, I headed into NoDa where I wandered the streets, finding little to be inspired by but I took a few pictures of trees beginning to bud and bloom. I quickly edited them and uploaded them with cheesy captions about the city feeling alive in the newly spring sunshine.

I'm packing up all my gear at the coffee shop when a text comes through my phone.

I grin, seeing Sebastian's name and open it.

Tickets are ready for you. Can't wait to see you later. Cheer loud for me.

I quickly type back, **Will do, hotshot.**

Immediately, I receive back a kissing emoji.

If I were a teenage girl, I'd squeal and hug my phone to my chest. Possibly scratch out our initials inside a heart with an arrow pierced through it. As it is, I'm in my late twenties and I still feel heat spreading to my cheeks.

Sebastian Hendrix uses kissing emojis.

Adorable.

When I go to slide my phone back in my satchel, I see the notification of my voicemail I haven't checked or cleared. It's probably nothing, but I always check voicemails just in case although usually it's only to hear about how I've won a free vacation, how I should make sure I'm registered to vote, or the most annoying of all... the grating tone from what sounds like an old school fax machine.

Still, ever since I missed my aunt's calls in Europe to tell me about my dad, I always check them.

I pull it up, and as soon as the voice starts talking, a rushing sound roars through my ears.

"Hi Georgia Barnes, this is Pam Wilson from Dr. Marie Connor's office. Our records indicate you were due..."

Oh dear God in heavens.

No.

No way.

I end the voicemail, blood racing through my veins and pull up my calendar app.

I'm not overdue for my birth control shot. It's supposed to be April third. I've known that since I made the last appointment.

Except.

"No." I blink repeatedly as I stare at the calendar and the appointment listed. The one I missed.

March fourth. Three-four, not four-three.

Holy freaking crap.

Almost a full freaking month late?

"This can't be," I mutter. This can absolutely not be right.

It has to be.

"It's okay. It's okay," I repeat to myself.

Sebastian can't have children.

He's clean.

But ever since that day in the shower, we started foregoing condoms. Which means we've been having sex. A LOT OF SEX.

And I was supposed to get my shot weeks ago.

Which still, it's fine. FINE. It can take several weeks past this for the shot to wear off. It's not like you miss it and you're instantly fertile myrtle.

Right?

Right.

I pull up my recent calls and call them back.

Ten minutes later, I have an appointment for Friday because they couldn't squeeze me in today or tomorrow and twenty minutes later I have a small box in a white bag shoved to the bottom of my satchel from a convenience store down the street from my apartment.

There's absolutely, positively, no way in hell I'm pregnant.

But I might as well take a test. Just to settle my nerves and confirm what I already know for a fact.

Sebastian can't have children.

Therefore, there's absolutely no way in hell I'm pregnant.

***

I'M squished between my dad and Steve, both of whom jumped at the opportunity to see the Ice Kings play live. The game is going on in front of us, fifteen rows up from center ice across from the team's benches. The seats are incredible. Low enough to feel the energy on the ice with the perfect views of both sides. I can still barely keep my eyes on the puck as it flies across the ice and every time a player is thrown into the boards, I jump in my seat much to Dad and Steve's amusement.

Why they insisted on squishing me between them is anyone's guess when they keep leaning in front of me to talk.

I've known from watching games on TV that the Ice Kings aren't only a great team, but that Sebastian is an incredible player. Seeing him live conjures an entirely different sensation in my stomach. He's *fast*. Strong. He has no problems checking an opponent into a wall and he's stolen several seemingly well-aimed passes, cleared the net and protected Maddox from having to save a shot on goal.

And still, with all the excitement, the energy around us and the happiness I feel at Sebastian's parting words, I can barely focus.

I have an unanswered text from him burning a hole in my coat pocket.

Tickets are ready for you. Your place or mine after the game?

What in the heck am I supposed to say to him? Should I tell him what's happening? Should I wait to see if there's anything to tell him at all? He leaves tomorrow for their last road trip before playoffs. I won't know anything for certain until I either grow a pair of lady balls and take the pregnancy test I bought this afternoon or go to my appointment on Friday.

By then, he'll be in Vancouver, making a quick trek across the western half of Canada before flying back home from Calgary.

Since I have no idea what to say to him and I know he'll catch on to something being wrong if I see him tonight, I haven't answered the text.

Does that make me a sissy? Probably.

Do I have a better option? I haven't been able to figure that one out yet.

Steven jostles my knee as he shoves forward in his chair. His hands are wrapped around his mouth, creating a megaphone while he shouts at the players, cheers for them. I only wish I could be this excited about everything.

It's only the first period. I have forty-five minutes left of the game tonight to figure out a response.

Forty-five more minutes to sit here, in the stands, wishing I was cheering on Sebastian with abandon like the rest of the home crowd, trying to figure out what in the hell will happen to me, to *us*, if I actually am pregnant.

It's torture.

I might be snuggled between two of the men who love me most in the world and in an arena of thousands, but I've never felt more alone. Or lost.

CHAPTER TWENTY-THREE

Sebastian

I CHARGE Maddox on the ice, slamming my body into his and almost taking us off our skates. It's Sawyer Chauncy, the third man to slam into our huddle but not the last that does it.

I fall onto Maddox and roll to my side, right before Mikah Lutzgo joins us and soon, the rest of the team has dog-piled on top of us on the ice right in front of the goal Maddox has spent the last hour defending with perfection. Tradition has us skating to the goalie after a win and slapping him on the helmet, but this game, this moment, is too big for a simple congratulations.

"We did it!" someone shouts.

"Hell yeah!"

"Championship bound, baby!"

We're all cheering and shouting at the same time while around us, the small amount of Ice Kings fans that have cheered for us in Calgary refuse to leave their stands.

Climbing to our feet, my cheeks have never felt so tight. It's this damn smile. This team and this season that does it. We've just beaten Calgary, securing a first-round bye for the playoffs. Two weeks off of practices and conditioning before we start round two of games with the home advantage in Charlotte.

This is it. Our moment.

Jason comes up and slaps the side of my face, pulling me to my feet as we skate to Calgary and fist pump gloves before they take off the ice.

We head down our own hallway, cheers echoing, congratulations being shouted from all the members of the Ice Kings who handle all of our behind the scenes work.

Tessa, who has traveled with us is there, tears streaming down her face, hands clasped together. Jason doesn't even break stride when he shoves his arm behind her, lifts her into the air and kisses her to even more raucous cheers and jubilation.

In the locker room, champagne is shaken and uncorked, glasses are filled. Bottles are dumped over Coach Woods before we have the time to remove our skates or helmets.

Fucking hockey. It's the best damn thing in the world.

"All right! All right!" Coach Woods shouts, champagne dripping from the tips of his graying hair, champagne glass raised in the air. "Y'all did this! And you should be proud of yourselves, right?!"

Everything he says is cut short by another whoop or holler that bounces off the walls in the vast space.

"Now. Take the night. Celebrate responsibly. Enjoy the long weekend off because next week, we're back to work so we can end this year the best!"

More shouts. More celebrations that eventually fizzle to a dull roar while guys start stripping off sweaty and now champagne-soaked gear before we're showered and re-dressed in suits, ready to catch the bus on the way back to the hotel.

During all of this, guys are on the phones, calling wives and girlfriends, and in my hand, I frown at the blank screen of my phone.

Gigi.

There's been a time change and while I'd like to blame our lack of conversation over the last week on that, it's bull-shit. For weeks while I traveled it was never an issue since she was usually at the bar so late anyway. We'd connect after my game, or before she went to work the next day.

I've barely spoken to her since the night I gave her tickets to my game. It was late, right after the game. I got back to the locker room when I got a text back from her congratulating me on our win, but saying she was wiped and heading home with her dad and Steve.

No invite to go to her place.

Which wouldn't have bothered me except since then, she's been distracted on the phone and while she's answered my texts, they've been brief.

Something is bothering her and for reasons I'm not willing to delve too deep into on a charter bus with dozens of guys, it's bothering me as well.

Holy crap.

I'm falling for Gigi. In a way that's been slow, and yet steady, taking minute steps forward until I don't know if I can turn back now.

That's why this hurts so much. Why it's kept me awake this week. Why I've done extra workouts to work the worry out of my brain before I take to the ice for games.

I don't just like Gigi.

Love, though?

It's too soon. Has to be. I'm only a couple months out of a divorce to the woman I loved over half of my life. It's not possible to be falling in love again so quickly, is it?

And what did we agree to? Something easy, something uncomplicated... because I was the one who didn't know how much I have to give.

Well. Shit just got a whole lot more complicated now.

I slide into a seat on the bus, smacking Klaus's forehead as I pass him. "You headed out later?"

He's grinning down at his phone, but when I smack him he flings his hand in the air and hits mine away. "Yeah, dipshit. Unless you keep assaulting me."

I grab the back of his headrest and peek over his shoulder. "How's Jillian?"

"Good." He swipes the text screen closed and looks up at me to glare at me. "Mind your own business."

"You get anywhere with her yet?"

Klaus and Jillian have been best friends for several years. They met at a signing we put on in South Park mall. She works for the company that has signed most of us to handle our promo gear. They provide the jerseys and hockey pucks and mature hockey sticks and we sign them and smile pretty for the camera.

Since that day, Jillian and Klaus have always been close. But I've seen the way he looks at her. I know he wants more. It's not the first or the thirtieth time I've asked him this question and every time he rolls his eyes and repeats, "We're just friends."

"We're friends," he says, on cue.

I roll my eyes and plop down into my seat as more teammates pass by. "Where we going out tonight?"

I ask it loud, for anyone who's planned anything. Across the aisle and a few rows up, Duke Fletcher throws his fist in the air and declares we're taking over the hotel bar.

Good enough for me.

For the first time in a long time, I'm ready to party and not drown my sorrows.

I'm in a pretty damn good place right now.

It'll be even better once I can figure out what's going on with Gigi. Take care of that, and then move us forward, closer... perhaps end this charade of *free and easy* during the season.

Playoffs start in two weeks and I can't think of anyone else I want at my side, cheering me on.

I'VE HAD TOO much to drink. Not enough to risk passing out in a woman's bed without remembering in the morning. Not enough to pass out in the elevator. I'm aware enough to know when I needed to stop tonight and I was having a good enough time with the guys that that was a while ago. Instead, I joined in seeing Mikah Lutzgo get drunk.

At twenty-three, he's the youngest player on our team. Sometimes that means we're dicks to him. Other times it means we're protective big brothers.

I've played both roles tonight which is why I have my arm thrown over his shoulders, propping him up as I get him back to his room.

"Holy shit, that was nucking futs."

"I think you got that wrong," he says.

"No. No. I said it right."

"Hm. It does not make sense to me," Mikah slurs.

He's only lived in the States a few years. Lots of things

don't make sense to him, especially American slang. If he was more sober, I'd spend time explaining the joke.

"How is Angelo?" He has a baby that has to be getting close to a year old or something now. It was dropped off at his doorstep, a one-night stand producing lifelong consequences.

He's loved him from the minute he showed up. I'm pretty sure that threw Madison over the edge for months. It might have been the final downfall of us before the final *final* downfall.

Whichever. I kick the thought out of my mind.

He grins up at me drunkenly and stupidly. Mikah doesn't drink much or very often. Which is part of what made tonight so fun. I probably shouldn't have bought him the last shot. But every man needs a slippery nipple every once in a while.

"You and Paisley are getting married soon, aren't you?" I don't pay that much attention to other guys' relationships, but when Mikah fell for his neighbor in his building, he fell hard and fast. And Paisley is sweet. They'd planned on waiting until she was done with graduate school but then decided not to.

Mostly, I'm just trying to keep Mikah from passing out in my arm so I'm trying to keep him talking.

His brows pull together and he shoves off me. "Yeah."

"Hey. I'm happy for you."

By now, the entire team knows what's been going on with me. Only took Jason running his mouth and definitely after I took off for Minnesota months back. I get strange looks sometimes, when the guys talk about their wives or girlfriends.

They don't bother me anymore. Not because I'm drunk.

Because I have Gigi. At least...I think? Shit. I need to

sober up so I can call her. All night long at the bar we've been hanging out, chilling, drinking way too much and eating probably all the food they have in the kitchen. While the time with the guys is a blast, so much like it used to be before I became a grumpy asshole, I haven't been able to stop thinking about her.

"Thank you," Mikah says. We stop at his door, and I wait for him to dig out his keycard. It takes longer than it should.

I prop myself on the doorframe while he fumbles with his wallet.

"When's the wedding?"

"August? I think? She is planning everything, and I am too drunk to think straight."

"You're too drunk to walk straight," I remind him. I take the keycard out of his hands. He's now tried to open the door at least three times and keeps getting the pesky red light. It takes me two times and when the light turns green, I open the door for him. "There you go, kid."

"I am not a kid," he mumbles, but he's already walking into his room, stripping off his shirt before it closes behind him.

"Drink water!" The door slams in my face and my vision blurs in front of me. Hopefully, he heard me.

Getting Mikah to his room took longer than I expected. Duke will be back to our room at some point. I left the bar early so I can have time alone with Gigi. The last thing I want is my FaceTime call going the way I want it to when Duke stumbles back into the room.

It takes me almost as long to open my door as it did Mikah and I pull a repeat of him when I talk through, stripping out of my dress shirt before the door is fully closed behind me.

Even though I quit drinking a while ago, I grab a bottle of water from the mini-bar and settle down into my bed.

It's one o'clock in the morning and we're two hours behind North Carolina. Hopefully she's awake.

Lucky for me, my phone only rings once before it's connecting, and then Gigi's sweet, but tired face is blurred on the screen. She has her makeup washed off, hair piled on top of her head so chunks of her teal tips fly out in every which direction.

She's covering a yawn as her photo clears and we have a decent connection.

"Hey. Did I wake you?"

"No." She moves a bit and I catch the hanging behind her bed, and my groin notices. She's in her bed. Probably wearing one of those skintight tanks of hers. Barely there shorts. Possibly no panties. Definitely no bra. "I was waiting up for you. Congratulations."

I'm still stuck on the possible no bra part, so it takes me a minute. "Right. Thanks. Sorry I'm late calling. Guys wanted to go party."

Her sleepy eyes crinkle at the corners. "You deserved it. Have fun?"

"I did. We got Mikah too drunk."

"Not nice," she says, but she's grinning. A cute little laugh follows her schooling.

"He'll deal. Mostly I thought of you and wished you were here with me."

Her eyes widen, surprised at the admission. This week has been... weird, to say the least. I thought after she came to the game she'd get that I want more. But then it seems like she pulled back.

So maybe I'm the one who's gotten wires twisted. Maybe she really does want easy.

"That's sweet. I watched all your games." She scoots back on the bed and yawns again, covering it with her hand with that broken heart tattoo and fingernails that are hot pink. "I'm sorry. Long day."

"Everything okay?"

She drops her hand and the typical, excited glimmer in her pretty eyes dims. Gigi almost always looks like she's having the time of her life. There's a sparkle in them that draws me to her, that pulled me in, and now it's missing. Especially when she doesn't answer right away.

"Hey. What is it? You can talk to me, you know?"

"I know. It's... nothing. We can talk tomorrow. When you get back?"

For the first time since we started hanging out, I get the distinct impression she's lying to me. Or brushing me off.

Either way, my chest constricts, like a fist is squeezing it, bringing back more pain than I've felt in several months.

I don't want her to leave. I want her to trust me. I want to know what all her looks mean. All her thoughts—good and bad. Tonight isn't the night to press. She's tired. I've been drinking.

"Our plane gets in at one. Can I see you?"

"Yeah. I can meet you at your place?"

"Sure. You're always welcome there." This conversation isn't going at all like I want it to, but as she fights against another yawn, this time I notice the dark rings under her eyes. She *is* exhausted. "I should let you go; let you get to sleep."

"I know. I'm sorry. I wanted to talk more, but like I said... long day."

"I get it, Gigi. No worries. See you tomorrow?"

"I'll be there." She grins and that grin disappears as she bites her lip. It's a nervous gesture, one that catches me by surprise. She always seems so sure of herself. "And I missed you this week. A lot."

That fist squeezing my heart finally loosens. Finally. I sigh and my shoulders slump. "I missed you too, Gigi. Probably just as much."

Her smile wobbles and she blows me a kiss. "Good night, Sebastian."

"Good night, sweetheart."

The last thing I see is her eyes blinking in surprise.

Sweetheart.

I've teased her with Georgia even though she finally admitted she doesn't really like the name, but unlike her nickname for her, I've never given her one.

Tomorrow. Tomorrow we'll talk. I'll figure out what happened this week, and then we'll move forward.

Hopefully, together.

CHAPTER TWENTY-FOUR

Gigi

MY SANDALS CLICK a rapid staccato beat on Sebastian's wood floor. I arrived early, hoping being in his home again before him will help me gather my thoughts and everything I need to tell him.

I'm pregnant.

How exactly am I supposed to tell him this when he doesn't think he can even make children and we're not even really together? There's no denying the grainy little gray blob on the small picture in my back pocket though.

It's been a week from hell. Between an all-day exhaustion setting in that makes me feel like I'm walking through a constant fog, and decisions I've made with my dad regarding the bar, everything has gone wrong.

Everything is changing all over again and a part of me, a large part, wants to do exactly what I did the last time things didn't turn out the way I imagined.

I want to slide on my running shoes and flee. I'd probably only get a mile away before I collapse from the exhaustion my body constantly feels, but I still want to run.

The only thing keeping me from doing it so far is needing to tell Sebastian. He has to know.

I only wish I knew how he was going to respond to this. I've imagined a thousand different scenarios this week. Multiple endings.

Only a couple of them end happily and the way I want to.

It's probably foolish. Completely.

We're not going to go from walks in parks and messing around to living together in a matter of months. And I don't want that just because I'm pregnant either.

Plus, there's so much that could happen before this baby is born. But there is no doubt, this baby is being born, assuming nothing bad happens over the next eight months.

On the couch, Bruiser sighs and stretches. He chased my ankles and my pacing for the first thirty minutes and then, with his little pink tongue lolling out of his mouth, decided a nap was a better use of his time. I've gone pee twice. Chugged two bottles of water and then dug through Sebastian's pantry for some crackers. I'm not nauseous, at least not majorly but too much water on an empty stomach doesn't feel so great these days.

My doctor assures me it's normal, and only the beginning.

I just pray this isn't the beginning of the end for Sebastian and me.

This potential tailspin of a day would have been so much more comfortable if I could have done it at my place, but it'll be easier to do it here. If he breaks my heart, I can leave.

Besides, if this is to be my last time welcome here, I

wanted to see his home one last time. As it is, I've gotten here early enough, already being given his security code before. In all my pacing, I've taken a trip through the house. And I can't help imagining being here. With Sebastian. Our child.

Raising him or her together.

Tears burn my eyes as I drop my hand to my stomach. There's nothing there, not yet, but I've found myself doing it a lot this week.

I'm having a baby. My vision blurs and I swipe my tears with the back of my hand.

God. This is so amazing and so horrible. My stomach churns as I anticipate Sebastian's arrival. If his plane arrived on time at one, he should be home any minute. I head to his hall bathroom to clean up, splash water on my face. If he sees my red eyes and dried tears, he'll instantly know I have bad news to share.

"Oh God," I groan, hands grip the edges of the porcelain vanity sink. If there's ever a time to throw up, it's now. I hold it back, and inhale slowly until the feeling goes away and until my legs don't tremble like a newborn fawn.

Once I'm feeling steadier, I run my hands through my fingers. I actually attempted to look decent today, full face of makeup. My hair has been blow-dried and hangs past my shoulders unlike my usual do of pulling it back from my face. Now it's just clipped with a small clip at the side, holding it back.

I look as good as I can be. If only I felt the same.

In the distance, Bruiser begins yapping and my stomach does another roll of unease. By the time I'm back in the entryway, Sebastian is walking through, suitcase being pulled behind him, suit coat draped over one arm.

He jerks his head in his eyes widen as he notices me. "Well hey! This is a nice surprise!"

He drops his suitcase and places his coat on top, coming immediately to me and when he reaches me, he doesn't waste a moment to press his hands to my cheeks and his lips to mine. I inhale his scent, revel in his taste. His beard scratches my lips and my cheek as he takes the kiss deeper. On instinct, I curl my hands around his forearms to hold him close to me.

Man. This guy can *kiss*. I savor it in case it's my last and when Sebastian wraps an arm around my lower back, pressing me even closer to his body, I settle into everything. Until I feel his hard length against my stomach and a deep rumble of delight rattles deep in his chest.

"Sebastian," I breathe against his mouth and pull back. "We should stop."

"No. We should take this to my room. I've been thinking of you and now I finally have you."

Oh goodness. Pleasurable shivers dance down my spine as I fight against them. This is what got us into this mess.

Summoning all my strength, both internal and external, I place my hand to his chest and push back. His heart is racing. Almost as much as mine.

I love that I can do this to him. Love that he likes being with me so much.

"We need to talk."

As if I've burned him, his hand falls from my back and my cheek. He steps back and frowns. "Talk? I don't think anything good starts with that sentence."

I cringe before I can hide it.

"I see," he says, and another foot of space gets placed between us as he steps away from me. His face goes as blank as it used to be, almost as hard as he was on New Year's.

"This have anything to do with why you were so distant this week?"

"It's not what you think."

"Right." He swipes his hand over his beard and mouth, and I hate what I see in his face. "Listen, Gigi. Just say what you have to say—"

The words I need to say lodge in my throat. "I wasn't lying. I had a really long week. My dad and I... well, we talked. And I decided not to buy the bar from him." At that, his brows shoot up. I'm certain he assumed I was going to. He practically encouraged me to do so, but instead, now I have something else more important. "I started looking for a job. A real one. Like in an office and everything."

I can't help the way my lip curls at the thought and now Sebastian's brows are more twisted than ever. "That doesn't explain why—"

"Because I'm pregnant."

I blurt it out so quick it takes *me* by surprise. Sebastian's face pales.

Then hardens further. "Excuse me?"

I step toward him, but he throws up his hands, immediately stopping me. "I'm pregnant."

I reach back into my pocket and just as my fingers brush against the slick photo, my body freezes when he asks.

"Whose is it?"

"What?"

"You heard me." He leans in a fraction. It feels like he's right in my face, his rage is so sudden. "Who else have you been fucking while having your fun with me?"

"No one. I swear." I can't even summon the strength to be upset by his accusation. "I swear it, Sebastian." I grab the photo and whip it out between us.

He doesn't move his steely, angry gaze from me.

My chin wobbles at what must be going through his mind. "I swear it, Sebastian. There's been no one but you since well, since I got home from Europe. I'm pregnant and it's yours. Ours. I swear."

"That can't be." He shakes his head and that fury rolling through him cedes enough for me to walk closer. "I can't. This…"

He trails off. I step closer. The photo in my hand shakes and trembles, I'm so nervous. "I thought I had to get my birth control shot done on April third, but instead it was supposed to be March fourth. So I missed it. And I swear, it wasn't on purpose and I didn't try. I just wrote it down wrong on my calendar but I got a call last week, right before your game that I was late…"

I can no longer speak. Something like hope bubbles in Sebastian's green eyes that makes me want to hug him and reassure him. Now that I've told him, the crushing weight of fear I've felt all week vanishes and relief slams into me like the harshest ocean waves.

He glances at the paper still trembling in my hand and as he reaches for it, so slowly it might take him a year to touch it, he looks at me. "You're pregnant."

"Yeah." I laugh. It's stupid. Not the time. "Apparently, my womb is ultra-fertile or something and it did something to those slow movers the doctors say you have."

He takes the photo from me and holds it like he already cherishes it.

"It's just a blob. That tiny gray thing." I point to it in case he doesn't know what he's looking at it and then the corner. "But my doctor said the heartbeat was strong."

The paper in his hand now trembles and I swear I hear him sniff but I'm too scared to look at him.

"How far along?"

"Six weeks. It's early. Super early. But since I didn't get that shot and then well... that day in the shower, I think..." I trail off. I've done the math and added the days and that first time without a condom had to be it. Or the next day. Regardless, it was one of those first times after I didn't get my shot. Which shouldn't even *happen*. At least not that soon.

He continues staring at the paper. Holding it like his dreams are pinched between his fingertips and any movement will shatter them forever.

Then, he lifts his head, and wet, blurry green eyes blink. Tears fall and then he smiles.

And it's so blindingly beautiful, so much better than what I expected him to do, I smile back at him.

"You're pregnant," he repeats. I don't blame him for not believing me. I still don't fully believe it and I've recently had something that resembles a vibrator shoved up my hoo-ha in order to double-check the pregnancy test.

"Yeah."

Before I can blink, I'm swooped up into a bone-crushing hug and he's moving, straight into his living room. He moves so fast he's sitting before I can wrap my legs around him to hold on and then I'm on his lap, crushed to him, my head to his shoulder and I hear him let loose a cry that's so filled with pain, so filled with hope and happiness, my own tears soak his dress shirt and I hang on tight.

I hug him back and hold him until his shoulders stop shaking and his tears stop soaking my temple.

"Sebastian—"

"What..." He swallows, eyes red, looking uncertain and scared for the first time I've met him. "I know it's your body. I know that well, I know we're not...we haven't talked about what we are... to each other or anything. But what... what do you think you'll do?"

"I wouldn't end something we created, Sebastian." My fingers run through his hair and his forehead drops to my shoulder. "I never even considered it. I'm terrified. My dad is probably going to kill me... or wait, he might kill you first." His shoulders shake and his lips press to my shoulder. "I want this, though. With you being as much of a part of this as you want."

"All of it," he whispers and lifts his head. His green eyes swim with a heavy emotion that I feel deep in my heart. "I want all of it."

I imagine him finishing it *with you* and kick that thought to the curb. He's talking about the baby. Not me. Not us. After all, like he said, there really isn't an *us*.

CHAPTER TWENTY-FIVE

Sebastian

GIGI IS PREGNANT.

I'm going to be a dad.

The natural, normal, boy meets girl and has a baby kind of way.

I can't express all the emotions tumbling inside of me, making my brain hurt and making my heart burst with gladness. This is... it's too much. Guilt, for getting her pregnant. For not being able to do that for Madison. Guilt, for thinking of Madison while Gigi is on my lap in the first place. I've held little back from her, and she's giving me everything.

Easy and uncomplicated has most definitely flown out the window now. There is absolutely no way Gigi will have my child and I won't work my ass off as much as possible to continue seeing if we can have the kind of relationship I wanted us to before finding this out.

God. This explains so much. Her exhaustion. Her

distance. This was not how I thought the words '*We need to talk*' was going to go by any means.

"I think I might have a heart attack, I'm so shocked." It's still hard to speak and my heart is racing so fast I press my hand there.

Gigi covers hers with mine. Those hot pink fingernails cover my hand and then slide into the gaps between my fingers.

"I thought I was going to pass out when I took a test."

"I wish you would have told me."

"You were leaving town. And I didn't know for sure until you were gone. I didn't think it right to share it over the phone."

"It wasn't. I still wish I could have been there. For you and for me."

"I'm sorry. About all of it. I mean, we barely know each other, and now... well, this is happening."

His green eyes darken and his hand at my cheek tenses. "Don't be sorry. You don't have anything to apologize for. Maybe give me a minute to process it."

"Good luck. I've been trying to do that all week and am still baffled."

"Your week. You mentioned you're getting a job? Why? You love the bar."

"Because I'm having a baby. Working there doesn't exactly give me stable hours, and I live above the bar. It's not the place to raise a baby. I need a job and better income."

"You'll have me."

"Sure, I mean. I know you'll help and I know you'll be involved, but—"

"You'll have me." I repeat the statement succinctly, letting her see how serious I am. What does she think is happening here?

"I know, but—"

"No. Listen to me. You'll have me. If you want to take over the bar, do it. We'll figure out the rest. If you want to get a job, wait and find one you'll love. The one thing I know we're going to teach this child is to chase their dreams and to go for what they want, and that won't happen if their mom is working a job she hates because she felt like she had to give up those dreams to have a baby. Whatever you need, *whenever*, I will give that to you."

"Sebastian—" Tears swarm in her eyes and before she reaches them, I brush them away with my thumbs. "We hardly know each other. And we're barely together."

I have nothing else to offer except for all of me, all my thought. Please, let be enough.

"I want that. Us together, I mean. I thought that while I was gone. I don't want easy and uncomplicated with you anymore, Gigi and I already knew that. Is this forever? I think that's way too early for us to know. But you are going to have my child which means we're forever united in this way and that means, I will *always* be there to help you, in any way you need, so you can be the best mommy to this baby."

She snaps her mouth closed.

It takes entirely too long for her to answer that my palms start to sweat.

"This is more than I thought you were going to say."

"I mean every word of it. And I'd help you and give you what you want because we're going to have a baby together, but I also mean it because I like you, and I want to see where this can go with us."

"I want that, too."

"Good. Now kiss me, help me out of my suit, and then show me how much you missed me."

She laughs, doing her head shake she does when she thinks I'm being cute. I lean in to kiss her but stop halfway.

"Unless you're not feeling well? I haven't asked. And you said you've been tired—"

She shuts me up with a kiss, upturned lips pressing to mine. "I'm not that sick yet."

"Thank God." I seal her mouth to mine and slide my tongue into her parting mouth.

***

HOT DAMN, she feels good. It's been a week, feels like forever since I've been inside her and I don't know if it's the time apart, admitting we want to be together, or the fact she's pregnant with my baby... maybe a combination of all three that makes this so intense.

Gigi straddles me, teal hair draped over her shoulders as her hands press to my chest.

From beneath, I'm the one in control though, arching my hips and thrusting into her. I have one hand on her hip, the other on her flat belly.

Pregnant. I've knocked her up and I want to pound my fists in the air in some caveman type victory shout. But God... to think it'd never happen and then have it be so unexpected... I'm not sure what I feel except the beauty of her tight sex taking me deep inside her.

"Sebastian," she cries and throws her head back.

I slide my hand from her belly down, finding her clit. "Come on, Gigi. Come for me."

She's close, pulsing around my dick, but I've already learned what it takes to throw her over the edge. As I play with her, I slam her down against me, force her to grind herself against my body. It's hard enough to hold back waiting for her even though I already gave her an orgasm with my mouth first.

"Get there," I grit out. And screw this. I want to be pressed against her, as close as we can get to one another. I sit up and wrap her legs around my back. Sliding my hand to her back, I cup the back of her head with my other and slam her mouth to mine.

Yes. Her tits. Her body. Her hips. Her colorful inked skin, but most of all her heart.

Shit. I am falling way too fast for this woman.

"Yes," she cries out against my mouth. "I'm going to... come."

She says it on a pant and I swallow her cries as her climax hits.

She's so freaking gorgeous, rocking against me, body trembling. I kiss her, bite her neck while she yells out my name and let my own orgasm hit, hard and fast.

It speeds down my spine, up through my balls and soon I have her body clamped to mine, my mouth and teeth at her shoulder.

I dig in, biting her while I squeeze her tight, giving her everything.

All of me. However much she wants, I'll give more.

"Shit," I pant and kiss where I've bitten her. It's enough to leave a mark and I like that. She'll have to hide it.

Or show it off.

Let everyone know she's mine now.

Possessiveness is not my natural inclination, but it's there. With the mother of my child.

My girlfriend.

My head swims from the events of the day, the early morning wakeup call and plane ride and all that's transpired since.

Shit. I'm pretty sure I say it again out loud, more of a breath against her heated flesh and let her comb her hands through my hair.

When I can think straight, I take us to my back and then roll us to our sides. I pull out only long enough to kiss Gigi's belly which earns me a smile.

"Stay here. Let me get you cleaned up."

"Thank God," she says playfully. She throws her arms to the bed and sighs. "Because I don't think I can move."

"Thanks. Make me feel good. Maybe next time tell me I'm the biggest and best you've been with."

She winks as I start to turn toward the bathroom. "You are. Definitely."

I laugh and head to the bathroom where I wet a washcloth. After I've cleaned us up, I climb back into bed and throw the comforter over us.

She's at my side, mermaid and butterfly tattoo at her shoulder I can't help but kiss.

"When do you have to get to work?"

"As soon as my legs remember how to work." I laugh against her shoulder. "I didn't think today would go like this."

"Me neither. But I'm glad."

She turns to me and kisses my temple. "Me too. I was so worried. And scared."

"Hey. Stop. We'll figure this out together, okay? All that's important is that we're together while we do it. At least to me."

"You're an even better man than I imagined you to be."

I've already told her I like her and want to be with her so I don't repeat myself. Actions speak louder than words anyway. I suspect we'll both have our demons from failed relationships we'll need to navigate soon enough.

"What are these tattoos for? I've always wanted to know."

She chuckles, this melodic low sound and slides her fingers through my hair. Pretty sure she likes my long hair more than I do, she plays with it so much.

"Is that why you always kiss them?"

"I've always wanted to ask," I admit. "And know you better. Know your secrets. What's so important to you you'll have it etched into your skin forever."

"Why didn't you ask?"

I pull back enough so I can meet her eyes directly. "I think I was afraid knowing would make me like you more than I thought I should."

She swallows thickly and I pull her to me. She has a small flower inside her other hip I can find in the dark at this point and script on her ribs that looks like a poem or a song. I run my hand there, across the ink I can't see.

"The butterflies and mermaid," I prod when she stares at me like she either wants to kiss me again or more. Not that I'm complaining.

"My dad calls me butterfly. My mom started it when I learned how to ride a bike. She kept telling me to spread my wings and fly and let it take me to wherever I was called. My dad says it all the time now. When I went to him about taking off to Europe he said, 'spread your wings and fly butterfly' and I knew I had his acceptance what I needed to do."

"I like that for you. That you had that and parents who gave that to you."

"I miss my mom. All the time. But I look in the mirror every day and know without a doubt what she'd want for me and it helps."

"I'm sorry you lost her."

Her breath shakes and trembles as she inhales deeply. "The mermaid I got in Germany. They have a lot of different symbolizations, but mostly it was for femininity, independence, transformation. I was just divorced, figuring out who I wanted to become."

I kiss her mermaid tail while she laughs and glances up. "I was also maybe a little lonely so I figured, what the hell."

"What the hell."

"I think I've always been someone willing to leap without looking."

"I like that about you, too. You'll keep life interesting."

"I hope so."

She shakes in her confidence so I do what I do best to remind her, how much I like her and want her, how much I believe we can do this. I roll her to her back and follow, and I don't stop showing her until she's clenching around me again, crying out my name, and digging her nails into my back.

Yeah.

Life with Gigi will be fun. Definitely.

CHAPTER TWENTY-SIX

Gigi

"YOU SURE ABOUT THIS?"

"I've had a lot of time to think about it, Dad."

I place my hand on top of his and the paperwork sitting on his desk. Last week, I told him I wasn't sure the bar was for me but not why. Given his concerns about the little he knew about Sebastian and me, to say I've lessened them is a lie.

He's more concerned than ever, but in the last week, Sebastian and I have done a lot of talking.

And I now have a plan, at least somewhat. Really, the only thing I'm certain of is there's no way I'll go back to a nine-to-five job in a cubicle.

Sebastian believes I can do this. More than that, I *want* to do this.

"I'll figure this out and I have lots of time. But I do have some ideas brewing which I'll let you know about once I look into them more." Plans like renovating and updating the bar, making the outside more welcoming. George's Bar is great for what my dad wanted it to be, but I want something different. A little more lively. I've been brainstorming ideas with Sebastian all week long and the more I consider what I can do with this, the more determined I've become.

"If it's yours, you don't have to clear anything with me."

"It'll always be your bar, and now, maybe it'll be the legacy we also leave to your grandchild."

He blanches. Tan and wrinkled skin turns to snow and I laugh.

"Dad."

He pulls his hand from beneath mine and like he's done every time I've reminded him I'm pregnant, he scrubs his hands down his face.

"You'll have to get used to that sometime, you know."

One of his eyes peers open. "Have you?"

"I'm getting there." And like I always do when I think of the baby growing inside of me, my hand settles to my stomach. "But I'm happy."

There's scared, nervous, fearful, anxious, elated, and joyful all joining my current mixed-up bundle of emotions over the last couple of weeks, but mostly, I'm choosing to be happy.

Mostly because Sebastian has decided to settle on ecstatic over the news, so it's hard to let worry and fear creep in.

"Then I suppose I should get used to becoming a grandpa, huh?"

"You have time."

"So do you," he says, bringing us back to the topic of the bar. "You have time to decide this isn't right for you for whatever reason and now that you've got something else to put first, I get it. You know that, right?"

"Like I've always said. If I decide to do something different, I won't hesitate to let you know, but this feels right. And I have time to figure out how to make it work so I can run and own the bar, but not be here all the time. Trust me, I'll figure it out."

He sighs, big belly jostling with the force of it. Leaning back in his chair, he settles his hands on his stomach, linking his fingers together. "Then I guess I need to start planning what I'm going to do with retirement. Can't move to Florida now and be too far away from watching my grand baby grow up, can I?"

Tears prick the corners of my eyes. "You can still take up golfing."

"Maybe tennis."

"And shuffleboard." He grimaces as he says it and lifts a hand. "Never mind. Maybe I'll just be the old, washed-up regular at George's and take a seat next to Steve."

"Or, you could go find something, or someone that makes you happy too."

"Let's not get crazy." He grins, but that sad look in his eyes every time I've ever mentioned him moving on and finding someone creeps in. "In all seriousness. You sure about this? Sebastian?"

"It's new. We're taking it slow, but yeah. I think so."

"Then I suppose I should invite the boy over for dinner sometime. Get to know the dad of my first grandbaby better, huh?"

I laugh at Dad calling Sebastian a boy. There's nothing boyish about him. Nope. My guy is *all man*. In body, in manners, and in heart.

"I'm sure he'd like that. I'll mention it to him when he gets here." Taking a quick glance at my watch, I crinkle my nose. "And speaking of, I'm running late. He's going to be here any minute and I still have to get changed."

"Go." Dad waves me off. "I'll keep an eye out for him at the bar and invite him myself."

"Thanks Dad."

I leave the bar and head up to my apartment through the storage room. There's a party tonight for the team at Jude and Kate's house about fifteen minutes away and Sebastian's asked me to go with him. At first, I balked, but when he asked me again, I realized how important it is to him for me to be seen with him and meet his friends. Of course I said yes. They're his family, too.

But, it's my first time hanging out with them outside the bar, so I've been fretting ever since he mentioned it. What in the heck do I wear to a party put on by professional athletes getting ready for the playoffs where they all make millions and drive cars like Sebastian's Maserati?

I have three dresses I threw on my bed earlier today, all black, all pretty casual. I grab one with loose sleeves, a wide boatneck collar with a thick band of waist. The bottom is short, barely covering my butt as I tug it down over my hips and drag my hair from beneath the dress, I'm grinning in the mirror.

In honor of playoffs and their first two games in round one being at home, I updated my hair to a brighter teal, streaks of blue and blond mixed in. My hair is the color of the team.

Sebastian laughed his ass off and then kissed me senseless when he saw it the other day.

Dressed and ready to go, I head back to the bar through the storage room. I already told Sebastian to meet me at the bar when he picked me up, but that was because I figured I'd be there already so I'm not the least bit surprised when I find him, sitting on the stool, chatting with my dad when I walk down the hallway toward him.

Like always, my breath stalls and restarts upon seeing him. He's dressed in dark blue jeans and a simple gray dress shirt.

His hair is down and wavy, brushing beneath his dress shirt color.

My heel *click, click, click* on the wood floor, getting his attention. Feminine pride suffuses my chest at the way he looks at me.

Like he's already mentally picturing stripping me out of the dress later.

Yeah. I made the right choice.

"Have a good night, Dad," I say as I reach Sebastian.

He's already standing from his stool, arm and hand outstretched to take my hand in his.

"You too. Be safe." He glances at Sebastian. "We'll see you Sunday then?"

"Wouldn't miss it. Have a good night, George."

"You too, son."

Sebastian's eyes widen and then he blinks. When he refocuses his attention on me, whatever caught him by surprise is gone. "You look beautiful."

"Thank you." I flush under his praise. "Ready when you are."

"I'm ready. Absolutely."

For what, remains the question.

JUDE'S HOUSE IS SPECTACULAR. Kate has given me the tour which has led to a movie room similar to Sebastian's, a library I could live in for days and forget to come up for air. The home, while as big as Sebastian's, is so much warmer. Kate has gone on and on how she had found some super cute antique and refurbished boutique stores on the Main Street where she lives. She said when she first moved in, Jude had a couch and television and the basics, but she's been spending time getting it decorated exactly how she wants it. Paisley joined us, claiming she needed to be walking so Angelo, her son in her arms, can fall asleep.

When I ask how old he is, she gives me the strangest response. "His birth certificate says July sixth. Mikah and I are planning a huge Fourth of July party for him, so make sure you and Sebastian are there."

"His birth certificate?" I ask. Let's hop right over the hope Sebastian and I are still together in three months.

"Oh, you don't know?" She flips a hand in the air and laughs. "That's how we met. Angelo here was dropped off on Mikah's doorstep and I was his neighbor."

She trails off, telling me the entire story of how they met, fell in love while bonding over the baby Mikah hadn't known existed with some puck bunny. My eyes grow so big during the entire thing they must be the size of saucers. Possibly dinner plates.

Wow.

"And you've made it work?" If I could suck back words before they reach someone's ears, I'd grab the closest vacuum. What a stupid question. Obviously they've made it work. She's sitting there with a ring on her finger and a baby in her arms but...

It's so oddly strange and crazy that more hope builds.

It *is* possible Sebastian and I can make this work, even if nothing has gone the way we originally thought.

"Well, yeah." Paisley kisses the top of Angelo's head and

leads me toward the kitchen. "I mean, I love the guy. And that accent? Ha. It gets me every time."

She wiggles her brows and I laugh. My stomach hurts I've laughed so much tonight.

I'm enjoying spending time with the team and their girl-friends, wives, fiancées. No one seemed surprised when I walked in, hand in hand, with Sebastian, so I'm guessing he told them to expect me. The women have made me feel welcome ever since we walked in hours ago and Katie told me where I could stash my purse and shoes if I wanted. Between the tour, hanging out on the patio with Sebastian for a while, and spending time with the girls I don't see nearly as often as the rest of the team, I'm having an absolute blast.

It's been so long since I've had good friends to spend time with, I've forgotten how much I love being social.

I've been carrying around a bottled water the entire time I'm here, but now that we're back in the kitchen, unease forces me to bite my lip.

"Do you like red or white wine? Or beer? We have a whole bar if you want something." Katie's standing behind the counter, uncorking a new bottle of red.

I stare at all the alcohol for a moment. "Funny. Usually I'm the one asking that question."

"I bet." Katie grins.

Hannah, the goalie Byron Maddox's wife, comes up and slides next to me. She reaches for a white wine bottle and holds it out for me. "Wine?"

"I'm good with water, but thank you."

She eyes me curiously. "Not much of a drinker?"

"Never really acquired the taste." Which is true. Also, I'm not exactly screaming I'm pregnant. Sebastian didn't say anything about mentioning it to his friends, so I'm not going to be the one spilling the beans by any means.

She winks at me and brings the glass to her mouth. "How odd. I don't know if I could survive."

"Then it's people like you who keep people like me in business."

"Happy to do my part for the economy," she says, both of us chuckling.

"Oh thank goodness," a new voice says, entering the kitchen, gaze on me and a bottled water in hand. I met her briefly before but don't remember her name. "Another knocked up woman who has to say sober with me. Thank goodness I'm ready to pop. I need a glass of wine like seriously bad."

"Um."

Every person in the room has laser-focused on me. Every single one has eyes the size of Texas.

"You're pregnant?" Katie asks, the first to seemingly remember how to breathe. Or speak.

"Oh shit. Y'all didn't know?"

"No, Debbie, and now you've made her look like she's going to puke." That comes from another woman, Paisley, I think. I'm too frozen to say anything.

"Maybe it's morning sickness," Debbie - is her name, says. "I puked *all* the time."

A warm arm wraps around my shoulders coupled with the familiar scent of Sebastian's cologne. "That was supposed to stay a secret, Debbie. Sawyer and his big freaking mouth."

"Oh. Oops." She shrugs nonchalantly and takes a drink of her water.

Katie is still staring at me. "You're pregnant? For real?" Her question ends on a squeak and then she slides her gaze over everyone who's now in the kitchen. "What the hell? You guys are too damn fertile for your own good!"

There's an awkward laugh. Not from me. I'm still frozen silent. I've become an iceberg in the middle of the kitchen and Sebastian squeezes me.

"Little does she know," he murmurs in my ear. "You're freaked. I didn't mean for this to come out. Not tonight. But it's good. They're happy for me. For us, I promise."

I nod although it feels forced.

"So when are you due?" Debbie asks like she hasn't dropped a bomb at my feet. "This guy is coming in May and I hope like hell it's not when Sawyer's playing an away game."

"December," I croak. "I'm due in December."

"*We're* due in December," Sebastian stresses in my ear and then kisses my cheek.

"Well holy hot damn!" Katie cries and throws her hands in the air. "This party just got even better. Congratulations!"

She gives me a fierce hug, pulling me from Sebastian's hold and protective gaze. I stumble from her hug only to receive similar well-wishes and congratulations from most of the players and wives who have now heard.

Among them is Jason, standing back, surveying the scene with lips lifted in a small grin but his dark eyes are so serious. Still holding that concern and worry he's been doing for a long time. While the attention turns to Sebastian, I go to Jason.

He tips his chin down when I get close. "Congratulations."

"You don't mean that." I say it nicely, but I'm pretty sure he doesn't. "And I get why. I also want you to know I really care about him and I know where he's at. I'm not pushing for anything or hoping for anything. I'm okay to see where this goes."

Essentially... you don't need to be worried about your friend, Jason. I've got this.

He must sense what I mean because he tugs me tight to his side. "You're good people, Gigi. I'm glad he has you. But take care. It's only been a few months."

"Trust me, I'm aware."

Madison is never far away even if she's living a half country away. I still sit in shock that Sebastian took this so easily.

Although, I'm giving him something he always wanted and something he stopped believing he could. Why wouldn't he be thrilled even if the circumstances make it seem insurmountable for us to work.

"I'll take care of him, Jason. Promise."

"Good. He's a good guy."

"One of the best."

He drops his arm from me and places his hand on my back, pushing me toward where Sebastian is headed our way, brows yanked close together, lips pushed down.

"What's going on?"

"Nothing. Happy for you is all." Jason slaps his shoulder.

"Just talk." Based on Sebastian's look, I doubt he'll be happy hearing his friend is concerned or giving me warnings about him.

"I think I've had enough talk for one night. Ready to head out?" He leans down to my ear and whispers, "And go do something that involves very little talking?"

Sign. Me. Up.

"THAT'S IT, Gigi. Slide it in nice and slow. Two fingers on your clit."

"Sebastian." My hips are rolling. He's driving me crazy with need and drawing it out to make sweat slicken at my hairline and down my spine. I'm on the edge of losing all control.

I have hit the jackpot for sexiest men I get to have in my bed.

Or in this case, on the FaceTime screen on my iPad. Propped against a stack of pillows at the end of my bed, Sebastian and I are currently mirror images of each other.

Him, on a hotel bed in Buffalo after their third game where they've won all three so far. He's also naked, propped against pillows and knees bent with his feet planted on the bed.

And let me tell you... the view is one I will remember forever. The light dusting of his hair on his chest that trims to a thin line between abs that are currently flexing. The muscles on his forearm while he works his thick, hard cock. The heavy weight of his balls beneath.

God.

I could watch Sebastian pleasure himself every day, all day, and never stop being turned on by it.

His teeth are gritted, eyes narrowed and layered in on me, sitting so much the same way as him, my vibrator shoved deep inside of me as I use it on myself, doing exactly what Sebastian commands.

"Please. Let me move it faster. Harder."

"No. I like the way you sound so needy."

Shit. This is hot. Nerve-wracking when we started as soon as he winked and told me to grab my toy from the nightstand. I didn't even know he'd found it until he told me to use it. Then he told me to strip and every piece of clothes that fell to the floor, he removed one of his.

I have to bite my lip to hold back my cries. At this point, I'm feeling so unhinged the people in the bar downstairs might be able to hear me.

"You're so damn sexy. I can see how wet you are for me. You like this, don't you? Love thinking of me while your fuck yourself."

"Yes," I cry out. "I like it more in person."

"Me too. Now be a good girl and move faster. Work your hips. Let me see how much you need to come, honey," he croons. He tightens his own grip and curves his other hand around his balls.

God, I want that in person. My mouth waters to taste him. My body craves the feel of him.

It's only been two days.

Sebastian has turned me into a sex-starved maniac in less than two months.

I close my eyes, picturing him taking me slow like this. Long, deep thrusts that hit the end of me while he presses my hand to the bed at my sides. When he uses his hips to put pressure on me so I can't move.

And God, the visual alone has me speeding up my movements, flicking on the vibrator.

"Sebastian—"

"That's it. Faster. Harder. Open your eyes and look at me when you come."

I manage to pry them open, gasping for breath, choking down my ecstatic cries and when I see the look in his eyes, from so far away but feeling so close, I fall over the cliff.

My orgasm hits, making my sex clench around my vibrator. My hips buck on their own volition, stomach tightens while I force my gaze to stay on him until he pumps his hand once, twice, and three times.

He grunts out a curse, jaw hard and tight, nostrils flared and he comes all over his stomach, leaving a trail of cream I wish I could lick up and taste.

Hot damn. My Hotshot should make covers for sexiest man alive. Except then I'd have to share him, and that's not gonna happen.

Ever.

I'm keeping the hockey hotshot who scored one goal tonight in his team's three to two victory.

"Well," he sighs, rolling to his side and peeling off some tissues in a container on his nightstand. "That was damn entertaining."

I laugh, tossing my vibrator to the side and sit up. I drape my bed covers over my lap and smile at the view.

Possibly it's better than any photograph I have hung on my walls.

Once he's cleaned, he tugs on his black boxer briefs and brings his phone close to him, running a hand through his hair. His cheeks are flushed, beard thick and messy due to playoffs.

I still want to slide my fingers into it and yank him down to my mouth.

"How are you feeling?" he asks, and while I know he's not talking about my orgasm, I can't resist.

"Sated. And still horny."

"I'll be home in a few days, until then, use that pretty pink toy of yours and think of me."

"Oh. I will." My voice goes deep and seductive.

He shakes his head, chuckling at my tone. "Seriously, Gigi. How are you doing?"

I'm roughly eight weeks. Other than extreme exhaustion and a sudden hatred of chicken, I'm feeling pretty well. And lucky, given the stories I've read about morning sickness.

"Tired. All the time. I almost fell asleep at the bar tonight and Dad made me take a nap in the office."

"You're not working tonight, are you?"

"Dom's here. I have some notices and ads out for another part-time bartender. I think once I'm through the worst of it, I'll be fine, but Dad and I still think I need someone else."

"I agree. You need to take care of yourself."

"I am. I promise." Man, he's so pretty. Some mornings I wake up and imagine the last several months have been one wild dream. Then I get a phone call or text from Sebastian and have to pinch myself to make sure I'm awake. "I really miss you."

Warm, lovely emotions rumble through me. This might be the first time I've shown him how much he means to me. It's not a love declaration, but it feels the same.

"Hey." Sebastian's face grows closer as he moves his phone and he frowns. "You okay?"

"Hormones, I think. I'm feeling sappy."

"I miss you too. A lot. More than I think should be possible, but you need to know that. When I'm here, or when I'm with you, you're all I'm thinking about. Well, you and the baby."

Somehow, I needed to hear this. I'm not sure how long I'll need the reassurance he's happy with me, not wishing this would have been him and Madison. No way am I asking either. I'm okay with being a chicken.

"I'll see you soon, right?"

If they win in two days, sweeping four games in the series, he'll get a small break before the third round.

"As soon as we win, I'll be home. And then we can do more shopping."

In the last two weeks, Sebastian and I have already started making lists of what we'll need. Two of everything since I'll be living alone.

I've started looking for new apartments. The baby deserves more than starting his or her life living above a bar. When I've mentioned that to Sebastian his jaw tightens and he nods. But it's not like I'm expecting to move in with him because of a baby.

That'd be crazier than anything that's happened to us yet.

"You know the way to my heart," I tease.

"I hope so, Gigi. I really do."

My jaw drops. Before I can say anything, the tip of Sebastian's finger comes into view as he traces my lips through the screen.

I blow him a kiss.

"I should let you go. Sleep tight, sweetheart, and I'll call you tomorrow."

"Okay. You too."

We hang up the call and while I get ready for bed and climb back into my covers, I repeat his last words.

I hope so. I really do.

Gosh. I might be falling in love with this man who's going to be the father of my baby.

I suppose crazier things have happened.

CHAPTER TWENTY-SEVEN

Gigi

I WAKE up to the soft snore of Bruiser curled up into my stomach and behind me, no Sebastian. He got home a couple days ago and I took yesterday and today off the bar so I can spend the entire time with him.

Man, dating a professional hockey is not for the faint of heart. I don't even know how he keeps track of his schedule, whether he's coming or going, or how in the heck they don't get sick from all their time spent in the air and adjusting to different time zones.

And playoffs are no freaking joke. I'm already exhausted from the constant hustle of them and they still have so long to go if they keep winning.

Which they're doing.

Because my guy is incredible.

It might have something to do with his team, but I'll give Sebastian the credit.

I stretch, waking up Bruiser who loves to cuddle up

next to me. He huffs and then bounces to my face where my first kisses of the morning are dog slobbers.

"Hmm. These are not the kisses I like to wake up to." I push his face away and sit up slowly. I'm learning if I move too fast in the morning, I get nauseous. Otherwise, besides the extreme exhaustion that makes me want to lay on any hard surface from three in the afternoon onward, I'm feeling pretty damn good. Granted, it's only been a few weeks since I found I was pregnant so anything can change.

Bruiser bounds off the bed, spins in his circles and trots off down the hallway leaving me privacy to use the bathroom and get cleaned up for the day. After, I go search for Sebastian, figuring I'll find him in the kitchen or living room. Possibly his weight room.

Instead, I find him in his office, doors open, Bruiser laying in the doorway outside. He's dressed in athletic shorts and a plain white T-shirt, his hair a rumpled mess while he sits at his desk in front of his computer. Sexy. Like usual when I see him, my stomach tumbles and excitement spikes.

He's just so delicious looking.

"Good morning," I mumble. I go straight to him, smiling when he grins up at me. He pushes his chair away from his desk and holds out his arm.

Good thing, too, because I'm cuddling up next to him whether he likes it or not.

I slide into his lap and he adjusts, swinging my legs over his thighs so my side is pressed to him and my head is at his shoulder.

"Hey, sweetheart." I melt a little every time he says that.

I kiss his throat. "What are you doing up?"

"Getting some work stuff taken care of."

On his screen is a picture of a house. A gorgeous beach

house given the ocean in the background. All white with eggshell blue shutters, it has a massive second-floor deck that looks like it wraps around the entire house.

"That's beautiful. What is it?"

He's kissing my temple when I ask and for a second, he falters. "Oh. It's... it's my house on Sanibel Island."

"You have a house on Sanibel Island?" My eyes grow wide as dinner plates and I glance at the computer screen, back to Sebastian, jaw dropping. "And it's this one?"

Sanibel Island is one of the areas on the coast where *all* the celebrities have homes. I can only imagine the people he sees out there.

"Yeah. But I'm selling it."

"Whatever the heck for?" Leaning forward, I grab his mouse and click through photos on Zillow. And holy cow. It's freaking amazing. I was right about the deck. But what I didn't see originally is that there's a massive, inspiring staircase on the other side at the driveway. It starts at two different sides, meet in the middle and then continues up toward two huge front doors, the same blue color as the shutters. Inside is even more breathtaking. I could live and die and never have to see another human being in this house.

His hand is at my thigh, sliding up and down, making goose bumps pop all over.

"Why are you selling it?"

"Because it was mine and Madison's, where we spent the off-season."

"Oh." My hand drops the mouse like it bit me. "I see. That makes sense, I guess. Is it... is it because of the settlement?"

"No." He makes a sound that's cold. I don't ask him about the settlement, or the agreement and he hasn't offered. I prefer staying in the dark when it comes to his now ex-wife and frankly, we're not at a place where his finances are any of my business.

Although a quick Google search a year ago tells me he has a lot. A lot, a lot. Like a number too high to count to in your lifetime, so the beach house shouldn't surprise me. He has to spend it somehow.

"She took very little. A modest amount. Hell, she makes about as much as my dad and it's only for two years so she can get on her feet."

"Oh." Seriously. What am I supposed to say? It's so nice the woman who left you and broke your heart didn't take you to the cleaners? "That's... that's nice of her."

"Mm-hmm."

Pretty sure that means drop it.

"So why the house?"

"Because I don't want the reminder of her everywhere I go, this house is enough." I'm not sure that's the *greatest* thing I can hear. Does he not want it because it's too painful? Like a good little ostrich, I stick my head in the sand.

"I like the beach." I can feel his smile, lips pressed to my cheek. "For real. This house is the prettiest thing I've ever seen. I'd sell my soul to see something like this."

"I like your soul. But if it hasn't sold after the season, I'll take you there. And if you want a house on the beach, we'll get a different one."

We?

My back straightens and I turn to him, smirking down at him. "You'd buy me a beach house?"

"I'd buy you a house in the mountains or at the beach or anywhere else you want so you and I and our child can have somewhere to go to make our own new memories. Yes. All you have to do is ask."

Well... wow. I shift in his lap, feeling his hard length at my hip. And then the wetness and warmth at my center.

God. This guy. I don't know if I've ever been so sexual, but I want him. All the time. Maybe it's the hormones. Maybe it's the fact we don't see each other every day and we're still new.

Possibly this moment could have something to do with everything he just said.

Or... he's just sex on a stick and a danger to my libido.

"I don't need a beach house," I whisper, brushing my lips against his. "But I love Topsail."

"Then I'll buy a house on Topsail as soon as I get rid of this one."

"You don't have to," I say, but the thought sends shivers through me. I'm dating a guy who can buy me a *house*. For fun. Is this really becoming my life?

I quit thinking about houses when his hand at my thigh drifts to my stomach. He lifts the large T-shirt of his I threw on when I got dressed and dips down, straight between my folds and then inside me.

"Oh."

"Gigi?"

It takes a hot minute to remember that's my name. "Yeah?"

"I don't want to talk about houses anymore," he says, kissing me, sliding his fingers in and out of me.

"What house?" I murmur back.

***

"THIS IS SUPPOSED to be really helpful."

"It looks like an egg."

I nudge Sebastian in the side and laugh. "It does look like an egg. But everything I've read so far tells me the moms love it. It's a swing or a bouncy chair."

Sebastian takes the registering gun out of my hand and clicks two.

"Hey!"

"You want it, we'll get it. Although I still don't like the idea of registering. Or doing it so early."

"I know, but I figure when it's time, you'll be playing and traveling next season and with the bar going to be mine, the fall will be a crazy time."

"Yeah, but our friends don't need to buy us stuff. I can do all that."

"Well then you kit out your place however you want, and I'll have them buy gifts for me."

He scowls at me, and I take the gun. He's been grumpy since we stepped foot into the baby store. And yes, I realize I'm out of my mind for doing this so soon, but everything I said is true. And Debbie thought it was a great idea. I can start a list now and add to it or change it, but it's giving me ideas on how much space I'll need for my new place or what I don't need two of.

"Come on. Let's go look at cribs."

His grumpy attitude is putting a pall on my day and frankly, he's the one who said we'd go together. I'm not sure what's messing with his head today, but I'm over it.

We reach the cribs and I start wandering, checking price tags more than checking the style. I need something for the baby to sleep in, not a fashion statement.

Next to me, Sebastian runs his hand down the top of an elegant, cream-colored crib that looks like it belongs in a palace.

"When is your next appointment?"

His question comes about of left field. "Two weeks, why?"

He looks at me, meeting me dead-on in such a way his eyes turn and I realize then what's been bugging him.

And a part of me is annoyed.

A part of me hurts for him.

He's probably had trips to the store or listened to a woman become so excited and ramble on about gear and the like. This isn't his first time talking with a woman about having a baby.

I look away before he can see how much that hurts, even if it's ridiculous.

"I'd like to be there with you."

I nod. "Sure. I'll double-check the date to see if it's when you're going to be in town, but of course you can come."

Walking toward another row of cribs, I'm no longer seeing anything but blurry floor and furniture.

He trails the other side, and both of us go quiet. This is not the day I envisioned.

"We should go," I say, stopping abruptly. "There's no point in being here. It's too soon and early and well, dumb I guess."

He eyes me warily. "Okay..."

"Okay then." I spin on my heels and head toward the entrance where I stash the little gun back in the registry area and decline printing out what we registered for. Hitching my purse over my shoulder, Sebastian and I walk out toward the parking lot toward his car.

"What happened in there? You were enjoying it."

"It didn't seem like you were."

"Gigi." He sighs and takes my hand and the *last* place I

want to have this conversation is in the middle of the parking lot. "It's early and it's scary and I keep worrying something's going to go wrong and we're getting our hopes up here and well... yeah... that was a little much."

"Our hopes up?" My brows rise as I ask and he flinches.

"Because you've had so many disappointments with Madison you don't want anymore."

He gives me a look that both crushes my heart and makes me ache for him.

"And maybe I've been kicked around enough when it comes to babies and pregnancies and hopes dashed that all of this... it just makes me nervous."

My frustration eases. I'm forgetting I have no idea what roller coaster he's been on for the last few years. And I saw him in the immediate aftermath. I need to be more aware of that.

He's still healing, even if he's moving on with me.

"Everything will be fine this time." I take his hand and press it to my stomach. There's only a bump at night before bed, and it just looks like I ate a massive Thanksgiving meal. "I swear it. The baby is healthy."

His lips roll out and then in. "I also don't like having to buy two of everything."

"Why not?"

His hand at my stomach slides to my hip and he pulls me close. Too close for public. Still, my heart races. "Because I don't like thinking of us doing this separately. I don't like the idea of you being alone with our baby. I don't like the idea of not being with you and him or her."

"Ohhhh." Is that why he's been so grumpy? Because I keep saying we need two of everything? But it's so soon, and I haven't considered when he said he wants us doing this together he meant *together* together.

I'm speechless.

"I'll let you think about that some, until then, can we wait on all this gear?" He bends down and kisses the tip of my nose and brushes his hand over my stomach. "Sorry, I ruined your day."

He just sent my mind twisting and turning like an upside-down roller coaster. "You didn't ruin my day."

"Good." He takes my hand and guides me toward his car.

Then he drives us to a local, traditional southern fried cooking restaurant where I gorge on all southern staples. Fried Chicken. Collard Greens and mac 'n cheese. By the time we leave, my food baby is making an earlier appearance except this time I know it's the food.

Definitely the food.

CHAPTER TWENTY-EIGHT

Sebastian

GAME THREE. Thirty-three seconds left. We're tied at two and Las Vegas has a power play thanks to Fletcher losing his cool and getting called with a hooking charge. It was a stupid move and I know he's already kicking his own ass for being sloppy. We've been holding off Vegas from scoring, but shit are we exhausted.

Pretty sure after we won at home the first two games, we got cocky since we were able to sweep Buffalo in four. Jason and Jude's little brother Joey is currently on the bench, but that doesn't mean the trash-talking during this game has diminished with him playing a different line than us.

He's fucking fast. So much better than the last time I saw him play. I think he even surprised Jason when Joey was able to get the jump on his big brother.

Still, we're tired. My thighs burn. Sweat drips off my beard and down my cheeks. It's gross, but I focus instead on the face-off at our end of the ice. Maddox has done an incredible job all play-off season so far, but even he looks tired, chest heaving as he braces his stick over his thighs while we wait.

I want this win. If we lose, it'll be hard enough to rally on the road but if we win, we know even if we lose the next one we head back home for game five with the advantage.

Damn. My desire to win burns down to my fingers inside my gloves. In my chest. My head pounds from the blood racing through me and I grit my teeth, waiting while the ref holds out the puck.

The Vegas winger jumps a millisecond too soon and the whistle is called, pulling us back to the face-off zone. I'm at the top of the goal crease, prepping to block anything to keep it away from Maddox. The wait is a killer, but when the puck drops again, skates and sticks go flying. Jude comes away with the puck, slapping it out to Mikah. He skates around Vegas's center and passes it off to Jason. Right before Jason snags it with his stick to slap it across the ice, a Vegas player comes out of nowhere, stealing the puck and moving so fast around me I can't even attempt to steal the pick from him.

Shit!

I hustle, try to chase him behind the net, but he's too fast and before Chauncy can get to him, he pulls back, aims, swinging it into the net.

The buzzer and lights behind the goal go berserk but it's not nearly as loud as the roar of the arena.

Game tied with seven seconds to play.

Damn it!

When the final buzzer blares seconds later, I slap Maddox on the helmet.

"My fault, man. Sorry."

"Shake it off, Hendrix," he mutters, but he sounds as dejected as me as we skate off the ice. We have a short break. Then an overtime period. Not what we need. Not on the road.

"It's all right. All right." Coach's encouragement falls flat. He's not much of a talker, but he stands at the bench as we skate off the ice, slapping us all on the shoulder as we hurry down the hall back to the locker room.

Reporters are out in the hall, calling our names, but I shove past all of them. No way am I taking a minute to talk to them even though I know someone will. Hopefully Jude or Jason. They usually don't mind. Tonight, I need my head focused.

God. Damn, I want this fucking win and if that guy hadn't just gotten around me, we might have pulled it off. Now we go into overtime, different than regular season, and we'll play a full-length period until the first team scores.

Vegas has scored first in the five of the nine periods we've now played so far in three games, so the odds are in their favor.

"Fuck 'em," I mutter and plop down on my bench. Water bottles are passed out and I rip off my helmet to cool down.

"That's right." Klaus holds out his now ungloved hand in a fist. "Fuck 'em."

"I didn't actually mean to say that out loud."

"Does not matter. We've got this."

"All right, Kings!" Coach enters the locker room, smacking his hands together. The assistant coaches fan out behind him along with the medical team and therapists. One goes straight over to Pierre, one of our second string wingers, and begins removing his skate.

Shit. The last thing we need are injuries, even minor

ones. I yank my gaze off that and focus on Coach, who's giving all the same pep talk stuff he normally does, barking out commands for the line.

I lift my water bottle in the air when he tells me to shake that off. Of course he hadn't missed it.

We just lost and it was my fault.

Damn it.

I stand and head to the bathrooms, stripping out of my gear enough so I can take a piss and get a minute of privacy.

I can do this. My life, which turned to utter shit almost half a year ago is now so vastly different I almost hate getting on the plane to leave Gigi.

I've had the shittiest personal year of my life and the best is on the horizon.

Sawyer, who's now a dad because Debbie gave birth, managed to squeeze in the delivery on our short break two weeks ago. The entire team has gone ballistic with excitement for them. We almost had to drug him to get on the plane to get his ass here, because he didn't want to leave Debbie and their new son, Abram.

I haven't had a baby yet, but the pull to stay with Gigi is strong enough I know this shit isn't going to end. Not anytime soon, anyway.

I'm pretty sure I love the woman and what I want, besides her and our baby to be healthy and happy, is to come back knowing we're about ready to win a championship, get the cup, and then have an awesome off-season we can spend together, growing closer, making love morning and night and some days in between. Where we can plan our future and enjoy ourselves.

Mostly, I'm feeling pretty damn good about where we're at in life, so when I stomp back on my skates into the locker room and the team is getting all fired up about kicking Vegas's ass, I join in.

Happily.

Because for the first time in a long time, I actually feel happy.

***

WE LOSE. Fifteen minutes into overtime and Joey Taylor of all the fucking players to score slides one past Maddox right between his legs.

Shameful. All of us.

By the time we're off the bus on the short trip up the strip to the hotel where we're staying, it's safe to say we're all exhausted. It's after eleven o'clock but between the game and the time change, it's surprising none of us crash on the short bus ride to the hotel.

As we trudge off the bus, heading into the private entrance of the hotel, I'm shocked as hell when Tessa, Jason's girlfriend, rushes to me with her cheeks flushed, iPad hugged close to her chest, and her eyes wild like she's seen a ghost.

"I'm so sorry, Sebastian. I tried to—"

"What happened? Is Gigi okay? The baby?"

Holy shit, my heart might explode.

Tessa swears and apologizes again, gripping my forearm tight. "No. It's not Gigi or the baby."

Jason has come to us, getting off the bus after me. "What's going on?"

"It's Madison," Tessa whispers in a harsh tone.

The hell?

"What's Madison?"

"She's here." Tessa keeps whispering, pulling me away

from the guys. At my back, I can feel Jason, probably Klaus and maybe a few others figuring out something's wrong. "I tried telling her you wouldn't want to see her, but she insists. So, she's here. Upstairs at the Lavalier Restaurant."

What in the hell? There is nothing, nothing that could prepare me for this. Has she heard about Gigi? That's not even possible. No one on the team would share anything about us to her or anyone else we might know. They certainly wouldn't rub it in her face. And honestly, she has no reason to be pissed if that's why she's here.

She left me. She divorced me.

My feet have somehow cemented to the carpet because I can't move when Tessa tugs on my arm again.

"Why?" I scrub a hand over my face. "Why would she want to see me?"

"I can tell her you're not interested," Jason says.

I peel open my eyes and shake my head. "This doesn't make sense. We're not even married anymore."

That was finalized months ago because I didn't fight it. I gave her the scraps she requested and signed everything like the good boy she expected me to be, even when I considered fighting it.

But now? So much is different. *I'm* different.

"Lavalier?"

Tessa nods. "It's on the second floor, and it's not near the casino floors, so you won't be seen."

"I don't give a shit if I'm seen."

Tessa's face scrunches. Next to her, Jason slides his arm over his shoulders and holds her close. He's a lucky bastard to be able to travel with his girlfriend all the time.

"You okay to do this, then?"

"What. See Madison? After months with no clue why? No." I hold out my suit coat and bag I use to carry my noise-canceling headphones. "Any chance you guys can take this to my room for me? I'll be up later when this is done."

"Yeah. Sure." Tessa takes it. "I can get an extra key, no problem."

"Thanks."

"Good luck," they both say.

I don't respond. There's a rush of noise in my ears, fogging my brain as I head to the elevator. I punch the second-floor button with my knuckle, wishing I could put my fist through the metal door. There's no reason for this, and Madison isn't one to cause drama unnecessarily. Hell, I've always given her what she wanted, the divorce included.

So, the only possible reason for her showing up in Vegas, thousands of miles from where both of us live, is if something's wrong.

By the time I reached the entrance to Lavalier, I've conjured up the worst possible scenarios. Something happened with her family. Something happened with *my* family. She's sick.

All of it means my heart is racing and my blood is boiling when I spy her in a corner booth, red hair gleaming from the chandelier hanging over the table.

My lip curls. This whole restaurant has a romantic feel to it from the soft gray booths and candlelit light. Chandeliers drip crystals from the ceilings and cream silks curve along the walls. Servers dressed in all black with sparkling white ties carry food trays with the obnoxious white towel draped over their forearm.

I want a beer and to get to my room and spend the night in sweats. Or meet the team at the sports bar downstairs. This pretentiousness has never appealed to me.

Waving off the hostess who offers to assist me, I move

like a rocket, straight for Madison, determined and fearful when I see her hands clasped on the table. She's fiddling with a ring, and my feet stall, jaw dropping.

She's wearing her wedding ring.

What in the hell is going on? As I stand there, gaping at her, Madison must realize attention is on her because she turns her head, notices me, and drops her hands into her lap.

Her smile trembles. Her nervousness is clear in the way she nibbles her bottom lip, blinks rapidly.

"Madison," I say her name and slide into the booth across from her. There are two waters on the table, the one nearest me covered in condensation and soaking the coaster beneath. She's been here a while. "This is a surprise."

Like always, she's beautiful. Her red hair looks recently highlighted and there isn't a strand out of place. The shirt she has on looks like silk, a bow loosely tied at the high collar at her throat, no sleeves. Her makeup looks like she could have come from a photo shoot recently. She looks like the Madison I used to know, not the one I saw in February. The only sign she's not completely in her element is the way she scratches her nose and then crinkles it.

Her nervous tell.

"Thank you for being willing to see me, Sebastian. You look great. Playing incredible, I see, too." She smiles, perfect white teeth shine through it. I remember the girl who had two crooked teeth next to her front two and a gap between those, back before driver's licenses and braces. Still, she's beautiful. It can't be denied.

Instinct urges me to pull her into my arms and hold her, tuck my chin to her shoulder to see if she still wears the gardenia-scented perfume that used to make me sneeze.

It's not the prevalent emotion, though, and surprise has me staying in my seat.

She's beautiful. Elegant. And that's it.

All I see is how much different she is from Gigi who dyed her hair to match our team colors for crying out loud. These two women can't be more different.

When I'm with Gigi, I laugh harder and more often than I can ever remember. There's a comfort in her presence. A simpleness.

It's *me*. She's meant for me.

"What are you doing here?" I drum my fingertips on the table. Now she's finally willing to see me and talk? It's about three months too late.

"I'm sorry." She blurts it out so quickly it takes me a moment to process. "I'm sorry, Sebastian. For everything."

She's... *sorry?*

Anger floods my veins, mixed with an acute pain so tight my stomach hurts from it. "You're sorry? For what? Being here? Leaving me? Ignoring me? Divorcing me? Not trying to be a jerk here, Madison, but you came all this way and I'm confused. Really fucking confused."

She flinches and then places her hands on the table. Fingertips spread out showing a recently done French manicure, her favorite. And that ring. It catches the light from the chandelier above us and glistens.

A snarl curls my lips and I refocus on Madison. The pain in her face. The worry.

I love her. I do. I still love this woman, but not in that way. I hadn't realized how much it had diminished in recent weeks, but it has. I'm still not feeling any reason to make this easier for her. She left me.

She licks her lips and nods. "I know. I understand you're mad."

"I'm not mad." Not anymore. Pretty sure I moved passed that phase back in February when I flew to see her and she said it was over.

"Okay. I'm seeing a therapist. And well, I've been doing a lot of thinking. A lot of work on myself over the last few months and I really, well I really wanted to come see you, and explain things now that I have more clarity, I guess."

"You're seeing a therapist? That's good." The pain in my stomach loosens and my shoulders fall. I wanted this for her.

"My dad said, after your visit, that I went to see a therapist or I went home to you. Those were my choices."

Ouch. I mean, way to go, Ben, but fucking *ouch.* "You chose the therapist."

"I know, and I'm sorry, Sebastian, I really am. I'm so sorry. I was hurting so much and in so much pain and then I was so confused and lost and it just felt like... it felt like the walls were closing in on me and I couldn't breathe and I couldn't think. I don't... I don't... I don't know how to describe it better than that, but I just..."

She trails off and blinks, staring at the wall next to us. I can't pull my gaze off her. Pain laces her eyes and her posture and there's that part of me that's always loved her that wants to comfort her but I can't.

She tugs on her diamond earring, one I gave her. Our fifth anniversary. Seeing them makes me cringe. She's decked out in my jewelry for a reason and that reason seems to settle when she says, "My therapist has helped me to start getting better, to find acceptance with everything. I guess... I want you to know that. That I think, I could now be at the place where I'm ready to accept everything won't go the way I wanted."

"Madison." It comes out as a sigh. Guilt curdles my

stomach like sour milk. Softening my voice, I remind her, "You divorced me. We're not married anymore." She opens her mouth, but I talk over her. This is the woman I loved for years. For half my life, and yet... now that love is different. Muted. It's changed and diminished and I don't think it even entirely has to do with Gigi or our baby. "I would have done that. I would have waited for you and gotten you the help you needed me. It kills me, it's killing me to see you now, looking sad, but you shut me out and when I fought for us, you pushed me away. I don't... I can forgive that, because I understand, I think I always did. But I can't go back to that."

"Sebastian—"

God. I *hate* hurting her. "I don't want to go back, Mads."

She flinches like I've stabbed her, curls her hand wearing my wedding ring into her other hand and squeezes tight.

"But I'm better. And it was a mistake. All of it was such a mistake. I was sick and not thinking clearly, and I think now, I'm getting better and I have help and know I need it."

"And it's killing me to sit across from you unable to give you what you want when I spent so many years trying to give you everything I wanted. I loved you, but I can't do this."

"Loved?" Her face pales and her eyes widen.

It takes me a moment to realize what's hurt her so much. And that's when it all comes clear.

I *loved* her. And it's not because I've fallen out of love with her that makes me want to end this... it's because I'm falling *in love* with Gigi.

Because she gets me in a way others don't. Because she lets me talk and she listens and she only offers advice if she thinks it's worthwhile. Because she follows her dreams and can take care of herself but she lets me do it when I need to. I'm falling in love with Gigi. She might not be everything the boy I used to be thought he wanted, but because she's everything the man I am today wants and desires—her passion, her humor, her excitement for life and hope for the future and her confidence.

All of it calls to me. Pulls me to her.

"I'm sorry this is hurting you. I really am. If you're getting help and finding your happiness that's all I've ever wanted for you, but I don't think... no, I'm sorry, I've always been honest with you. I can't give you this."

"But Seb—"

"I've met someone." And God, the pain was bad before but now tears instantly swell in her eyes and she gasps such a wretched sound I hurt from it. "I'm not trying to hurt you, swear to you, Mads, you know I don't want that, but if you came here to be honest, I need to be too. I've met someone, and she's special to me."

Pretty sure I'm in love with her and not because of the baby. Because Gigi is life and happiness and hope and new beginnings, and goddamn, I want to call her and tell her.

There's no point in mentioning Gigi or the baby. I won't hurt Madison unnecessarily.

I lean onto the table, pressing my forearms to the table top, careful to keep my hands from hers. As much as I'd love to hold her hand and promise her things will get better, I won't.

"I'm glad you've been working on your health and you're getting the help you need, but I've been working on me, too, because I didn't have a choice, and I've moved on."

She sobs and months ago I would have vaulted over the table to wipe away her tears and promise I'd never do anything to make her cry again. But I can't. It's not my place anymore.

"This was stupid of me, wasn't it?" She pushes tears away and her chin wobbles when she asks.

"It wasn't stupid." It was just three months too late. "I'm sorry for hurting you. I really am."

She blinks away more tears and I finally hand out the cloth napkin that's been folded around silverware near me. She takes it from me and I relax on my bench.

"This is goodbye then, isn't it?"

Goodbye was when she told me that standing in her parents' basement when she looked a wreck. At least physically she's back to her vibrant, healthy self. I hope the therapy continues.

"I think it has to be."

She sniffs. Looks over my shoulder, still uncertain. "Can I get a hug goodbye then?"

"Anytime." This I can do. At least this ending is more pleasant than the last one and maybe I need this too. To know she's okay. That we can be divorced and possibly, someday, when I'm back in Minnesota and our families run into each other, it can be pleasant.

I slide out of the bench and then, for the first time in months, I hold out my hand to Madison. She places her palm in mine, smiling sadly at my soft touch.

I feel nothing but fondness for the woman I loved when I hold her. When I pull her into my arms and press her gently to me, not tightly, not romantically. I hug her like I'd hug my mom or my sisters or one of my teammate's girl-friends, and I know she can tell the difference because she steps back and drops her arms, clasping her hands together.

"I see," she says. "It really is goodbye."

"Yeah." I wipe away a tear on her cheek and then I lean

in, kissing her forehead. "It is, Madison. But I'm still glad you came. It's good to see you looking healthy, knowing you're getting the help you need."

"Yeah," she cries and it comes out more of a hiccup.

"You going to be okay? Do you... do you have a room? Or something?"

"I'll be fine. I don't think I'm yours to help anymore, am I?"

She's not. I'd do it because I can't not take care of her, but she's right. And mixed signals at this point would be too painful.

"Take care, Madison."

"Bye Sebastian."

I slide my hands into the pockets of my pants and walk out of the restaurant, straight to the elevator and back to my room.

I'm exhausted, and it's not from the game. And yet, I'm hopeful too, because Madison and mine's ending might be painful and tragic and it might still clench my chest and make me hurt—but I have a future to look forward to, with a woman I love—

And I can't wait to get home and tell her.

Twenty-Nine
Gigi

"MUSIC BINGO?" Steve asks, sounding aghast at the horror of my idea.

"Yes. I've looked into this. People flock to bars for either regular bingo nights or something fun like music bingo or trivia. I think it'll be fun."

He gives my dad a wide-eyed look. "I might have to find another bar."

I slap his shoulder, laughing as he winks at me. "You can still come and *not* play. Although I don't know why you'd be such a party pooper."

I give him a look, barely holding back from sticking my tongue out at him.

I've been spending the last few weeks while Sebastian's traveling so much for playoffs, researching local bars in the area that draw a consistent and fun crowd, but doesn't aim for the twenty-something club hoppers. I have no intention of turning George's into a nightclub with flashing lights and a dee-jay, but I want to build on the small town, family and community feel I love about our area and this bar so much.

It's where I grew up, and I want it to feel like home for others even if they only come in once. But the idea of adding special nights that cater to the older crowd, those who need a few drinks away from kids and responsibilities but still wraps up at a decent hour. I figured I can alternate the nights once we get going and see what's more popular, but when I heard of music bingo, I was sold.

Heck, if everyone wasn't so busy right now, I'd call up some of the Ice Kings who I've had the pleasure of getting to know. I'd love to hit up a music bingo night.

Music? Bingo? *Prizes?* I am *so* in.

"Besides," I tease Steve. "Isn't Bingo something all you old farts like to play? I know you have a few lucky trolls hidden somewhere in your house. Let me guess, you bring your own stampers and everything."

"What? Are you... you can't be..." he blusters through a series of threats while I laugh, winking at my dad. "Did you just call me an old fart?"

I shrug and fill him a fresh drink. "If it walks like a duck and talks like a duck..."

"I changed your diapers."

"And I am thankful for that. Anything else you need?"

"Yes," Steve grumbles. "For you to go back to the age before you could speak. That was fun."

Dad and I laugh and with my glass of lemon water, I tap it against Steve's glass. "Love you, Steve."

"Even though I'm an old fart?"

"Especially because you are." I kiss his cheek and turn to Dad.

He's been silent while I share my ideas with Steve.

He's not entirely sold on these ideas either, but while he still owns George's, he's letting me begin making the decisions. That way, once I officially take over when I'm ready, I'll know exactly what to do. We've agreed that can be anytime between today and after the baby's born, whenever I'm ready for the full responsibility.

For now, outside looking for the future, I'm in immediate need of another bartender so he and Dom can alternate nights and weekends giving me a break and more time with Sebastian once their season ends.

Which I'm hoping isn't until late next week when they finally win the Cup.

They have game four later tonight in Vegas. Sebastian's been quiet since their loss the other night and has been ultra-focused. I have plans with a bunch of the girlfriends and wives to watch it at Mikah and Paisley's place. Mostly, I plan on hogging Debbie's new little boy all night.

The door opens to the bar and I face it, ready to serve whoever would wander in here this early and my jaw drops.

"Hey! What are y'all doing here?"

As if I've summoned them, Debbie, Paisley, and Katie saunter in, purses thrown over their shoulders, dressed to kill in their Ice Kings shirts and jerseys with jeans or shorts.

"You're in a good mood," Katie strangely says.

"Why wouldn't I be?"

Paisley's gaze slides to Debbie and then Katie. An eerie sensation prickles the back of my neck.

"What's wrong?"

"Nothing's wrong," Katie says too fast. Much too fast.

The way her gaze slips to Debbie and then Paisley makes that prickle at my neck heighten and slide down my spine. "What is it?"

"You don't get Google Alerts for Sebastian?" Debbie asks, even more weirdly.

"Uh. No. Why would I?"

"I have an alert set for the Ice Kings."

I glance at Paisley and Katie. "Is this normal? For everyone?"

"I have one for Jude," Katie says, "But I don't really pay attention. Debbie thrives on gossip though."

"So, why would Google Alerts put me not in a good mood?"

"Because of this." Debbie grabs her phone and types in her password. While looking at her screen and flipping through something on her phone she says, "But I figured you would have already seen it, so really we came to make sure you were okay."

She hands me the phone and I'm already reaching for it. What I see makes my brows pull together.

"Who is this?"

In the photos she's pulled up, there's Sebastian. He's in a restaurant with chandeliers and wearing a dress shirt and I assume his dress pants. He would have worn a suit to the game the other night. And in his arms? A stunningly beautiful woman with red hair.

"It's Madison," Katie says, lowering her voice. "She's in Vegas."

"What?" Something cold falls like a rock in my stomach. "She's there?"

"Or she was the other night. Like I said," Debbie says, voice softening to a tone I don't like. It reeks of pity. "I didn't know if you'd seen it, so we wanted to make sure you were okay."

"I haven't seen it."

And I've talked to Sebastian several times since then.

He's had opportunities to tell me he saw his ex-wife. He's had chances to tell me he hugged her. Kissed her.

God. I see it. His lips at the top of her head, her holding him tightly. The way her manicured fingernails are digging into his biceps. The upturn of his lips on her *skin*. It's burned now into my brain, and I see it when I close my eyes. The image of Sebastian. Kissing. Another woman—a woman who he was married to up until only a few months ago.

And it's a woman he's been in love with since he was fifteen.

He's had tons of time to tell me he saw her when he called.

Is this why he's been quiet?

"I..." I shake my head, try to gather my thoughts. "He didn't say anything." And I hate the tremor in my voice.

The emotions bubbling. The fear. The worry.

"Why wouldn't he tell me?"

I glance up and jolt. I've practically forgotten they were there, and when I see the concern lining their eyes, that rock in my stomach turns to something sour.

"I think I'm going to throw up."

I drop the phone to the bar and hurry to the restrooms. My stomach churns and my hand goes to my stomach.

Oh God.

I fling open the stall door and drop down to a squat.

Sebastian's now having a child. *His* child. What's stopping him from going back to Madison and having everything he could possibly want? The woman he loves *and* his own, flesh and blood, child.

"I'm so sorry, Gigi. I didn't... I didn't think this would upset you so much." It's Debbie and I barely register her presence in the bathroom until the stall behind me opens and a hand rests on my back. "I wasn't thinking, but when I saw the photo, I just wanted to make sure you were okay. If I would have thought you hadn't known I wouldn't have done this."

"It's fine." I croak like a frog. There's nothing in my stomach to throw up, but I'm dizzy and that sour ball in my stomach grows and thickens.

"It might not be what it looks like. I wasn't trying to jump to conclusions about anything, honest, I just thought you should know."

"He didn't tell me. We've talked for hours. That night after the game. He's been quiet, but I just figured it's the game. My God."

I fall back and rest my ass on the floor, knees bent, back to the wall.

Debbie crouches down in front of me and sighs. "Maybe it's nothing."

I drop my head back to the wall and close my eyes. "That night he got the divorce papers? It was New Year's. He came here and got so trashed. So drunk I had to haul him upstairs and he passed out on my bed." I don't know how much he's told the team, but I haven't said a word about that night until now. "It wasn't even six months ago. And he's told me he's loved her since he was fifteen. Why else would she be there if she didn't want him back?"

"That doesn't mean he'll *go* back."

I shrug, unable to think that's a possibility. I've seen the way he looks when he's talked about her. Wanting her to be happy. And us? We were supposed to be easy. Maybe me getting pregnant made both of us think things that weren't real... or at least him.

Because if I didn't know before now, the way my heart is shattering into pieces inside my chest, teaches me one thing... I've gone and fallen in love with a guy who might not actually be mine.

"What am I going to do?"

"I'd say drink, but since you're pregnant and don't like alcohol, that's probably not a good idea."

"No." I laugh quietly. "Probably not."

"Then take the afternoon off. Come hang out with us. Watch the game and trust that when Sebastian gets back tomorrow, you two will figure everything out."

"Right. I'm sure we will. But no offense, I'm not all that excited about the game anymore."

"I know." She stands and holds out her hand. Pulling me to my feet, she tugs me toward her and hugs me. "I know you're right. But a night with friends always helps."

"Maybe."

Except if Sebastian is going back to Madison, I'll lose my new friends, too. And that sucks. I was starting to really like them.

"What are you doing here, anyway? Where's Abram?"

Abram is the cutest and she just had him a couple weeks ago. She should be home, resting. "He's at Paisley's. Her parents are in town, so they're watching Max and Angelo."

***

IT'S ANOTHER CLOSE GAME, the game tied at four with only a few minutes left. The game is so brutal, Sebastian's already been in two fistfights, complete with helmets and gloves tossed to the ground before being separated. Both Jason and Sawyer have also spent time in the penalty box, and I've lost track at how many goals they've tried to make that Vegas's goalie has stopped.

You can practically feel the frustration pouring off the Ice Kings players as they line up for another face-off down on their side of the ice.

It's so similar to the last game, I've chewed off half of my fingernails. Katie and Paisley don't look any more relaxed.

"Come on," Debbie says, leaning forward. She's quiet due to the fact Max apparently *really* likes to eat, so even though I agreed to come tonight, I've barely been able to hold the little guy.

She did, however, give me the honors of changing a blow-out diaper, laughing while telling me I need to get used to it.

That was an hour ago, and he's been on her boob ever since, sleeping while suckling.

It's the cutest and oddest thing I've ever seen. Gross, poopy diaper that went all the way up his backside, it only makes me more excited about what's to come, despite my nerves about Sebastian.

I'm focusing on the game, not on later. Not on what will happen tomorrow. Debbie and Paisley both made excellent points.

It might be nothing.

It could be everything.

I won't know until I know and the stress won't be good for me, so I'm trying to enjoy Paisley's parents who hover over the babies like they're made of the finest glass. My time with my new friends.

And biting my lip as Vegas gets the face-off, skates down the rink. Jason catches up to him, shoves him into the boards where Mikah gets the puck back and under control. He flings it over to Jude, up to Sawyer.

We're all on the edge of the couch watching, counting down the last minute while men get shoved aside, knocked off their skates, pushed into boards. It goes from a Vegas player to a King, back and forth, and finally, with less than a minute to go, Jude gets a hold of the puck, pulls back and slams it at the goalie. Who misses it go through the far top corner of the goal.

"Score!" all the girls shout. I cry out too, clapping, with the rest of them.

They can do this.

They can win it all.

The question is... what will I end up with?

CHAPTER THIRTY

Sebastian

THIS SERIES IS A KILLER. We're tied at two and two, heading back to Charlotte for another game tomorrow. Traveling is the worst part during playoffs. Two games here, two games there, and then every other one until the series is over, back and forth through time zones.

It forces everyone, exhausted at the end of an already long season, to push through all the pain and discover our mettle.

How strong are we really?

Add in all the emotional and family problems I've had this season and when I pull into my driveway, Gigi's Jeep Wrangler bright blue and in the driveway already here, I almost don't care if we win any more games.

I'm bone-weary tired, in need of a long, hot bath to soak my muscles and a few hours in the sauna to sweat the rest out. I need a night of quiet, curled up with Gigi on my couch, listening to her tell me about her week and grin as she excitedly prattles on about her plans for the bar.

God.

Yes.

This. This is what I've been missing for so long—excitement in my veins at coming home. Gigi gives me this in a way that's effortless and easy to hope it can be forever. I want that. With her.

I might not have known it until early this week, but sitting across from Madison, mourning what I had for the last night, it took that moment to show me what I have now, and what I will have in the future.

Gigi is laughter and love and adventure, and she's all mine in a way I want to keep her there.

Which means I park my car in the garage, hit the button to shut the door and enter the drop zone where I drop my suitcase and kick off my sandals, intent on finding her so I can tell her all of it.

Everything I feel for her.

"Gigi," I call out, stepping into the kitchen, already searching for her.

She's at the couch, standing as I enter and my grin, all the things I feel for her and want to say crash to a slamming halt when I see the look in her eyes.

"What is it?" I ask, hurrying to her.

To my utter shock, she steps back, hands clasped together. We talked last night and everything was fine, outside her being tired.

Or was it?

"What's wrong?"

"How was your trip?" She stresses the word trip with a look.

She saw the games. It takes a second for it to click.

I take a step back, a cool fist gripping deep inside my chest cavity. "Did Tessa call you?"

She tilts her head to the side. Face blank. No. She's not void right now. She's hurt. I've done that by not telling her I saw Madison. "Interesting that's your response."

"I didn't think you'd find out."

And ouch. She flinches and I feel that pain lash so deep so quick I'm already apologizing for that. "Shitty. That was shitty and sounds bad. It was nothing. For me, Gigi, it was absolutely nothing."

Tears wet her eyes and she nods, pressing her lips together. She pulls up her phone and holds it out.

"This doesn't look like nothing."

I don't want to see the damn photos. But now I know it wasn't Tessa. Which I should have known. She probably would have assumed I told Gigi right away, which in hindsight, I should have done. Mostly I wanted to push Madison's visit out of my mind.

"What did she want?" Gigi asks, still holding out the phone. "Because I've been trying, trying to trust what you're telling me right now, but I have to tell you it's difficult considering the way you're looking at her, and knowing how much you love her."

"I don't love her. Not in that way. Not anymore."

Screw this. Seriously, screw this. I take the phone from Gigi's hand, glance at the photos and cringe. It does look bad, but I know why she's insecure and worried right now.

Because I haven't been honest with her in a long time.

"What did she want?" she repeats.

I toss her phone to the couch. While she watches it fly through the air, I'm there in her space, hands to her cheeks, forcing her to tilt her head up and look at me.

"Listen to me, Gigi."

"What did she want?"

"Don't do this. Please, just listen to me—"

"What—"

Fine. "She says she made a mistake and she wants me back."

She jolts at that, which I expected, so I hold her tight, not allowing her to break from my hold on her. "You wanted to know." Frustration leeches through my tone. "I didn't tell you because it's not happening. It didn't matter. It was hard to see her. Hard to listen to that and not be able to give her what she wants—"

"Because of the baby?"

God. Is that really the kind of man she thinks I am? She's hurt. I get it. I know she doesn't think that of me, does she? That I'm only with her because of the baby? "No. Not because of the baby. Because of you. Because Madison chose to walk away from me and when I was at my worst, you were there, and when I started accepting she was gone, it was *you* I wanted to spend time with. And maybe I should apologize for not telling you about Madison, but yeah, I didn't think you'd know. At least not before I could get home and we could talk about it because I would *tell* you, but because I walked away and pushed it out of my mind. It was never going to happen, Gigi. And mostly that's because it wasn't until I was sitting across from Madison that I realized how crazy in love with you I am."

"What?" Her eyes widen and lips part.

If I wasn't so frustrated with myself for not telling her sooner, or for her not trusting me more, I'd kiss away the stunned look on her face.

"Yes. You. I love you and I should have figured that out sooner so I could tell you so you weren't standing here now doubting me, but make no mistake, it's *you* I'm in love with.

Madison is my past. You, and our family we're making, you will be my future and I *want* that."

She blinks rapidly and tears fall down her cheeks. I swipe them away quickly.

"I would think you'd want that for me, Gigi. Madison might have flown to Vegas for other reasons, but I have full closure. I firmly, permanently, was able to close the door to my relationship with Madison the other night in a way I have no regrets."

"I'm sorry," she says, chin trembling. "The girls came to the bar and showed me and then I was so worried and went crazy... and well... I don't think I realized how much I love you until I saw them and it hurt. Seeing you holding and kissing another woman hurt."

"It will never happen again. This I promise you." It takes a beat. Then two for what she said to me to settle in. "You love me?"

"Of course I do."

For the first time since I walked into my home, her eyes are shining.

I grin down at her. "Did you hear me say I love you?"

"Yeah." Finally, she grins. A laugh bubbles from her. "Although I wasn't expecting that, so you might have to repeat it."

"Every day. Multiple times if you need to hear it." I bend and brush my lips over hers. "I love you, Gigi. I swear it. And I'm sorry I didn't tell you about that night, but I told her about you."

"About—"

"No. Not the baby, I didn't want to be cruel."

"Okay." She chuckles and her wet lashes blink. "I'm sorry I didn't trust you."

"Maybe you would have if I would have realized how much I love you before then."

She grins up at me then and smiles so bright it's almost blinding. "So... we're in love." She chuckles and shakes her head like she still can't believe it. "And we're having a family."

"And I hope that you're in agreement with me, when I say, I want us doing all of it together. As a family. Living together."

"When should I start packing?"

That's my girl. She gets hurt and lets things go. And now, she's as vibrant as she always is. "As soon as we make up and this time, since you were the one who's mad, I think you should do all the work." I swoop her up into my arms and carry her into my bedroom. Our bedroom soon, hopefully.

Because we might have bumps along the way. Miscommunication. Poor communication. But it's a part of life and it's a part of loving someone.

When I set Gigi on the bed, she crawls to her knees and rips off her shirt. Her stomach is slightly swollen now, and my gaze stalls on her stomach where her hand rubs lightly. "I think, since I'm the one carrying your child, you should do all the work."

"Deal." Making love to Gigi my way is not a hardship.

And then I lunge.

SEVERAL WEEKS LATER, my team wins the Stanley Cup and we spend a full week celebrating with parties and parades.

Three weeks later, Gigi moves in with me.

Six months later, she officially takes over the running of George's Bar. It's a smashing success with all of her months spent planning and marketing. I screw her on her new desk, bent over it since her belly is so grown. I'm so proud of her I can't wait until we get home later in the night.

One month after that, on December twelfth... Samson George Hendrix is born.

Nine months later, before the next season begins, I cry when I see Gigi at the end of the aisle, dressed in white, headed my way.

I kiss her at our wedding and we spend the night dancing under the stars, our wedding reception at our home, around the pool and the acres of land beyond. We celebrate with friends and family and teammates and all the tiny Ice Kings toddling around.

The next day, we leave Samson for a week with my parents and head to Europe, where we make love in our hotel along the French Riviera and Gigi spends two weeks showing me all the places she loves the most.

And me? I can never picture my life without her in it. Without her unfailing love or her steady confidence in us and her joy in the world around her.

She's everything I never saw coming, and everything I need.

EPILOGUE

I STARE at the piles of suitcases and gear.

Next to me, Gigi drops another small bag.

"Do you think we packed enough?" The pile at my feet I'm somehow expected to fit into the back of our Navigator keeps growing. I foresee a game of Tetris-like packing in my future and curl my lip.

"Well, it's the beach. But what if it gets cold at night? Or what if Elijah gets fussy? I mean, we don't have the pack 'n play there or bouncy seat so I can't leave them behind, and then there are books for me and you and—"

I shut my beautiful wife up with a kiss. I've learned over the years that when it comes to our kids, she's a wee bit over-protective and slightly neurotic.

However, I don't tease her for it... much... I still like to get laid on the regular.

And regular I do.

Who knew after three years of being married and two

kids, I'd still get hard multiple times a day by my wife's simple presence and silliness.

"Are the boys sleeping?" I murmur.

She slaps my arm and tries to push me away. I move closer instead. We bought a new house on Topsail Beach in North Carolina last summer, but then the season started and we spent most of the winter and spring renting it out instead of enjoying it.

"Elijah is. Samson's in the movie room."

That means they'll be out for the time I need.

"Come with me. We should go check the bedroom, make sure you've packed everything we need."

"I have..." I kiss her again and she grins against my mouth. "Oh. Yes, I should probably do that. Give it a quick look."

"It'll be slower than quick."

"Quick is all we have. Remember yesterday?"

I remember. Gigi was on her knees in our bathroom, greeting me happily by reaching for my dick when I stepped out of the shower. I was almost ready to orgasm when Samson started banging on our bathroom door. She'd pulled off, leaving me hard, panting, and somehow, laughing my ass off while she went to take care of him... and I finished myself off.

"We'll lock the bedroom door this time."

"Deal." She turns on her heel and runs through our house, grinning at me over her shoulder when she reaches the top of the stairs.

I take my time. Her ass has grown some over the years and I enjoy the way it shakes.

Four years ago, I never could have imagined my life. Everything changed the moment Samson was placed in my arms, and I experienced a love I never understood. So much bigger and deeper than anything I expected. A year later, when we tried for another, was a dark period.

For six months, I watched Gigi frown when her period came. All that old guilt, the weight of what I'd been through before threatened to pull me under and it was once again Gigi who saved me.

She climbed into my lap one day, naked, and placed her hands to my cheeks and said, "I'm perfectly content with Samson. If you want more, we'll adopt."

Right before the last season began, we brought Elijah home to us from China. It was a long process. A frustrating one with its own twists and turns, but he's perfect. We fell in love with him the moment we saw him, and when he was placed in our arms, it felt like he'd always been meant to be ours.

Even cooler is the town we live in has a Chinese Immersion School. We'll all be able to learn about his heritage and his culture and language together.

As for Samson? He adores being a big brother. At three and a half, it's mostly head petting and bottle grabbing and helping stick pacifiers in Elijah's mouth. But it's a beautiful thing to witness.

I follow my wife to our bedroom, where I remember to lock the door, and when I don't see her in the bedroom, I find her in the bathroom.

She's naked.

Cheeks flushed... both sets.

Her hands are braced on the counter, and she's smiling at me over her shoulder. "Show me what you got, hotshot."

I'm naked in five seconds, inside of her in two more, groaning at how wet she already is.

Yes. Gigi might have been the surprise I never saw

coming when I was absolutely at my worst, but she's the best chance I've ever taken.

We've built a family based on a strong foundation of love and a whole lot of fun.

And me?

I never imagined life could be this beautiful.

THANK YOU

THANK YOU for reading Hooked On Her! Interested in what I'm working on next?

Be sure to sign up for my newsletter so you can stay up to date on more books in the series releasing this year.

www.staceylynnbooks.com

ACKNOWLEDGMENTS

HUGE thank you to Hilary and all of Social Butterfly PR for throwing your full enthusiasm and support behind each and every book I write. I have loved working with all of you and can't wait to see what's ahead! Hilary, I miss you most of all. ;-)

Ellie and Virginia, as always, thanks for putting up with my mess and spit-shining each manuscript until it sparkles. Thank you especially during this crazy time in our world for your flexibility and your extra hard work.

Shannon, you're the best. Always. Forever. Your talent is astounding and I'm thankful I can call you a friend.

Special, enormous thank you to my family who is always here, cheering me on and being so patient when I'm in my office. Your support is everything to me and I love you all with all of my heart.

To my Sweeties! I love you ladies and your excitement for my books! Special thanks to you this time for coming up with Brenna's name for me. It fits her perfectly.

To Lauren and Tamara – I'm so thankful our moves brought us into each other's lives!

To all the bloggers who devote their time and passion into reading books, book tours, release events, leaving reviews, promoting and pimping – you are all rockstars! Thank you for all the love over the years.

My family— I love you all to the moon and back. I don't know what I would do without you in my corner, cheering me on every step of the way.

And last but definitely not least – to you the reader. I'm blown away with every release how much you adore my books. You have made my dream a reality and I hope I can cheer you on with yours.

Weekend Fling

The Fireside Series

His to Love

His to Protect

His to Cherish

His to Seduce

Just One Series

Just One Song

Just One Week

Just One Regret

Just One Moment

Tangled Love Series

Entice

Embrace

Enflame

The Luminous Series

Dominate Me

Crave Me

Long For Me

The Nordic Lords Series

Point of Return

Point of Redemption

Point of Freedom

Point of Surrender